SUMMER AT THE CORNISH FARMHOUSE

ALSO BY LINN B. HALTON

SUMMER AT THE CORNISH FARMHOUSE

Linn B. Halton

An Aria Book

First published in the UK in 2023 by Head of Zeus,
part of Bloomsbury Publishing Plc

9 7 5 3 1 2 4 6 8

A catalogue record for this book is available from the British Library.

ISBN (PB): 9781804546406
ISBN (E): 9781804546475

Cover design: Head of Zeus
Typeset by Siliconchips Services Ltd UK

Printed and bound in Great Britain by
CPI Group (UK) Ltd, Croydon CR0 4YY

Head of Zeus
First Floor East
5–8 Hardwick Street
London EC1R 4RG

WWW.HEADOFZEUS.COM

To my fabulous four... you are my inspiration!

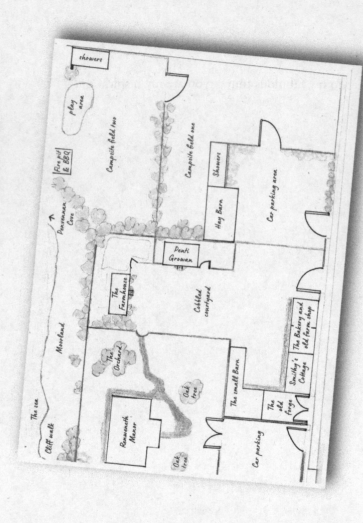

Renweneth Farm, Cornwall

Prologue

My hands shake as I press the call button but the moment Grandma's voice fills the room my throat closes over.

'Jess?'

My chest is so tight I begin to panic.

'Darling, what's wrong?'

'My... my world is falling apart, Grandma, and I...' With my emotions in utter turmoil, I struggle to pull myself together.

'Take your time, lovely. Try to slow down your thoughts and focus on breathing.' Her tone is soft, so gentle that it's like a hug and I find myself nodding my head even though she can't see me.

Pushing my shoulders back with a sense of determination, I clasp my hands together firmly in my lap as I stare down at the phone lying in front of me. Moments later the tight band of pain around my ribcage gradually begins to ease and I reach out for a tissue to dry my eyes. *Enough*, I silently berate myself. What's done is done, now it's about survival.

'Sorry. I just... I don't know what to do and I can't even think straight.'

As if leading me, what I hear in response is the sound of Grandma drawing in a deep, deep breath, then slowly expelling it before taking another. I follow her example for several minutes until my jaw unclenches and my shoulders relax, helping to take the pressure off my chest.

'Thank you, Grandma,' I reply, my voice barely audible.

'Now, start at the beginning.'

'Ben has been distant lately. No… we've both been distant with each other, is the truth. And yet, I don't know how it happened… how we got to this point.' I mutter an involuntary groan as my husband's face flashes before my eyes. 'Ben insisted on taking me out for dinner last night; just the two of us, something we haven't done in quite a while. I was a little anxious but also relieved. I thought we were finally going to sit down and talk honestly to each other, like we used to do. We get so little real quality time alone together these days. And when we do the timing doesn't seem right somehow. There's always some little upset to spoil the atmosphere. Silly things that don't really matter, or so I thought, can feel like invisible barriers and I was happy that he wanted to clear the air. You know, get us back on track.'

I take a moment to steel myself before I repeat those fateful words that passed his lips. As it turns out, there are some things that you can't put right because once it's lost, it's gone forever. I saw the pain reflected in his eyes even before he started speaking and it was gut-wrenching.

'He told me…' I gulp down the lump that begins to rise in my throat. 'Ben admitted that he's not in love with me anymore and he said he was sorry for messing up our lives. He wants a divorce.'

'Oh, Jess. My poor darling. I can feel your pain and my heart goes out to you.'

An icy chill begins to course through my veins. I rang Grandma because she often notices things other people don't pick up on. She says little, but she's a people watcher and it's the words she chose not to say in response that tells me she'd already sensed that something was wrong.

'How did I not see it coming?' My voice has an edge of desperation to it.

And then Grandma lets out a sigh that emanates from deep within her and it sends a little shudder through me. 'Because in your heart you know the truth, Jess, and you've probably known it for a while, but you aren't ready to accept it.'

Suddenly, it's as if scenes from my life are flashing before my eyes in quick succession. Ben's eyes smiling down into mine and I can actually feel his love wrapping itself around me. And the birthday when I arrived home after an exhausting day at work to a trail of rose petals leading from the front door to the bathroom. Inside, there were tealights everywhere and a fragrant bubble bath awaiting. He appeared some five minutes later carrying a tray with a dish of handmade chocolates and a bottle of champagne. As he slipped into the bath to join me, my tiredness simply faded away. That was in the early days, when happiness was something I took for granted.

'It's over and there's nothing I can do about it,' I gasp as the reality continues to sink in. 'I remember Ben standing in front of the window with Lola in his arms the night she was born. He had tears in his eyes as he talked to his daughter for the first time. He still looks at her that way, Grandma. But when he looks at me his eyes haven't lit up like that for a long time now. I told him we could fix it... see a counsellor, but he said he can't change the way he feels...' I choke down a sob as my words peter out, my mind wandering.

'Jess,' Grandma's voice brings me back into the moment. 'What is your heart telling you?'

I pause and my stomach churns as the truth is almost too painful to bear. 'That it's over. It's been over for a while and I ignored my biggest fear because I knew there was no going back.'

'Then your focus must be on building the future you want for you and Lola.'

'How do I do that when my heart feels like it's been shattered into a million little pieces? My life no longer makes any sense.'

'So, you're what? Just going to fall apart?'

She's right. I have Lola to think of. I don't even know how I'm going to tell Mum and Dad. Then it occurs to me that Grandma might not be the only one who could see the cracks forming in my marriage. Now I feel foolish and angry with myself. I thought that if I gave Ben a little space and some time, he'd sort himself out. It was just a phase he was going through, I told myself.

'No. Lola comes first, always,' I reply, meekly. Wallowing is a luxury I know I don't have.

'There you go! That's the Jess we need now; strong and determined. It's hit you hard, my love, but life goes on. It's time to build a new dream and gradually the wounds of disappointment will heal. But understand this, Jess. If, deep down inside, you'd felt there was a chance of salvaging your relationship you would have immediately leapt into action. People change over time, Ben just changed in different ways to you. It's no one's fault.'

'Our life became mundane. If only I'd…'

Grandma interrupts me. 'Don't do that to yourself, Jess. It changes nothing to think like that.'

'But when you know someone isn't happy, I mean… it wasn't your idea to move to Cornwall, was it?'

Grandma gives a little light-hearted laugh. 'Your grandad's dream was always to live near to the sea. We all know that after Cappy left the navy he settled in Gloucestershire for my sake, because that's where most of the family were living. I knew you'd all come and visit if we moved to the farm, as who doesn't love the sound of the sea?'

Grandad's nickname, which family and friends now use with great affection, harks back to when I was small. I asked Grandad Gabe what he did when he was away. He said he was the captain of a ship. I wasn't good with 'T's' and from then on he was known as Cappy.

'You made his dream come true, though.'

'Well… partly,' Grandma admits. 'There's still a lot of work to do to bring the farm and the buildings back to life. He won't rest until it's all done but then I want him to buy a boat.' Her voice lifts and I know she's smiling.

'A boat?' I repeat, thinking I might have misheard her. Cappy has never mentioned a word of that to me.

'Once a captain, always a captain,' she says, happiness radiating from her tone. 'And why not? Even if he only goes mackerel fishing, he'll be back on the water again and that's his spiritual home.'

Now that's true love.

'And what's your dream, Grandma?'

'To see him wearing his captain's hat again. He'll want to take you and Lola fishing, of course. But he told me once that looking back on the land from the sea changes the way you look at life. He said that, give or take, the earth is seventy per cent water and only thirty per cent land. How amazing is that?'

No, Grandma. How humbling is that – the way you always put Cappy first.

'And what's your dream for the farm, Grandma?'

There's a long pause. 'I want it to be a comfort for him, for you all.'

An uneasy feeling descends upon me. 'It is, and you're happy there, too? Aren't you?'

'Yes,' she instantly responds.

'And Renweneth Manor?' I ask, unable to stop myself.

'Now the farmhouse is in better shape and once the farmyard outbuildings are brought back to life, the boat comes next. After that... well, we'll see.'

'But you love the manor house and the beautiful gardens and orchard surrounding it.'

'It's been standing a long time, Jess. That old house will wait its turn if it's meant to be. The point is that this isn't about one person's dream but building something for the future. When life gets tough it's all about options. The farm is just one of them, something that might... well, who knows what tomorrow will bring? But that's the exciting bit about life, Jess. How many times do we look back on something bad that happened, only to realise that it changed our course, which turned out to be a good thing in the end.'

I fall silent, knowing there's a message for me somewhere in those words and feeling frustrated I can't see it right now. 'What if I make the wrong decision along the way, Grandma?'

She laughs, softly. 'No one gets it right first time, Jess. We can plan all we like, but the key to surviving the ups and downs of life is to be like a willow. Know when to bend and flex, don't let your ego make you dig in your heels for the wrong reasons.'

That makes me smile. 'I hear you.'

'Good. When you know something is right you'll feel it in your gut, Jess. There's nothing to fear in losing face, or even losing your pride, but there's a lot to fear in doing something just because you're too scared to take a risk. If you get it wrong it's a learning experience, that's all.'

As the long process of establishing a life without Ben by my side began, that conversation with Grandma was often on my mind. When, almost six months later, she died after a short and unexpected illness, I awoke from a dream one night thinking I'd heard her repeat something she'd said about the farm and Cappy. 'I want it to be a comfort for him, for you all.'

Did Grandma know she was ill when we spoke? Or did she instinctively know that her life was drawing to a close? Either way, her words stuck with me as if one day I'd understand exactly what she'd been trying to tell me.

ONE YEAR LATER

JUNE

I

Those Tricky Little Four-Letter Words

Buying paint, I'm discovering, can be as complex as finding love. It should be easy, shouldn't it? I mean, you meet someone, fall in love and live happily ever after. And buying emulsion to paint a wall is just a case of plucking a tin off a shelf. Except that nothing in my life has ever turned out to be straightforward and today is no different.

The next item on my list simply says *blue paint*. It's for my daughter Lola's bedroom and she told me exactly what she wanted. However, none of the pre-mixed colours on the shelves come close to her exacting description. After a lot of deliberation, I walk over to the impressive Colour Selection Zone and my heart sinks. There's a vast wall display with tiny colour charts. The blue section ranges from a mere hint of a tint that's so subtle it's hard to detect, to the darkest, densest navy. In between are hundreds, literally hundreds of nuanced shades.

I find myself sighing. As with love, I'm probably heading for another fall from grace. For an eight-year-old, Lola has an old head on her shoulders. My instructions this morning as I dropped her off at school were that it should be cornflower blue, like the flowers on the edge of the meadow we walked through last summer.

'That warm shade, Mum,' she'd added, intently. 'Not the way they looked after our picnic when the clouds were dark grey, and they made everything look cold.'

My stomach started to churn. I tried to transport myself back into the moment, picturing us sitting on a blanket, munching contentedly on sandwiches and cake. The truth was that I couldn't even remember what flowers there were around us that day. I'd been too caught up trying to make a happy memory before I broke the news that Lola's father Ben, and I, were officially divorced.

The move to Cornwall was imminent and, in a way, I'd wished the confirmation had come through after we'd left Gloucestershire. Lola knew it was coming, of course, but the reality of it felt harsh. As the sun slipped behind the gathering clouds and it started to rain, it seemed appropriate somehow. How dare the sun continue to shine when our world was about to be turned upside down? A period of mourning had begun. As we'd rushed to gather everything up and head back to the car, the questioning began.

'We're really going on our big adventure then, Mum?' Her eyes had searched mine, looking for reassurance. Was I really doing the right thing? I'd questioned myself. Lola had already been through so much since Ben moved out and I was running on empty. That didn't bode well when it came to taking on a project that was going to require a lot of energy and motivation. My nerves and emotions were frayed because, stupidly, I'd thought... hoped... that Ben would suddenly have a last-minute change of heart and beg us to stay. Or even better, come with us and start over again in a place that held so many wonderful memories for us all. A decade of family birthdays, Christmases and summer holidays gathering together to celebrate the happiest times in our lives. It was the right thing to do and I knew it.

'Yes, and it will be amazing, Lola,' I'd replied with every ounce of positivity I could muster as we bundled everything into the boot of the car. Instinctively, I'd reached out to help Lola tuck a few stray strands of hair that the breeze had whipped across her forehead, behind her ear.

'But Dad loves Cornwall as much as we do, Mum.' Lola's eyes had reflected the anxiety that she felt about leaving her dad behind.

'I know, my gorgeous girl, and it is sad, but it's important that we're all happy. Once Dad is settled in his new house he'll come and spend some time with us, you know that and Dad never breaks a promise, does he?'

'No, Mum, he doesn't, but Cappy's old farmhouse is a bit... spidery and dark.'

I'd stifled a laugh, wrinkling my forehead and putting on my serious face. 'Between us, we're going to get out the paintbrushes and make it light and bright and spider-free, don't you worry. And Cappy will be so happy to come and visit because your great-grandma Maggie would be pleased to think of the two of us living there. We all had so many wonderful family holidays, didn't we? It holds a lot of special memories, Lola, and we're about to add to them.'

The happy times were put on pause when Lola's great-grandma died and Cappy moved back to Gloucestershire to be close to my parents. Being at the farm without her by his side was simply too much for him to deal with. He struggled to pick up and make sense of the shattered pieces of his life. For a while it was a struggle just to get through each day; he looked lost and bewildered. Appointing a manager to run the camping and caravanning business kept things ticking over, but no one talked about the longer-term future.

However, we all missed a place that had become a huge part of our lives and that applied to Lola, too. She isn't a child to sulk as she has a sunny, effervescent outlook on life, but the day of our picnic was a poignant one at that time. Aside from our home in Gloucestershire, there was only one other place she felt a strong connection to and that was Cornwall. Oh, I know Ben will always be there for us, but taking Lola away from her friends and her school to make the move was still a risk. In my darkest moments I'd realised that neither of us were adjusting to the inevitable, that three had become two in terms of living our daily lives.

Now, here we are... nearly a year has passed since we made the move and the last room of The Farmhouse is going to be a masterpiece if I can get just the right shade of blue to please my daughter. But even as I rifle through the swatches, my mind won't switch off. If only I'd put as much thought into choosing a husband as I am into decorating Lola's new bedroom, maybe we'd still be a happy family. Then it dawns on me that if I'd married someone else I wouldn't have my beautiful girl. In that split second my face lights up and as I glance around my eyes alight upon the perfect shade of sun-kissed cornflower blue.

There's a lot riding on this because Lola has been battling with separation anxiety. As daft as it sounds, every tiny detail of her new room matters. If you take a baby bird out of its nest it feels threatened, vulnerable and disorientated, so this isn't just about decorating a bedroom, it's about creating Lola's little sanctuary.

Perching cross-legged on my favourite window seat, I stare out at the sea as it extends far into the distance. The trees are thinner here and frame the scene so perfectly it could be a painting. If I think back over the many times I've sat here with Lola, the pictures that fill my head are like charting her growth. From a babe in arms to a boisterous toddler, and now we often sit here side by side, just losing ourselves in the view.

It's cathartic and a reminder of how wonderful nature is; nothing upsets the rhythm of the seasons and today it's gloriously sunny. There's hardly a cloud in the sky and it's impossible to distinguish from here where the water ends and the sky begins on the horizon.

My phone kicks into life, shattering the silence, but when I see that it's Ivy, I immediately put it on speakerphone.

'How did the paint-buying trip go?' My best friend since pre-school asks.

'It was a bit of a nightmare but I'm hoping Lola will think I've nailed it.'

'Thank goodness for—' The sound of alarm bells going off in the background stops Ivy in her tracks. 'Sorry, Jess. The fire alarm is going off again,' she yells down the line. 'I'll ring you back shortly.'

Oh dear, Ivy sounds at the end of her tether. 'Speak soon!'

As we disconnect, I stand, staring at the large test square of *wildflower blue* I've just painted on the wall. I think it's pretty, but I have no idea if the vision in my head will match what Lola is picturing. When my phone kicks into life again I grab it, assuming it's Ivy, but to my delight it's Mum.

'Hi darling, just checking in. Is this weekend still on?'

'It is. The chippings are being delivered later this morning. Are you and Dad okay?'

She chuckles. 'I'm fine and Dad is... Dad. He's in his greenhouse loading up trays with plants for your new patio area as we speak.'

My smile grows exponentially. 'Aww... bless him! Going for the quickest and cheapest option to tidy the area behind The Farmhouse isn't ideal, but it will transform it.'

'Is Ben joining us?' Mum asks hesitantly. My parents don't get to see him very often now and it takes a while to adjust to that. They miss him too, which is only natural as he's been a part of our lives since I was eighteen years old and that's a little over ten years now. Following the divorce I decided to keep my married name, telling myself that it was for Lola's sake. Maybe at first there was that element of wishful thinking Ben might come back to me at some point, but now I know that isn't going to happen, I still think it was the right thing to do.

'No. Sadly he's working tomorrow. He did offer to drive down afterwards and stay overnight so he could give a hand on Sunday, but I didn't think that was fair on him.'

'Oh well, it's the thought that counts and it was good of Ben to offer.' Mum's voice is upbeat, but the extra pair of hands would have been a boon and we both know it. Ben is an antiques furniture restorer and used to shifting heavy items of furniture around. When he let slip that he wouldn't be coming alone, I panicked and rejected his offer without even thinking.

'The good news is that Ivy has talked her lovely husband into coming.'

'We haven't seen Adam for ages,' Mum gushes, instantly perking up.

Adam is a builder and he's solid muscle. His second home is the gym and while I have no idea how much work is involved decanting twelve one-ton bags, my parents, Lola and I really do need all the help we can muster.

'Well, it certainly put a huge smile on my face when she broke the news.'

'It'll be fine, Jess,' Mum reassures me. 'Goodness, I've carted enough compost down the path to your dad's kitchen garden over the years to know anything is do-able. I might not be able to manage a wheelbarrow but with the right size buckets we'll be fine. I'll also bring a smaller one for Lola, as she won't want to be left out.'

A beeping sound emanates from my phone.

'Thanks, Mum... I have an incoming call from Ivy, so I'll love you and leave you. See you in the morning.'

'Bye, darling. Give Lola a hug from us!'

As Ivy's voice looms up, she sounds frazzled. 'Another false alarm. Seriously, Jess, if the electrician doesn't get this sorted soon we're going to lose customers and money. Each time we evacuate the café we have to offer everyone a replacement hot drink. Thank goodness we don't serve hot food yet or we'd be sunk.'

'Is the landlord still messing you round?'

'Let's just say that he rarely returns my calls or my emails and if he can't get the alarm sorted out, what chance do I have of getting his permission for me to install a new streamlined kitchen? I'm seriously considering starting to look elsewhere, because there'll be no point renewing the lease in October if this continues.' Her sigh of exasperation is tough to hear.

Poor Ivy. She's been rushed off her feet setting up a new business and while it's in a prime spot in the centre of Stroud, in Gloucestershire, space is at a premium. She can seat sixteen people inside and, fortunately, she's allowed to put up six further tables outside when the weather allows. But it's always packed and she's constantly turning customers away. I can't help but wonder whether it's the right place to invest in though. Turning The Cake and Coffee Emporium into a full-blown café offering hot and cold lunches is a risk. It's a great idea to grow her business, but if people sit and linger over their meal rather than eating and exiting, how long will it take her to recoup the outlay for her dream catering kitchen?

'You could always write to him and send it recorded delivery. He can't ignore that, surely?'

'Hmm,' she groans disparagingly, 'if he treats all his tenants like he treats me I suspect he gets a lot of those. Anyway, ignore my moaning. Trade is brisk and I can't complain. So… the dreaded paint situation. You sounded quite confident just now.'

'I am,' I reply, smiling to myself. 'We've chosen some lovely pieces of furniture to up-cycle and she's even drawn a floor plan.'

'It's good to hear that Lola really is ready for this at last, Jess. It's wonderful news.' Ivy knows what a big deal this is for both Lola and me.

'When we move her bed out of my room and into the newly decorated one, we're going to put some voile drapes around it. She's very excited about that.'

'That's a clever idea. When she's all tucked up in her own little space she'll be comfy, cosy and, hopefully, start to let go of that anxiety. I remember calling in to see you at the old house and Lola was curled up in a ball, sobbing. My first instinct was to panic.'

It tears me apart how unsettled Lola has been since we moved to Cornwall. Sleeping in my room was supposed to be a temporary thing, but she didn't show any interest whenever I suggested we make a start on her bedroom. Now with everything else sparkling and comfortable, the time has come. She's fine at school and has made some good friends, but when we're home alone together every little sound sets her on edge.

'I know. Thankfully, Lola's meltdowns are few and far between now. Her feelings often overwhelmed her, and all I could do was to offer to sit and hold her in my arms until she calmed down. Sometimes she simply wanted to be left alone and that scared me. She couldn't put what she was feeling into words and it was as frustrating for her, as it was for me. Ben missed all that, of course.'

Ivy sighs. 'Moving to Cornwall was a courageous move, Jess, but the right one.'

'Thanks, Ivy. I think so, too. It's a pity Lola's best friend, Daisy, lives a good ten-minute car drive away but they're like the terrible twins when they're together,' I chuckle. 'They're boisterous, they shriek a lot and it's so good to see.'

Lola is used to living on a small housing estate, within easy walking distance of the school. It's the sort of community where children are safe to play together in the cul-de-sac because the inhabitants drive slowly, expecting the unexpected like a ball appearing out of nowhere, or kids playing chase and forgetting where they are. Here, there are no friends living on her doorstep to play with unless we arrange a play date. In winter, we look out on to the inky blackness of the moor and dense swathes of trees. In the distance is the sea and when it's blowing a gale, the wind coming off the water can be scary even in the mildest of storms.

'The worst is behind you now, Jess. Keep your focus on the future.'

'Lola moving into her own bedroom is a major milestone for us and I hope she can finally relax and enjoy having her own space again.'

'The upside is that you'll be able to get rid of your double bed and get a decent-sized one in your room.'

'I'll have you know it's very comfortable,' I point out. 'Besides, a king-size bed isn't in the budget.'

'But what if at some point in the future you want to entertain?' Ivy teases me.

'I think I've done all the entertaining I want to do for a while,' I scoff. 'A long while.'

'Aww... one day you will let go of your feelings for Ben. Don't rule out a second chance to find someone new to share your life with.'

I groan. When the man you love falls out of love with you, it's hard to accept. It's true to say that I'm not ready to move on but each day I am getting a little stronger in my resolve not to think about Ben, or what he's doing. 'Well, let's just say that I have enough problems on my plate to keep me fully occupied for the foreseeable future. Is Adam still coming tomorrow?'

Ivy chuckles. 'He sure is, and he's looking forward to it. He calls it a free workout and you know him; he loves showing off his muscles.'

That's very true, but he's also a man you can rely upon, knowing that he'll step up every time. He's like the brother I never had and Lola adores him. From day one he didn't begrudge my close friendship with Jess and now he too is regarded as a part of our extended family.

'It's been a while since he visited so he'll notice the difference. And tell Adam that I've made a large batch of Cornish pasties for lunch. There are also some bottles of Proper Job beer in the fridge with his name on them.'

'Jess, you make me look bad when you spoil him like that!' Ivy quips, laughing. 'I like to keep him on his toes, not inflate his ego. I mean, his favourite Cornish beer and homemade pasties. And what about me?'

'I'm a mum who cooks, you're a pro. Anyway, you're sorted

as unlimited coffee/refills are on hand and Lola and I made a batch of traditional Cornish fairings. Oh, and we can pick as many homegrown strawberries as you can eat!'

'Okay. I'll let you off. We'll be there bright and early. I must go, we have a queue and I need to give the girls a hand. Love you guys!'

2

Where There's a Will, There's a Way

As I watch the crane on the back of the lorry lift the giant bags of chippings off one by one, the driver can see from my reaction that I'm a little overwhelmed.

'Don't worry, your builders will soon get this lot laid.'

His brow furrows as he works the controls of the handheld device. 'It's a bit of a squeeze,' he acknowledges as the last of the twelve, one-ton bags is inched over the high stone wall into an area to the right of the second of the two cobbled courtyards.

'We're laying it ourselves,' I admit.

'Oh. I see. You have a strong team on standby then.'

Hmm… not exactly. 'What we lack in muscle, we make up for in determination. We're hoping to get this lot shifted in two days,' I comment, drolly, and he raises his eyebrows.

The first holidaymakers to rent the newly refurbished Penti Growan – which Cappy told me is Cornish for Granite Cottage – are due next Saturday. I know it's a tall order. There are still some bits and pieces to do to get it ready but as it's adjacent to The Farmhouse, I want to make the outlook as charming as possible.

'In a week's time this sea of chippings will cover the newly created patio to the rear of The Farmhouse and the large corner garden. Then the space the bags are occupying will be transformed into a colourful garden for the rental property, with space alongside to park a car. I'm going to fill it with an array of colourful potted plants and create a little oasis.'

'In which case, I hope the rain they're forecasting for late Saturday doesn't materialise. You're going to need all the luck you can get as that's quite a job. It's a pity the gate isn't wider so I could have dropped this lot a bit closer.'

I nod in agreement, but it is what it is. As for more rain, after a very wet and windy May, I'd hoped June was going to be dry and quite a bit warmer. It has certainly started off with some beautifully sunny days, but the wind can still be biting up here on the moor at times.

'They don't always get it right,' I reply, determined to think positively. 'Anyway, thanks, and this is for you.' Since I moved here I've discovered that for some rather bizarre reason tradesmen aren't always comfortable taking a tip from a woman. The guy stares at me awkwardly.

'That's very kind, but you paid extra for delivery you know.'

I stretch out my hand a little further and he reluctantly accepts it, tilting his head in acknowledgement.

He hesitates for a moment before making eye contact. 'If you ever get stuck,' he adds, 'I'm a carpenter by trade but I can turn my hand to a bit of general building and plumbing. I work at the builder's merchants when they're short-staffed, mainly driving the lorry. My rates are reasonable and I can supply references.'

He pulls a card from his pocket and I take it, gratefully. 'That's useful to know, appreciated.' I hold out my hand.

'My name is Riley, Riley Warren.'

I glance down at the card which says: R. *Warren, Home Repairs – no job too small*. When I look up, his friendly smile reassures me he's genuine and not being pushy. He comes across as an honest, hardworking guy. He's certainly strong and his handshake is firm.

'I'm Jess,' I reply.

'Well, good luck, Jess. I'm sure you'll continue to breathe some life back into Renweneth Farm. For many years they had a permanent farmer's market here and folk came from all over. They sold a bit of everything, and it was a real draw.'

'I didn't know that, Riley. What a great idea.'

'Lots of the more remote places have fallen into disuse. The youngsters go off to the big cities where they can earn a lot more. That's life, eh? What attracted you here?'

'It was becoming a bit much for my grandad to manage now he's on his own.' Truthfully, I'm beginning to think it's a bit much for me too.

'I didn't know you were related to Cappy. I was terribly sorry to hear about his loss, but he's no doubt glad to hand the reins over to you. There's a lot of potential here. Right,' Riley pulls a folded piece of paper from his pocket. 'This is your delivery note… Jess. There's a code on the bottom giving you ten per cent off your next order.'

I burst out laughing. 'It might be a while until I need another load, depending on how it goes, but I'll remember that Riley, thanks.'

The lorry disappears from view and I gaze around at the collection of empty and unused outbuildings. Updating my grandparents' four-bed farmhouse and the two-bed rental has been relatively easy. Aside from employing a plumber, a plasterer and an electrician, I turned myself into a DIYer. Learning a few new skills has been cathartic and keeping busy got me through what has been a painful period in my life.

As for Renweneth Manor in the adjoining courtyard, and the three stone outbuildings opposite Penti Growan, it's true that none of them is beyond saving but all will involve a serious injection of cash.

When my grandparents first arrived here, ten years ago, only the farmhouse and the cottage were habitable, albeit tired-looking rental properties. Once the builders finished the renovations, Cappy and Grandma focused on turning the first of the two large fields that came with the farm into a handy little income stream. One of the attractions of this place was that while the farm complex is a sprawling collection of buildings, it didn't come with untold acres of land. With the abandoned manor house sitting in an orchard the other side of a high stone wall, the dream was to convert the buildings around the vast cobbled courtyard and turn this place into a holiday complex with onsite amenities.

Phase two, several years later, involved getting planning permission to turn Renweneth Manor into bed and breakfast accommodation, and approval for change of use for the row of smaller stone buildings and the small barn to be used as commercial retail space. My grandparents envisaged a farm shop, a second rental cottage and an indoor market which would be a mere walk away for the campers. Much to their annoyance, the application dragged on and on. Then one day, after submitting the fifth set of plans, they finally got the green light. The builders were all lined up and a start date agreed, then Grandma got sick. When a loved one's life is suddenly turned upside down, all you can do is get through it one day at a time and priorities change. The longer-term plan is in place, but that's as far as it's gone.

Cappy and I sat down and did some number crunching. The problem is that while I walked away from my marriage with a lump sum after selling our family home, and a monthly contribution from Ben for child support, it's a lot to juggle. Admittedly, it was my decision to give up work to take over this place and if I hadn't, then Cappy would have sold up. He said it was my inheritance either way. Maybe I didn't want to disappoint him, or perhaps I was just running away and desperate for a lifeline – I don't know which, but Lola and I saw it as a big adventure and a fresh start.

Cappy suggested I think about using both fields to grow the income from the campsite. The outlay for that mainly involved extending the shower and toilet facilities and taking down a part of a stone wall to access the second field. With the work now completed, doubling the number of pitches available has also allowed me to employ a full-time site manager, Arthur Preston.

In my first year here, the rental pitches made a respectable profit, but the new summer season is already looking promising with a bumper number of bookings secured. It will allow me to plough forward but I need to spend every penny wisely as I'm well aware that Renweneth Farm could end up being a money pit.

Still, once the chippings are laid it will instantly tidy what is currently little more than a mud bath when it rains and an ugly eyesore when the sun shines. It's vital because it spoils the ambience and could put people off coming to stay in Penti Growan. Besides, I'm also hoping that this weekend will give me the lift I need to keep my motivation levels up, as I'm flagging a little.

'One day,' I muse out aloud, spinning around, 'this courtyard will be the hub of Renweneth Farm.' I intend to turn it into a place where not only holidaymakers, but equally as importantly, local friends and family will be eager to visit. However, patience is a virtue and I must be patient, because it isn't going to happen overnight.

Glancing at my watch, I see that it's time I jumped in the car for the afternoon school run. Today I'm picking up Lola and three other children we'll be dropping off on our way home. That's what I love about living in the countryside, my neighbours might be scattered around but help is simply a phone call away.

Each day is getting a little easier, but there's still a long way to go until Lola and I feel at home. By that, I mean safe in the knowledge that we're here for good. There are still days we both waver; and nights I spend tossing and turning, wondering whether I made the right decision.

Come on, Jess, that inner voice pipes up. *You were a budget manager for a property developer, so making the figures work is what you do best.* In theory it's not beyond my capabilities, but in practice... well, only time will tell whether I have the stamina, as this isn't a task for the faint-hearted. I do hope I can pull it off, because everything I have is on the line here and my dream is to make a good life for Lola and myself.

'Grandma, Pops!' Lola shrieks, as she runs towards my parents, arms outstretched.

I hurry over and Mum looks up to give me a welcoming smile, as Lola isn't in a hurry to let go.

'My you've grown, young lady!' Dad declares to Lola's delight, as he widens his arms for me to join them. 'And you've got some colour in your cheeks I'm glad to see, Jess.'

'I've been building a stone wall around the new patio area,' I inform him.

'We've got to take a look at that, then. Come on Lola, give me the tour.'

Lola finally releases her hold, grabbing Pops' hand and steering him towards the picket fence in the far corner.

I lean in to give Mum a hug. 'It's good to see you. We'd best tag along. Lola is very proud of herself, she helped me by doing some of the pointing.'

Mum raises her eyebrows. 'She did?'

'Yes, and between us we did an okay job.'

Mum and I link arms and she turns her head to study my face. 'But you're under pressure, I can see that.'

I sigh. 'If this weekend goes well, then I'm in with a chance of getting the finishing touches to Penti Growan done. It's going to be close, though.'

'Everything doesn't have to be perfect, Jess. Just looking around I can't believe how lovely the farmhouse and the cottage look now. It's been four months since our last visit and I'd say you've more than turned the corner.'

'Pulling all the old climbers off Penti Growan was a nightmare of a job and filled several skips, but a quick wire brush and I'm pleased with the result. There's still a bit of painting to finish off inside. Plus, a table and chairs to be unboxed and assembled in the little patio area where the chippings have been off-loaded,' I groan, 'but I'm hopeful it will all get done in time.'

'Well, we've come prepared to make a start.' I glance at Mum's old jeans and her gardening fleece. 'And Dad has brought a whole stack of pots and plants ready to pretty up that side patio. It's a pity Cappy is a bit under the weather, but your dad managed to fill every inch of the car.' Mum stops to stare at the enormous bags and starts laughing. 'Hmm... that's a bit daunting, isn't it? I'm so glad Adam is joining us!'

We chatter away as we catch up with Lola and Dad. They're inspecting our newly built low stone wall.

'I did this bit all along here, Pops,' Lola points out, her face a picture of satisfaction.

'All by yourself?' He stands there looking seriously impressed and her smile grows exponentially.

'Yep!'

'You did an amazing job. All it needs now is for us to fetch the pots from the car to plant up that raised bed. Shall we make a start?'

'Dad... don't you want to come inside for a cup of tea, first? Or at least bring in your overnight bags?' I check, but he's already walking hand in hand with Lola back towards the car.

'We couldn't get to them if we wanted to, the car's packed with plants. Just bring me a mug out here,' he calls over his shoulder. 'We've work to do, haven't we, Lola?'

'Maybe cast your eye over the membrane I laid, Dad. I pegged it well as you said and overlapped the joins, so fingers crossed it'll stop the weeds from coming through.'

The sound of another car arriving has Mum and me turning around, as it's only just coming up to eight o'clock.

'It's Ivy and Adam,' I remark, as I give them a wave. I wasn't expecting them for at least another hour.

'You go and greet them, Jess, and I'll put the kettle on. It's so lovely to get together again... like old times.'

As Mum and I go our separate ways, the words rattling around inside my head are: *yes, but without Ben*. At least it isn't with Ben and his recently acquired girlfriend, Naomi. I just couldn't stomach that right now. Not here, at Renweneth Farm.

'Jess!' Ivy leaps out of the passenger door the second the car stops moving. 'OMG... this is all looking fabulous! No more creepy vines obscuring the windows – it's so pretty now!'

We hug like long-lost sisters, as she gazes over my shoulder at The Farmhouse. 'You pulled it off, Jess. I knew you would. And I'm so glad you kept that wisteria.'

'I simply couldn't bring myself to cut it down to ground level.' The way the main stems intertwine beneath the sitting room window and then branch out either side, forms a perfect heart shape. The now much smaller canopy of new growth runs along above the top of the ground floor windows and the front door, making the front of the old stone farmhouse picture perfect.

'It takes my breath away!' Ivy sighs.

'Oh... it's so good to have you here again. It feels like forever and yet what is it... five months?'

'Yes, I'm really sorry,' she responds, pulling away. 'I'm at the Emporium six days a week. Sundays I'm wiped out. I can only take time off when I can get someone to cover for me, I'm afraid.'

'I understand, Ivy. You don't have to explain.'

'But I promised you I'd help whenever I can,' she beams at me.

'And you are. We've that little lot to shift and there's no one else I could ask, is there?'

Adam walks towards us, smiling. 'It's like a different place already!' he remarks, closing in for a hug. 'It's good to see you thriving here, Jess, and Lola is growing like a weed. It must be all that wonderful country air.'

I gaze across at her as she trots along next to Dad, carefully carrying a tray of six plants as if they're as fragile as hen's eggs.

'Yes, she is, Adam. How are things with you?'

He lifts his right hand, rocking it from side to side. 'The company I'm contracted to have a new guy in charge and he's piling on the pressure. A job takes as long as it takes but he thinks we could work more efficiently. I swear if I hear that word one more time I'm going to explode.'

Glancing up at his face he does look a little hot and bothered.

'I've been there and have the T-shirt. Don't take it personally, Adam.'

'I keep telling him the same thing, Jess. Bosses come and go, so—'

The sound of a tooting horn as yet another car pulls into the farmyard makes all three of us turn around.

'Oh, it's one of my neighbours, Erica. Go on inside, Mum's in the kitchen making tea and coffee. I'll be straight in. There's been a change of plan as Cappy wasn't feeling up to travelling. You're staying in Penti Growan, if you want to put your things in there.'

'We can do that later,' Adam replies, looking purposefully at Ivy. 'I'm up for grabbing a coffee and making a start. After three and a half hours in the car, I'm raring to go.'

'I guess we'll get the tour to see what you've been up to at lunchtime then, Jess,' Ivy rolls her eyes as I head off to see Erica, Lola's best friend Daisy's mum.

Erica opens the boot of her car and disappears from view as I call out. 'Morning.'

She appears in front of me carrying a tray covered in a tea-towel. 'Jess, it seems I've arrived just in time. Daisy and I baked these for your visitors. We figured they'd need something hearty before the work begins.'

'Oh, bless you, Erica!' I reply gratefully, taking the tray from her.

'Saffron buns and my grandma's recipe buttermilk scones. It's just a little thank you for doing the school run all week with Daisy.'

'It's no problem at all. How's your mum doing?'

She pulls a face. 'On the mend but she's not one to listen to advice. Her biggest gripe is her hair. Apparently I don't have the knack and that arm won't be fit to use for a few weeks yet. Bones don't heal overnight, so I'm taking her to the hairdressers later this morning.'

'It can't be easy for either of you,' I empathise. I can imagine that Erica's mum isn't exactly a *patient* patient, I muse to myself. She's a woman who doesn't hold back if she isn't happy about something.

'These are double wrapped, so they might still be warm. I'll leave you to it. My...' she glances at the mass of jumbo bags of chippings, 'you've certainly got your work cut out for you. Charlie says if you need a hand just give a call. He's working night shifts this weekend but if you get stuck he said he can surface at noon tomorrow and is available until five o'clock.'

'Ah, that's really kind of him, Erica. I'll bear that in mind but I'm sure we'll soon make a dent in that little lot.' Charlie Godden is a paramedic, and the night shift can't be easy, especially as it's a long one. 'As soon as Lola's room is finished, Daisy must come for a sleepover to christen it.'

Erica gives me a wink. 'I told you not to worry and the day would come. I'm seeing the changes in Lola with each passing week, Jess. Anyway, the sun is shining and you'll be eager to set your team to work. Hopefully that tray will fuel them!'

3

Avoiding a Drama

With stomachs pleasingly full, we all trail outside. Dad and Lola are looking smug, perched on the new stone wall, drinks in hand and each munching on one of Erica's saffron buns.

'What d'you think, Mum?' Lola asks.

The long, narrow raised bed we created against the tall stone wall that looks out over the narrow strip of moor now has a row of small pops of delightful colour. Ruby red geraniums intermingled with small clumps of greenery, some sporting tiny blue flowers and others white, is a real transformation.

'It's beautiful. What are these?' I ask Dad, stooping to examine the flowers as I don't recognise them.

'It's called *campanula*.'

'Which is simply the Latin name for "little bell",' Mum adds, as Dad is the only true gardener here.

'Precisely,' he takes over. 'It gives good ground cover and the trailing flowers will spill over the edge of the wall to soften the landscaping. It loves a sunny aspect and is hardy and evergreen.'

'In other words,' Mum interjects, 'you don't need to fuss with it.'

'I had a rather special surprise in the back of the car, didn't I Lola?' The two of them exchange a mirthful look.

'You did, Pops.' But instead of blurting it out, she runs her fingers across her lips zip fashion, grinning at me. 'We've put it in the small barn, Mum, and you're not allowed to go in there until Pops and I say so.'

These two love their secrets, but Adam is already rifling through the assortment of spades to find the biggest one and Ivy is wheeling the barrow down to the gates.

At least making an early start it means we can break off for a nice, leisurely lunch. Goodness knows I think we're all going to need it.

'Lola, I brought two little mini tin buckets for you that you can fill with a trowel.' I leave Mum to instruct Lola on the importance of bending her knees and keeping her back straight before she lifts them up. It makes me chuckle to myself, as Dad had me lifting large rockery stones at about her age and Mum would have had a fit if she'd seen the size of some of them. But that's Dad and it's no wonder he often puts his back out, but fortunately I inherited Mum's common sense and somehow managed to avoid the pitfalls.

'It's a pity these couldn't have been dropped a bit closer to The Farmhouse,' Ivy reflects as Adam starts shovelling and she grabs two of the large plastic buckets to follow suit.

'I do feel bad about that, but the lorry was too wide to get through the gate,' I explain.

'They didn't have lorries that big when this was built,' Adam chuckles, which at least makes me feel a little less guilty. 'He did well to get the bags over that high wall into this compact space. Anyway, less chat and more shovelling ladies, as it's going to get hot later on.'

As Mum, Dad and Lola join us, the trek back and forth begins. It seems never-ending and it soon dawns on us that the wheelbarrow isn't a good option. As Dad trundles it along the chippings spills out unless it's less than a third full and, exasperated, he gives up and at one point Mum stops to take a photo with her phone.

'It's like watching worker ants.' She's right, we traipse in a straight line across the courtyard in front of Penti Growan Cottage and through the wooden gate into the L-shaped garden.

'Great job, Lola, but I think it's time to find your sun hat. Anyone else in need of a cold drink? I know I am.'

Mum instantly offers to sort us out.

The chorus of yeses sees her and Lola scuttling back to the kitchen. I put my two empty buckets down next to Adam and pick up a shovel that's half the size of the one he's using so effortlessly.

'How much of this do you think we'll shift today?' I ask.

He stops to lean on his shovel, one hand grazing his chin with his fingers. 'Half of it if we're lucky. Six tons in a day is no mean feat given the distance we're carrying the buckets.'

'And the fact that it's over cobbled ground,' Dad adds, as he's about to set off all loaded up.

When he's out of earshot I turn to Adam and Ivy. 'My concern is that today we're all fresh and tomorrow most of us are going to ache in places we didn't even know we had,' I laugh.

Adam's brow wrinkles. 'It's do-able if it doesn't get too hot. I can always come out and shift some more this evening.'

'No... it's nice to have everyone here and we must make the most of our downtime. Lola and I miss you all. I'll make sure Mum and Lola take frequent breaks, but Dad won't stop. He says he's a workhorse and proud of it. Nothing slows him down.' I roll my eyes and Adam chuckles. At fifty-four Dad acts like he's in his thirties, but he's used to manual labour as he was a landscape gardener for twenty years.

'I hear his business is doing well,' Adam remarks. 'It's quite a change for him spending so much time indoors, I should imagine.'

Dad went self-employed to combine his love of computers with his gardening expertise. Now he works with a national network of smaller contract gardeners, liaising with their clients to design the garden of their dreams. He provides both the visual representations for the customer, as well as a list of all the items, including plants, ready for the guys to start work and make it happen.

'Admittedly he misses getting hands-on but it's less strenuous and he loves it. Mum says he spends every hour he's not working in the garden, anyway. Personally, I think the changes were harder on Mum than Dad.' My lips twitch and Adam's eyes are full of laughter, but he says nothing.

As I finish topping up my buckets, my brain is still ticking over. It's good of everyone to help out but I don't want them all going home totally exhausted. What we need is an extra pair of hands.

After almost three hours of non-stop back and forth, I give Mum a nod.

She glances at her watch. 'Right. I'm heading into the kitchen to warm up the pasties and make a salad for lunch,' Mum states. 'Lola, will you give me a hand setting the table, sweetie?'

'Yes, Grandma.' Lola has been sitting in the shade reading a book for the last half-hour and looks pleased to have something different to do.

'Harry, why don't you dig out our bags from the car and put them in the guest bedroom? Jess can then take Ivy and Adam on a tour of Penti Growan and give them a bit of time to settle in before lunch is ready. Let's say forty minutes guys, and lunch will be served!'

Bless Mum, she can see we're all beginning to flag a little, having had only two short coffee breaks.

'I guess we've had our orders. It's time to down tools.' I lower my voice as Mum disappears. Dad shrugs his shoulders and then strides over to the car to rescue the overnight bags.

'Well, I'm more than ready for a break,' Ivy declares, leaning back and stretching her arms up into the air. 'Don't your muscles ever ache, Adam?'

'I'm used to it. This is no different to a light session in the gym. But this is more fun.'

'Fun?' I question, raising an eyebrow at him. 'Seriously? Come on, it's time to put down the shovels and check out my handiwork.'

Ivy and I link arms, heading to Penti Growan, leaving Adam to fetch the bags from their car.

'You did a great job with the front door, Jess. There's something about a traditional old oak door that says welcome, isn't there?'

'All it needed was a good sanding down and a couple of coats of oil applied with a lint-free cloth. I bought the door knocker at an antiques fair in Polreweek. It needed something in keeping with the rustic look, and a wrought iron lion's head is traditional. As you can see, I wasn't able to do the same with The Farmhouse's front door. There were a few rotten bits that needed chiselling out and filling, so I had to paint it.'

'That is a shame,' Ivy says, turning to stare at it. 'But it's a really pretty soft blue.'

I shake my head, smiling. 'Let's not talk about blue and anyway, it's French grey.'

'What was Lola's reaction to the test square in her bedroom?'

As I push open the door to Penti Growan, I put my thumb up in the air triumphantly. 'It looks a bit odd until I can do the whole wall, as the rest of the room is white. I had to do two coats to cover the awful racing green, but her bed is now in situ and I'm sure she'll show you around after lunch.'

Ivy mutters a 'Wow,' as we step from the small hallway into the sitting room at the rear of the rental cottage. 'This doesn't even feel like the same place. This is glorious and so cosy, Jess. And what a bonus to look out on to those bay hedges to the rear.'

Ivy turns on her heels, to walk over and run her hand over the mantelshelf above the small wood burner.

'I found that piece of wood in one of the outbuildings,' I

admit. 'Mind you, the carved wooden corbels to support it cost fifty quid from the local joiner's, but they were still a bargain.'

'And you put this up?'

'Yes. I'm now a dab hand with a drill, but it took two of us to lift the wood up to sit on the mounts.'

'How... who did you get to help?'

'The window cleaner. He saw me struggling to get it across the courtyard with the sack trucks and even though I said I was fine, he was very insistent.'

'I'm not surprised. You shouldn't be doing stuff like that on your own,' Ivy lectures me, as Adam steps through the door.

'Like what?' he asks.

'Lifting that mantelshelf into place,' Ivy states, pointedly.

'Jess, seriously?' Adam shakes his head at me.

'I didn't do it by myself, I just said I'd intended doing it by myself. Moving stuff with the sack trucks is easy and I was going to jack it up to the right height with the help of some wooden crates.'

'Fair play to you for having a go, Jess, but you have Lola to think about. What if you'd hurt yourself?'

At the time I knew I was attempting the impossible but getting help for small jobs isn't easy around here. Finding a builder is equally challenging.

Ivy is still trailing around the room, taking in every little detail.

'Did you do all of this yourself?' She sounds amazed.

'I had an electrician in to do a couple of small jobs. Moving three sockets and putting up a couple of complicated light fittings. And a kitchen guy to install the traditional double butler's sink. Now he was handy, as he showed me where the isolation valves are and how to mend a washer.'

Ivy laughs, still intent on taking in the little details. 'Ooh... I love these curtains.'

'Lola chose the fabric.' Tiny hares run and leap across the soft cream background and it's fun, as well as giving that country vibe.

'Oh, Adam... wouldn't it be lovely to live somewhere like this?'

Adam stares at Ivy as if she's lost her mind. 'Like we could afford it.'

But Ivy's mind is elsewhere and it's time to leave them to it.

'Inside there are still a few items on the snagging list I need to sort out, like the lock on the bathroom door which keeps sticking. I haven't had time to oil it yet, so beware. The keys are on the windowsill in the kitchen. See you in a bit then, and thanks for coming. Not just to bail me out, but it's so good to see you both, it really is.'

I beat a hasty retreat as a lump is rising in my throat. I was speaking from the heart.

After lunch, Lola insists on taking Mum and Ivy upstairs to see her bedroom and explain what else we have to do to get it finished. Adam says he'll take a look at the dodgy lock in Penti Growan for me, and Dad suggests the two of us have a wander. Which means there's something he wants to say while Mum is out of earshot.

Stepping over the threshold of The Farmhouse, I follow his lead. The path bears to the right, which takes us through the stone archway into what I call the main courtyard, and the garden surrounding Renweneth Manor.

'The grass is nice and tidy,' he remarks. 'The car parking area down by the gate needs a good weeding I see.'

'I know. There's a guy who comes round with a sit and ride mower on a trailer. He does the two fields as well, but I really do need to employ a gardener. The problem is this side of the wall is out of sight and I keep forgetting.'

'I'm not criticising, the important thing is that you're keeping the ivy at bay on that side wall, which is a good thing. It destroys the pointing between the stonework if you let it run amok.'

Dad tells me that every time he visits. The building is structurally sound, but inside is another story.

'And those two oak trees need a bit of attention. If you were closer I could get mates rates for you, but I don't know anyone down this way. I could ask around though.'

'Thanks Dad, but it's fine. One of the locals will no doubt recommend someone when I can get around to it.'

'And I'm just pointing this out, but once the chippings are shifted if you're going to use that area as parking and a private patio for Penti Growan, it'll need fencing off. Your holidaymakers won't be wanting to see strangers walking past them when they're sat at their garden table eating, will they?'

'It's on my list.' I know he's right, but first things first. It's time to change the subject. 'Is everything okay at home?'

'Champion. Our next-door neighbours are watering the garden for us this weekend.' He draws to a halt, turning to face me. 'This is a lot you've taken on, Jess. It's not for us to interfere, but you know me, I'll always say what I'm thinking and offer advice whether you want it or not. It's how I am. It's just that it worries your mum and me, not just the pressure on you, but the way you're pushing yourself. Cappy's not expecting you to realise his dream, you know.'

'What is it you want to say, Dad? Just spit it out.'

'When he suggested you sell off this plot and Renweneth Manor, he meant it.'

I glance at him, appalled by the thought.

'I don't know why you're making that face, Jess,' Dad states, firmly. 'Unless you step through the archway you honestly don't know it's here. If that was filled in, with the parking down by the gates, the orchard off to the side, and a large tidy garden to the front, it'd sell easily. Even as it stands. And there's a sea view from the back. Someone with a pot of cash could end up with a comfortable six-bed property that would be worth a bit. Think about what you could do with the money.'

Once a week, right up until a couple of months before

Grandma died, she'd unlock the heavily carved front door to Renweneth Manor and wander around each room. She was happy as long as there were no new holes in the ceilings from falling plaster. The joy for her was in appreciating the beautiful and irreplaceable features, like the original inglenook fireplace in the kitchen with its own bread oven set back into the wall. That's the real reason I come over most mornings before I start work to potter in the garden. Just yanking off the ivy and grabbing a few weeds makes me feel close to her.

'Look, I know you're worried but finance is my thing, Dad. I'm being cautious about what I spend precisely because I don't want to sell anything off unless I'm left with absolutely no alternative. Being my own boss means I'm here for Lola if she's unwell and we get to spend way more quality time together than we did before. And yes, our first winter wasn't easy but we were adjusting to our new lifestyle and the... um, change in circumstances.' I really don't want to bring up Ben's name. 'Lola has made some lovely friends and now that Penti Growan is getting bookings, we'll have guests a stone's throw away as well as our happy campers. This is going to be a marvellous place to grow up.' That makes Dad smile.

'Your mum warned me you wouldn't listen. It's not that we doubt you, Jess, we just don't want you running yourself into the ground. We could always move here, you know, so we'd be on your doorstep. That's the beauty of working online.'

My parents moved home when I was eleven years old, so that I could walk to school with my friends. We lived a bit further away and it would have involved a car, or a bus journey for me. Dad left behind a beautiful garden and had to start over again. Now he works from home, my parents regard working on the garden together as their quality time. Mum is happy to spend hours alongside him, toiling away like an apprentice as he instructs her on what he wants done. It never occurs to him that she does it out of love more than interest; personally, I think she'd rather spend more time with her nose in a book, or cooking. Anyway, I have no intention of letting them make that sacrifice for me again.

'Dad, we'd drive each other mad you and I, and we both know it.'

We grin at one another. 'All right… I know when I'm beaten. At least your mum listens to me on occasion, even if you rarely do,' he moans, playfully.

'What did Grandma used to say? Something about people who live in glass houses shouldn't throw stones, I think.'

'Cheeky! I'll back off but the offer stands, Jess. And… this is a bit of a favour really, but Cappy was gutted he couldn't join us today. That's three trips in a row now he's backed out of, even though he misses you and Lola so much. He assured your mum that he's on the mend, however, I think it would cheer him up to come and see for himself what you've done before too long. I won't poke my nose in anymore, for now anyway.'

I think what Dad is trying to tell me, in a roundabout way, is that Cappy isn't quite ready to face the ghosts of the past by coming here. Perhaps it would be easier if, for his first trip back to the farm since Lola and I settled here, it was just the three of us. I can understand that, so I'll think of something.

Dad wraps his arms around me and I know that if I ever have a problem, he and mum would be in the car without giving a thought to anything else – their precious oasis of a garden included.

'Hi, is this Riley?' I ask, pressing the phone to my ear as I can hear the sound of cars passing in the background.

'Yes. Who's that?'

'Jess Griffiths from Renweneth Farm.'

'Oh, hello Jess, how can I help?'

I wave the card he gave me back and forth in my free hand nervously. 'I'm in desperate need of some help tomorrow. I don't suppose you're free, by any chance. Even if it's just for a few hours it would—'

'I'm installing a new handbasin and toilet in a cloakroom, but I can easily put it off until Monday evening. I have a key as the couple are away on holiday.'

I squeeze my eyes shut and mouth a silent *yes*. Now for the difficult part.

'You have no idea how grateful I am. Having enticed family and friends to Cornwall for the weekend, I'm in danger of sending them back home utterly exhausted. There's still quite a lot to do, as it's not just chippings. My dad brought a carload of plants. Knowing him, he'll want to pot them himself.'

Jess! That inner voice berates me. *You're rambling. Get on with it.*

'The thing is that I have a whole list of jobs that need tackling and I'd just like you to consider.' I pause to take a deep breath. 'Not all at once, obviously, but it would go a long way to reassuring my overly caring visitors that I have some regular help. Does that make any sense to you?'

He clears his throat, probably stifling a laugh as I'm making a complete fool of myself.

'Okay. Just so I don't mess up your little plan, I turn up out of the blue to what... check how it's going, then roll up my sleeves and get stuck in?'

'Yes. Exactly that. Everyone thinks I'm in over my head, which I am but I don't want them stressing over it. And I'm not joking about that list of jobs. There's enough to keep you busy every moment you can spare but I realise I can't monopolise your time.'

'Don't worry, we'll agree an hourly rate and take it from there. I believe in being fair. If you present me with something I can't tackle, I'll tell you up front. If I get an emergency call I'll expect you to understand, it's quid pro quo.'

I like that he's being up front, even if it means I have to wait my turn sometimes.

'And I hope your visitors have their waterproofs ready for tomorrow, rain is incoming. I'll arrive fully equipped. A little rain doesn't stop me; I've lived in Cornwall long enough to know it has higher rainfall totals than the rest of the United Kingdom.'

'And why is that?'

'That would be down to its location on the southwestern tip of the country.'

Hmm. Obviously that means something, but it's lost on me. 'Of course… and thank you, Riley. You have no idea what a weight you've lifted off my shoulders for tomorrow.'

'That's what I'm here for. A lot of my clients call me Mr Fix It behind my back.' He laughs and I'm not sure whether or not he's joking. 'I'll be there around ten o'clock, as no doubt your visitors will want to enjoy a relaxing breakfast before day two begins.'

'Well, if any of them are aching as much as I am tonight, then I have no idea how jolly they're going to be in the morning. And thanks for rejigging your schedule.'

'You're Cappy's granddaughter, it's no problem at all.'

4

Many Hands Make Light Work

Peeking out of the window at six o'clock on what is a decidedly grey Sunday morning, my spirits immediately sink. After a wonderful evening with Adam and Dad manning the new outdoor barbecue, Mum, Ivy, Lola and I sat back praising their skills. We were grateful to rest our legs ready for today. It looks like Riley is right, the grey storm clouds are already gathering and if I was a betting person I'd say it'll start before we break for lunch.

'Ha!' I mutter to myself, glancing around quickly to check that I haven't disturbed Lola. Then I remember that she slept in her own room again for the second time last night. It's little short of a miracle as it isn't even finished so she's using the rollout bed. Maybe this means the worst of her problems really are behind us.

Annoyingly, I'm wide awake now, although I have no idea what disturbed me. Maybe I was missing the familiar sound of Lola's breathing interspersed with her constant squirming around. In the still of the night, I did find the silence slightly unnerving as I seem to effortlessly slip back into that ingrained city mode. Although I don't miss the jarring sounds of motorbikes and cars with big bore exhausts that make the walls vibrate, it's rare to hear vehicles passing the farm in the early hours of the morning.

Pulling on my summery cotton dressing gown I quietly make my way downstairs. Instead of putting on the kettle and risk waking up the entire household with its whistle, I put a small pan of water on the range to boil. A sudden creak has me spinning around, teaspoon in hand, only to see Mum standing there looking floral in her best white silk kimono covered in cherry blossom.

'The birds woke me and I've been lying there hoping you'd stir. It's like old times, isn't it, Jess?' Mum remarks in a half-whisper.

She walks towards the oversized scrubbed pine table. It's not exactly antique, but it's probably older than I am. Every little dent, and ding, is a part of its history.

I nod my head in agreement. 'Tea?' I check, although I know full well Mum will only drink coffee first thing if she's feeling a little jaded.

'Please. I love this time of the morning before your dad is awake. I envy the fact that he can drift off to sleep easily and seems to have an internal alarm clock that wakes him naturally around seven each day.'

Carrying the mugs across to the table, as I lower myself on to the seat next to Mum I groan involuntarily, which raises a smile.

'My shoulders are aching this morning,' she confides in me. 'How are you doing?'

'Same here, and also my calf muscles,' I admit.

'You were relentless, Jess. Try to pace yourself today. Still, the half of the patio area we did manage to cover lifted the space instantly, didn't it.'

My face brightens. 'Do you want to take a sneak peek at our hard work in the light of a new day?'

'I'm game if you are. I'll grab my jacket on the way out, though, as it looks a tad chilly.'

We bundle up, but as soon as we step out it's definitely a lot more blustery than either of us imagined.

'At least the mud pit is gone,' I whisper as I gaze around. Albeit that the black membrane still to be covered seems to stretch out endlessly. That's more than half of the area and I can only hope I got the maths right when I ordered the white Chard flint.

On the air I can smell the distinct bitterness from the geranium leaves intermingling with what I assume is the merest hint of a perfume from the campanulas.

'It's an instant garden, Jess, and you made the right decision.'

We saunter along, talking quietly, and end up in the far corner looking across at Penti Growan, but there's no sign of movement.

'I fancy Adam wasn't quite his usual jolly self yesterday,' Mum remarks. 'They're not having problems, are they?'

'No. Nothing like that. Just work worries. Hopefully it'll sort itself out.'

'Dad didn't go overboard when he had his little chat with you, did he?' Mum's eyes sweep over my face, her brow furrowed.

I shake my head. 'No. I know I get het up because things aren't moving along quite as quickly as I'd hoped, but a stroke of luck means I've found a local tradesman who's a bit of an all-rounder.'

'You have? That's wonderful news, Jess. Did you tell Dad?'

'Oh, I forgot to mention it.'

'Well, you have no idea how delighted he'll be to hear it. You know he gets hung up on the minutest of details sometimes. If he says anything about those two oak trees to me one more time I'm going to stick my fingers in my ears. They've been there well over a hundred years, and I have no doubt they'll be around for a few more. They're healthy and strong, so don't let him panic you. Another year's growth won't make that much difference and by then you'll have more time to turn your attention to getting them thinned out a little.'

Dad always implies that Mum is the only worrier, but he worries about Mum worrying about me. Annoyingly, I'm equally as impatient as Dad, constantly wanting to speed things up.

'And he has good credentials, this man?'

I raise my mug to my mouth, taking a slurp and giving a little nod of my head. The least I say the better, but the builders' merchants wouldn't employ Riley if he wasn't trustworthy and reliable. I have no reason to believe that he won't turn up later this morning, but my parents won't be the only ones uttering a sigh of relief if and when he does. And not just because with the odd spot of rain already being carried on the wind, the more muscle we have the better; I want to ensure everyone sets off for home by four o'clock at the latest. With a three-hour-plus drive ahead of them, I don't want Dad or Adam driving home worn out and tired.

By ten o'clock breakfast feels like an age ago already. It's hot work and the fine drizzle seems to seep its way into every little nook and cranny of the waterproofs. Lola thought it was great fun at first and it was, because everyone's spirits were high. We laughed off the damp but now she's pouty and I encourage Mum to go back inside with her.

'She's bored, bless her, but she's done well. I'll get Lola to dry her hair and change her clothes, then we'll start prepping the veggies for lunch,' Mum says, out of earshot of anyone else.

'Thanks. Everything's in the fridge, including a large joint of beef. Lola knows how to make Yorkshire puddings, just make sure she remembers how many people will be eating. What if we aim for lunch at one o'clock?'

A small white van drives through the gate and Mum looks at me, her eyes lighting up. 'Is this your builder guy? I guess that will make seven for lunch then, perfect timing!'

Riley is already striding towards us, a big smile on his face.

'Morning! I thought I'd drop by and see how it's going. Do you need an extra pair of hands?'

Our little team stop what they're doing to check out my visitor just as the heavens decide to open. Mum acknowledges Riley with a little wave before grasping Lola's hand and making a dash for The Farmhouse. The rest of us tighten our hoods, although it's probably a waste of time.

'That would be great, thank you. This is Riley, everyone. That's my dad, Harry,' I begin the introductions and while the handshakes might be a tad damp, Riley's appearance seems to have revitalised the general mood.

'I'm Adam and this is my wife, Ivy.'

Ivy gives Riley a smile, her interest piqued.

'It's great to meet you all,' he replies. 'Right, put me to work.'

'That would be great if you have time. I thought you had a plumbing job today?' I can see that Dad is wondering what's going on and it needs some sort of explanation. 'And, um... I have that list of jobs ready for you Riley, but it's inside.'

'Oh, it's no problem, Jess. There's been a delay so I can't do the installation until tomorrow.'

'That's our gain then, Riley. You couldn't have timed it better as we had a bit of a late start.' Dad hands Riley the shovel Mum was using. 'We're winning, but no one wants to be hanging around out here longer than need be.'

Riley takes the shovel, giving Dad an affirming tilt of his head, and seconds later we're all hard at work. Ivy keeps glancing at me, curious about the stranger in our midst. However, there's no time to stop and talk and even when the rain eases off again the drizzle doesn't stop.

As noon approaches the sun puts in an unexpected appearance when there's a sudden break in the clouds. It's heartening and, to be honest, it's such hot work that we'd all be feeling a little damp and bedraggled anyway. With the end in sight it gives us that final burst of energy, thinking longingly of a hot shower and dry clothes.

Half an hour later, we can all stand back and there's that satisfying moment when you know that a job has been well done. The Farmhouse now sits in an attractive, low-maintenance garden. It looks loved now; colourful and quaint in a way only a beautiful old building like this can. For many people, moving to the country is an aspiration which never comes to fruition. For those who do take the step, it changes your life forever in ways you can't even imagine.

'Well guys, you've all more than earnt a slap-up Sunday roast and I might be biased, but I think my mum makes one of the best. In thirty minutes it'll be on the table, so I suggest we all go inside, grab a shower and some dry clothes. Riley, naturally you'll stay for lunch but um...'

His face lights up and he points to the van. 'I always have spare clothes on hand and I never say no to a meal I didn't cook myself.'

This man is a total star and I can see by the look on Dad's face that he's curious to know more. However, no one is in the mood to hang around as it's a huge relief knowing the job is done. In fairness, Dad's daughter and his granddaughter live in a cottage on the edge of a moor and I guess it's reassuring to know there's someone on hand if I get a burst pipe, or something. It's fortunate, too, that Riley is the sort of man who's instantly likeable and he's not a complainer.

Ivy pipes up. 'Riley, why don't you head over to Penti Growan with us? There's an en suite shower in the second bedroom going free.'

Oh no... this is her excuse to get him chatting. I give Riley an anxious look, but as our eyes connect I can see he has my back as he gives me an almost imperceptible wink. 'Thanks, Ivy. I'll collect my things.'

Ivy looks extremely chuffed with herself but there's nothing I can do about it. Adam insists on folding up the empty jumbo bags and putting away the tools while Dad and I head inside. I can only hope that good manners will mean my loved ones won't give Riley a grilling during lunch. But what is heartening is that even though Dad will insist on potting up the remainder of the plants to make Penti Growan's parking area more attractive, the clouds are beginning to drift away. Hopefully we're on target to see the mass exodus by late afternoon and Riley certainly played a part in that. What a result!

Mum's cheeks colour up when Adam is the first to clear his

plate and she asks if he'd like seconds. She glances at Riley questioningly, and he offers up his plate too.

'Best Sunday roast I've had in a long while, Celia. That certainly hit the spot, thank you.'

'It's my pleasure, Riley. It's been quite a weekend and I'll admit I was flagging and ready to quit. Your arrival meant I could leave the action with good grace,' Mum chuckles.

'Ah, but few people can cook like that. What do you say Adam?'

'He's right, Celia.'

'Hey, what about my homemade Cornish pasties?' I join in, pulling Adam's leg.

'Oh, they're fabulous but...' he grins at me. 'Sorry, Jess, nothing beats a roast lunch and those Yorkshire puddings, Lola, were a-maz-ing!'

The banter around the table reminds me of Christmas Day when everyone is in high spirits. Riley just seems to fit right in and everyone assumes he's the guy who's been helping me out. In truth, I've employed a string of tradesmen with varying levels of success, as none of them were multi-skilled. The first plumber turned up once and then wouldn't return my calls, even though he'd left the job half-done. The electrician was better when I could actually get him here, but it would take numerous phone calls and delays due to *emergencies*. One day I was at the end of my tether, and I left him a message to say that my job was an emergency because I was about to blow a fuse. He knew exactly what I meant and was there promptly at nine o'clock the next morning.

'Pops, will we have time to do that surprise for Mum?' Lola blurts out, her eyes gleaming mischievously.

Dad leans forward, gaining her full attention. 'I do hope so! I think she more than deserves it, don't you, Lola?'

All eyes are on me now. 'Well, today I'm really grateful to you all for rolling up your sleeves to get me to that finish line,' I murmur, feeling a tad hot and bothered by the scrutiny.

'It's also good to know you have someone like Riley here on hand, Jess.' I glance at Dad and he looks like he's just getting started. Goodness knows what he's going to say next, but just as I'm about to interrupt, Mum takes over.

'That's the wonderful thing about living in a rural community, I'm assuming you live locally too, Riley?'

'I'm originally from York, but now I live about a twenty-minute drive from here. Who can resist the lure of rescuing an old cottage and turning it from a ruin into a home? It's the dream, right?'

Dad looks suitably impressed but that's a complete surprise to me.

'Well,' Ivy muses, 'I'm sure Jess will be able to keep you busy for quite a while, Riley. But watch out… she picks up things quite easily and she'll be looking over your shoulder and gleaning whatever she can.' Ivy stares directly at me, holding my gaze for a few seconds. 'She's certainly mastered a few surprising new skills, that's for sure.'

Now she's curious about how long Riley has been around and I need to nip this in the bud.

'Mum,' I interject, diplomatically changing the subject. 'Can I give you a hand serving dessert?'

Everyone's eyes light up when Mum informs us all that there's apple pie and custard, and if anyone wants seconds there's plenty to go round as she made three of them. Seriously, any calories I've worked off are about to be heaped back on, but I'm happy; this couldn't have gone any better if I'd planned it and I owe Riley big time.

I've learnt two things this weekend. Friends and family will go to great lengths to help someone they love. However, as kind and generous as it is for them to offer to come and help out, it's not fair of me to encourage it. What I desperately need is quality time with my family and friends, not stressful weekends where I end up feeling guilty for sending them home in need of a few days off to recover. I want this to be a place they come to relax and have fun.

The second thing is that, for some inexplicable reason, sometimes a stranger like Riley can understand the dilemma that causes. I can only thank my lucky stars that our paths crossed, as I need whatever professional help I can get. I don't want my family thinking *poor Jess* because that isn't the case. I just need a builder who will turn up when he says he will and it looks like I might just have found the right man.

5

Finally, We've Turned Yet Another Corner

'Welcome to Renweneth Farm. I'm Jess and this is my daughter, Lola.'

'Hi Jess and Lola. My, what a beautiful setting,' the woman gushes. 'We're so in need of a break and we're really looking forward to some long walks on the moor and down on the beach.'

Her husband disappears to fetch the luggage, as I hand over the keys to Penti Growan. It's been a hectic five days doing the finishing touches, but I got there in the end.

'I hope you'll make yourself at home. The courtyard garden and car parking space to the side of the cottage is for your exclusive use. Lola will call in every day at five o'clock to water the pots. The fridge is stocked with milk, eggs, and bacon from Treeve Perrin Farm. Their produce is organic, and they also sell fresh vegetables and a whole range of various meats, cheeses, chutneys and jams. If you want to eat out, there's a list of restaurants within a thirty-minute car ride in the folder on the kitchen worktop. Any problems, day or night, my mobile number is on the inside cover.'

Lola was a little disappointed that our first guests in the cottage are a couple and not a family. Luckily, today she's made some new friends, a boy a year older than her and his sister, who is two years younger. They arrived the day before yesterday and hired a caravan pitch for a week. As luck would have it, when they pulled up I was talking to my site manager, Keith, and ended up having a little chat with them. They're a nice family and I said I'd take Lola over to meet them. She invited them to a picnic tea in her treehouse this afternoon and we're about to hurry back to the kitchen to take a batch of cupcakes out of the oven.

'Mum, why is it that some kids get to take time off to go away when everyone else is in school?'

Is it my imagination, or are Lola's questions getting more challenging these days? I reflect, casting around for a suitable response.

'I'm sure there are lots of reasons, Lola. Unfortunately, not every parent can take time off work during the school holidays. We're lucky, because we live here, but like the lady we were just talking to, sometimes people need a break and can't wait.'

Opening the picket gate to the side garden and walking around to the rear of The Farmhouse, Lola is deep in thought.

'Riley told me he has a little boy named Ollie. Did you know that Mum?'

It's so typical of Lola to flit from one topic to another. 'No, I didn't.'

'Riley said he doesn't get to talk to him very often.'

As she follows me into the kitchen I can see that the conversation isn't going to end there but judging by the wonderful smell wafting out the cupcakes are ready. I make a beeline for the range.

'He's about the same age as me,' she continues.

Grabbing the oven gloves, I slide out the tray and place it on the cooling rack.

'It's not really polite to ask people personal questions, Lola.'

She looks at me, frowning.

'Maybe it's best to talk about other things, Lola. When Riley's here working he would probably appreciate being left alone to get on with whatever he's doing.'

Riley has popped in twice after work to do a couple of small jobs, like putting in an outside tap over by the small barn and clearing some weeds that were blocking the guttering on the side of Renweneth Manor.

'But he's our friend, Mum, isn't he?'

It's hard not to sigh. 'Yes, Lola, and it's perfectly fine to say hello. But we must bear in mind that he's a really busy man.'

'Okay, Mum. I understand. Can we paint my new chest of drawers tomorrow?' And just like that, much to my relief, she's on to the next thing.

'Of course we can. That's the last job on our list, isn't it?'

She puckers up her face. 'Can I have some bookshelves above it?'

'I thought you liked using the windowsill for your books?'

'I do, but last night when Daisy came for the sleepover we piled them up on the floor and then put one of my snuggle blankets on it instead so we could use it as a seat. The floor was lava,' she explains in all seriousness.

'It was?'

'Yes.'

Obviously it's a game they were playing and will probably play next time Daisy stays over again.

'Right, I see. In which case, let's turn it into a window seat with cushions and I'll sort out some shelves.'

'Thanks, Mum. You're the best! Can we paint them white, though, as I want to decorate the edges with the glow in the dark stars Grandma gave me last weekend.'

Scooping the cupcakes out of the baking tray, I make a mental note. Wood for shelves, brackets and fixings. Oh, and a piece of foam and some fabric to make a seat for the windowsill.

'While these are cooling, can you mix up some icing sugar please Lola and I'll make the sandwiches.'

'Will do, Mum.' She trots off to the larder, leaving me marvelling at the change in her. It was so the right thing to discourage Ben from coming down when my parents, Adam and Ivy were here. However, I know that I can't put him off for much longer as naturally Lola misses her dad and weekly video calls just aren't the same.

The truth is that I don't relish the idea of Ben and his girlfriend sleeping under my roof, even though he was always close with my grandparents. It's wrong, just wrong and I'm not sure how I'm going to get my head around it. Surely he can understand that.

With Lola deciding to add cocoa powder to the icing sugar, she's in full-on concentration mode as she uses the hand whisk to smooth out the powdery lumps. My phone starts to ring and when I glance at it, it's Ivy.

'Hey, you. How's it going?'

'Awful.'

'Really? What's gone wrong?'

'Everything!' Ivy's voice is wobbly and it's obvious she's walking as she talks.

'Where are you?'

'I've just left work. I'm going home early as I have a really bad headache that I can't shift. Oh, Jess... I don't know what I'm going to do. Everything is beginning to fall apart, including me.'

'Hang on a second, Ivy.'

I put the phone close to my chest and wave my hand to attract Lola's attention.

'I'm going to have a quick chat with Ivy, I'll be just outside the back door if you need me, all right?' I whisper.

'No probs, Mum. I'm going to do icing swirls on the top.'

A few seconds later as I put the phone back up to my ear, it's obvious Ivy is stifling a sob.

'Are you crying?'

'Just snivelling, but people are beginning to stare at me so I'm heading back to the car as fast as my legs will go without actually running.' Her breathing is erratic and she sounds distraught. 'Adam walked off a job this morning after a row with his new boss and, as if I wasn't stressed enough from his call, this afternoon the alarm in the café went off twice within an hour.

I swear I was on the verge of grabbing the scissors and cutting the damn wires until someone pointed out I might electrocute myself. I'm on my way to have it out with my landlord, but really I want to go in search of Adam.'

This is one of those occasions when what Ivy needs is a reassuring hug, not platitudes.

'Slow down, Ivy, and take a few deep breaths. Come on… get yourself back under control.'

I give her a minute or two and wait until I can no longer hear that awful, raspy sound. 'That's better. Now, start at the beginning. What sort of frame of mind was Adam in when he called?'

'He's done with it, Jess. This is the third company he's worked with in the last four years. Oh, it all starts out well because they need hard-working guys who don't let them down. He's never late for work and rarely takes a day off sick.'

'That's a problem, is it? I mean, I assume that as a contractor they only pay him for the hours he works?'

'Yes, but some of the guys do jobs for more than one firm and if they can get a higher rate elsewhere, they'll call in sick.'

'Oh, I see. But Adam wouldn't do that.'

'No. He plays fair, but they don't play fair back, Jess. I have no idea where he is. Adam rang to say he'd quit and that he'd see me at home tonight. Then he switched off his phone and I've heard nothing since.'

'Oh, Ivy. Adam isn't a quitter and he must really have been at the end of his tether. He needs a little time to cool down, that's all. He's got a lot of contacts in the trade, so perhaps he's doing the rounds in person to get some leads.'

'But he walked out on a client because of a call he received from his boss. That's a different thing altogether. The homeowner had no idea Adam had just been told that instead of being paid for the full five days' work, he was going to be docked a day's wage.'

'Why?'

'Because this new guy wants to up the profits. Each job will be allocated less time in future. All of the contractors are complaining but no one walks off the job, it's not professional. Word will get out about what Adam did and it'll be made to look like he's unreliable. His mates are up in arms about it, but everyone has bills to be paid and it's not the first time this sort of thing has happened. Then customers wonder why corners get cut, it's ludicrous.'

I get her drift because when all is said and done it's not the client's fault.

'But he's still self-employed, so can't he approach some of his former clients direct?'

'He hasn't taken on any private jobs now for a couple of years. When he started up it took him a while to get a list of regular clients and after that it was word of mouth recommendations that kept him busy. It would be like starting all over again.' Her voice begins to waver.

'Look Ivy, just get yourself home and have a strong cup of tea while you wait for Adam to return.'

'He thinks he's let me... us, down, Jess. It's not his fault though. I have no idea what we're going to do. We can use the nest egg we've saved towards a deposit on a house to supplement my income for a while, but that will devastate him. He'll end up taking a labouring job on a building site or something just to make ends meet, I know him.'

'All you can do is be there waiting for him when he returns. He's going to have a lot of pent-up emotion to shed before he'll be able to think clearly about what happens next. If you need any moral support, or a listening ear, I'm a phone call away. Stay strong for him and try not to panic if he says some wild things first off. Adam's got a good head on him and he's not a defeatist, so he'll think of something. If you get a chance, text me later on to let me know how you're doing. You're both in my thoughts, Ivy, and sometimes things happen for a reason. It's hard to assess it at the time but looking back things becomes clearer. Not unlike my situation. It hasn't been easy but I'm beginning to see what I couldn't see before.'

'Which was?' Ivy sounds confused.

'That Ben fell out of love with me quite a while ago, I just refused to believe it. When something isn't working it needs fixing.'

After a few seconds of total silence, we sigh in tandem. 'Life, eh?' Ivy moans. 'It's a good job we're all made of strong stuff. Thanks for listening, Jess. What would I do without you? I'll be in touch later. Mwah.'

True friends are few and far between, but Ivy is one of the best and I'm here for her because she's always had my back.

With Lola and her two new friends settled into the treehouse in the orchard next to Renweneth Manor, I'm working in the garden behind The Farmhouse and within earshot. I can hear them chattering away as they tuck into their picnic.

Dad's surprise when they visited was that he'd bought me an olive tree. It's something I've always wanted but never got around to treating myself to. Here I have all the space I need and while Dad wanted to plant it himself, there simply wasn't enough time to fit everything in.

Today's little project is to give it a home in front of the six-foot high stone boundary wall. It will add a little colour with its silvery-grey leaves, but also some height with that bushy head and robust stem. Yesterday Lola and I carried a pile of stones from a stack leaning up against the small barn. They're all relatively flat, so they were probably set aside for a reason. Some are covered in a pretty green moss, so they've obviously been there for a very long time. I'm going to have a go at building a low dry-stone wall, as I want to turn it into a feature. And it's easier than having to mix up cement, as I had to do with the random-shaped stones I used for the flower beds.

The sound of the kids' excited voices as they talk over each other is a real tonic. I kneel and begin the task of what is, in effect, a stone jigsaw puzzle to sort out. It's a case of layering them up so that they don't list to one side. If I can get them to interlink it will give the wall stability. It reminds me of the hours that Lola and I spent building all manner of things with those little plastic bricks before she got into arts and crafts.

I love doing jobs like this, it gives me time to think. With so many campers coming and going during our peak season, Lola is definitely more open to making new friends which is a huge positive. The problem is that although the campsite is on our doorstep, it's not close to The Farmhouse. Behind Penti Growan there's a wide corridor of trees that run the length of what was formerly the farmyard. It's now a general car park that's hardly used. At the far end there's an enormous hay barn and adjacent to that are the gates to the site. It's great on one hand, as it cushions any sound, but it does rather isolate the cobbled courtyard. I only tour the facilities once a week when my site manager, Keith, and I do a walk around.

Keith's Cornish wife, Vyvyan, set up the Renweneth Farm website for my grandparents shortly after they arrived here and she's run it ever since, dealing with the online bookings and enquiries. It's because of her that Keith ended up taking on the role of site manager when Cappy went back to Gloucestershire. Between them they keep things ticking over nicely. On Keith's days off, another local man – Len – covers for him and I told him to seek me out if there's ever a problem. Cappy thinks the world of Vyvyan and she is a gem, but I do find Keith to be a bit frosty on occasion. On reflection, I wonder whether he felt a bit threatened when I first arrived, because all I seemed to do was ask questions. And then, of course, I started making big changes. Things are finally beginning to settle down, but I think he was much happier taking his instructions from Cappy.

'Mum!' Lola calls out and I instantly look up. Three smiling faces peer through a gap between the clusters of leaves. 'Is it okay if we come in and get some ice lollies?'

'Stay there and I'll bring them around to you.'

'Ta, Mum. Can you bring my favourite board game too, pretty please!'

'All right,' I laugh. 'I'm on my way.'

Peeling off my gardening gloves, I head inside and gather a trayful of items. When I swing open the front door, Riley is just about to reach out for the door knocker.

'Hi, Jess. Here, let me give you a hand with some of that.'

'Oh, um… thanks, Riley. This little lot is for Lola. She's in the treehouse in the orchard.'

He grabs the three bottles of water and the board game wedged beneath my arm, leaving me to carry the ice lollies, a bowl of apples and a game of snap.

As we traipse across the courtyard and through the arch into the garden of Renweneth Manor, it's like entering another world. I do miss having grass, even though the back of The Farmhouse looks out on to moorland and the sea beyond, but it's full of rocky outcrops and doesn't have that manicured look.

'I didn't mean to interrupt but I've been giving some thought to that list of yours and—' As we approach the largest of the gnarled apple trees, the kids come running towards us and Riley turns his head to grin at me. 'It doesn't take much to put a smile on their faces, does it?'

'No. But I think it's the ice lollies they're focusing on right now,' I retort, as I hand over the tray to Lola.

'No running around with lolly sticks in your mouth and don't forget to drink the water,' I instruct them all.

'Mum, we're not babies you know. Hi, Riley. How are you today?'

'Fine, thank you, Lola.' He seems pleased to be acknowledged but seconds later off they go again and we make our way back to The Farmhouse.

'Do you have time for a cup of coffee or are you on your way to a job? There's some homemade cupcakes Lola iced that need eating.'

His eyes light up. 'It's a tough job but someone has to do it. Actually, I was hoping to have a bit of a chat with you as my situation has changed a little since we last spoke.'

That doesn't sound good.

'We'll have to take our drinks outside so I can keep an ear and an eye out for the kids, if that's okay with you?'

'Of course. It doesn't pay to let them totally out of your sight these days.'

Walking through to the kitchen, Riley opens the patio doors. He stands just outside like a sentry, his eyes firmly on the treehouse as I make the drinks and put some cupcakes on a plate which I hand to him.

'Here you go, help yourself. Every single one you eat is one temptation less for me,' I joke. 'Right.' Grabbing the mugs I follow him over to perch on the wall with our backs to the sun. The screeching laughter coming from the orchard is wonderful to hear as the board game gets under way. 'My dreaded list,' I groan. 'Did it horrify you?'

His mouth is full, and I wait patiently for him to finish. 'Sorry, but nothing beats a homemade cake. Lots of icing, too. Lola did a great job!'

Yes, and some of it has dribbled down on to your T-shirt, but I'm not about to point that out.

Placing the mugs between us, I stretch out my legs and grab a cupcake. Just the one, I tell myself, offering the plate to Riley, who has no intention of refusing another one.

'Anyway,' he continues, a cupcake halfway to his mouth. 'It is quite a list, I'll grant you, but aside from the electrical work there isn't anything there I can't tackle.'

'That is such good news, Riley.'

'I'm not a bringer of problems, just solutions. It is a lot of work, but I can offer you a minimum of two full days a week if you can be flexible and some weeks an extra day or two.'

Out of four builders I approached, only two turned up to take a look and one of them said he couldn't give me a firm start date.

The other sounded positive, but still hasn't submitted a quote. The problem is that I can't afford to have everything done in one go, which means the bigger companies aren't interested. They'd bring in a team and turn it around in just a couple of months. On the other hand, the smaller set-ups are swamped with work and usually juggle more than one job at a time. I can't deal with that sort of approach. The last thing I want is someone who turns up for a day, then hares off to another job leaving me with no idea when they'll be back. I like to plan in advance and know exactly what's happening and when. It's even more crucial now that I have paying guests on site. As I'm mulling it over, Riley interrupts my thoughts.

'The truth is that I'm really looking for steady work to tide me over the next few months. At the moment I'm only needed to drive the lorry two, sometimes three, days a week as they recently took on a new part-timer. It would make life a lot easier for me to have a period where I'm working in one particular place for a while, rather than having to dash around in between doing lots of little jobs. What with the cost of petrol and travel time involved, to be honest it's not really profitable.'

Popping the rest of my half-eaten cupcake into my mouth I sit back and consider Riley's proposal.

'My daily rate is probably the cheapest you'll find around here and if you can guarantee me work over the summer, I'll knock an extra five per cent off.'

'Really?' Every little helps and at least I can be confident that he'll turn up when he says he will. 'That's very generous of you.'

I can also see that he's in earnest. Riley glances away, his eyes straying to the treehouse. 'I have a son who is a few months older than Lola, and bills don't pay themselves.'

Given his expression I don't think he intended to share that with me, but obviously for whatever reason he's struggling financially.

'That could work to our mutual benefit, but it would help

me to make a decision if you could give me a rough estimate of how long each job might take. I understand there are a lot of unknowns, but I'm prepared to be hands-on and am happy to do the general clearing up and whatever you think I can handle. Not least because I'm keen to pick up as many skills as I can along the way. But I'd hate to come to an agreement, then find I'm being too ambitious and have to end up calling a halt for a while.'

Riley seems to appreciate my honesty.

'I fully understand the position you're in, Jess, but if you don't mind me saying, without looking at the plans Cappy drew up I'm working in the dark. I'm fine with building regulation compliance and can file those forms for you. I did all that for my own cottage and the inspectors know me quite well from other jobs I've worked on, which usually helps.'

'Mum, Mum!' Lola's voice filters through the air. 'Are there any more cupcakes left?'

Riley looks at me and smiles as I call back, 'Yes, I'll bring them around, just give me a couple of minutes.'

'Are you happy to move forward on that basis?' Riley is keen, I'll give him that.

'All I'm doing these days is tinkering with things, rather than pressing forward in a significant way, and there's no time to waste. As long as I balance the income versus the expenditure, this could be the perfect solution.'

'At any time at all you can choose to slow the programme down if things get tight and I can pick up a few little jobs here and there to keep me ticking over. I'm more than happy to be flexible because this is an exciting project.'

'Okay Riley, that sounds good to me. I'll email across a full set of plans and we can discuss it further when you've taken a look. Now, I'd better sort out Lola and her gang before they come storming over here.'

We drain our coffees and as I say goodbye and make my way around to the orchard, my phone pings. It's a text from Ivy.

Quick update. Adam is angry with himself. He's helping a mate out on Monday. Just labouring, but at least it will keep him occupied. I'll let you know how it goes. 😔 x

It's easy to say, but I think Adam did the right thing. The problem is that if other contractors don't do the same, nothing will ever change.

The irony isn't lost on me that here I am about to employ Riley, but if Adam and Ivy lived in Cornwall my builder would be sorted.

6

One Door Opens and Somewhere Else Another Door Slams Shut

Among the various groups of parents clustered around the school gates, I spot Erica and head straight over to her. She greets me with a warm, Monday morning smile.

'Hi Jess. I could have dropped Lola back to save you the journey.'

'That's really kind of you but we're going straight from here to the DIY store to pick up some shelves to finish off her bedroom. How are things with you?'

Erica is certainly looking a lot less stressed than the last time I saw her.

'Life is gradually returning to normal, well our new normal for the next few weeks. Mum is back in her flat and I'm calling in twice a day to give her a hand. She said she missed her sea view.' Erica's brow lifts as she grins back at me. 'All I can say is thank goodness for that.'

'Nothing beats the sound of the sea, it's very calming.'

'You're lucky being a short walk away from the cliff path. It's one of my favourite trails,' Erica replies.

'Ours too, but life is getting busier by the day and I can't remember the last time Lola and I took a wander.'

She pulls a long face. 'We need more hours in a day.'

That makes me laugh. 'I know, but I don't think I'd have the stamina to use them anyway. I do, often, sit on the window seat late at night and gaze out of my bedroom window. If it's open, I can hear the crashing of the waves when the wind is in the right direction.'

'I bet it's amazing. Who wouldn't want to look out on to a wild strip of moorland sloping down to the clifftops. How are things back at Renweneth Farm?'

'Bookings are way up and now I'm also letting out Penti Growan, which Vyvyan tells me has had the phone ringing off the hook. She's amazing, isn't she?'

'Yes, a real gem.' But as Erica says that I notice a hint of a frown creasing her brow. 'She's a saint to put up with Keith. He blows hot and cold, that man.'

'I had noticed,' I admit. 'Ooh, while I think of it, I've been meaning to ask if you know Riley Warren.'

Her face instantly changes into a beaming smile. 'Mr Fix It has made a few hearts flutter, I can tell you, but it all goes over his head. Riley is a mate of my Charlie's; they occasionally go hand-line fishing down at the cove. Why?'

'I'm thinking of getting him to do some work for me. He says he's a bit of an all-rounder. Would you recommend him?'

'Most certainly. Riley's done quite a few jobs at our house. And, from what Charlie told me, Riley's done an amazing job on the almost derelict cottage he bought on the other side of the moor.'

'Thanks, Erica. That's good to know. It's not easy getting someone to come and price a job, let alone give a start date. What I consider quite a big job doesn't seem to interest the builders I've contacted. But Riley is keen and he's already helped me out at short notice.'

The sound of the school bell sees a sudden exodus of children come flooding out of the building. Both Erica and I crane our heads searching for Daisy and Lola.

'Riley's a good man and trustworthy,' Erica confirms. 'Charlie knows more about him than I do. Moving to Cornwall on your own is a brave move. It's not easy to start over from scratch. Most people come here for a better quality of life in their downtime. You know, taking advantage of the walks and the wonderful sea views. Riley just wants a quiet life and work is what seems to keep him going.'

'Mum, Mum!' Lola runs towards me, carrying something in her hand. 'I got a merit award from Mrs Saul for keeping the classroom book corner tidy. I love doing it, Mum.'

Erica gives me a parting smile as she spots Daisy and I stoop to give Lola a congratulatory hug. 'Well done you! Right, let's go and buy some shelves. It seems I might have a budding librarian on my hands,' I state proudly.

It strikes me as ironic that Lola doesn't always hang up her clothes without a reminder, but she never leaves her books hanging around. They're her pride and joy.

'Mum, what does a librarian actually do?'

'Come on, we'll talk about that when we're in the car.'

There's a gentle tap on the sitting room window and I hurry into the hallway, my footsteps hollow on the flagstone floor. Riley is a little earlier than I expected and when I open the door his voice is hushed. 'I didn't like to use the door knocker in case Lola's asleep.'

'Thanks, that's thoughtful of you. I've just tucked her in. Her eyes were closed and the book she was reading had slipped off the bed,' I half-whisper, as I turn to lead Riley into the kitchen.

'She's a bright girl and books fire up a child's imagination,' he continues.

'Yes, and she's inquisitive, which means it's an effort trying to curtail her seemingly endless stream of questions,' I acknowledge. 'Do you fancy a drink? Hot, cold... a beer perhaps?'

'A beer would go down really well, thanks.'

'Stressful day on the job?'

'No, it was a good one. Just the same old problems going on

in the background… you think something is sorted and all of a sudden it raises its head again. How about you?'

'I had a brilliant day actually,' I reply.

While I grab a glass and a cold beer from the fridge, I indicate for him to take a seat at the table, then I pour myself a small white wine.

'It looks like you're in a celebratory mood,' he reflects as his eyes scan my face.

I take the seat opposite him and raise my glass. 'I am, and I hope you are, too. You've got yourself a labourer come apprentice and I've found myself a Mr Fix It.'

His grin grows exponentially.

'In that case, I'd like to propose a toast of my own.' He pauses for a moment, glass raised in the air. 'Let's hope that whatever problems we find turn out to be easily fixable to please my new boss.'

As we chink, I chime in with, 'I'll second that.'

'But there is one annoying little thing I should probably mention.'

I glance at him, cagily. 'And that is?'

'When planning approval is issued there's usually a date by which the work has to be started.'

My face instantly falls. 'Darn it! I remember Cappy saying something about that. His filing system isn't the best and it's probably better that I give him a call. I bet he'll be able to put his hands straight on the relevant paperwork. To be honest with you, I thought I'd be further ahead with the programme than I am, and it probably hasn't crossed his mind either.'

There's no point worrying about it until I know for sure and for the next half an hour we relax and generally chat about the work ahead. Riley says he can't wait to cut back the massive Virginia creeper that is threatening to consume the far end of the row of stone outbuildings. It hadn't occurred to me that would need to be cleared first, even though the renovation work will start at the other end. Riley explains that it depends where the roots are concentrated and if there's any structural damage that should really be addressed first. While it's yet another potential little complication, it reassures me that Riley knows what he's doing and that he won't cut corners for convenience's sake.

When my phone pings I glance at the clock, it's just after nine-thirty and I've been anxiously awaiting a text from Ivy.

'Sorry, Riley, but do you mind if I see who that's from?'

'Sure, go ahead. Actually, it's time I headed off. Thanks for the beer and don't worry, it all sounds labour-intensive, but once the greenery is cleared back we can start the transformation.'

'My fear is that the climber is the only thing holding the last of the stone outbuildings up,' I admit, pulling a long face.

He gives a reassuringly dismissive laugh. 'Oh, there might be a few cracks, but those stone walls are thick. Cornishmen know how to build something to last, so don't you worry, because we'll fix whatever we find. Anyway, I'd best leave you to it.'

As I see Riley out it crosses my mind that the old adage is true, a trouble shared is a trouble halved. But first I need to check with Cappy that my revised timetable isn't going to grind to a halt because of a technicality.

Anyway, first things first. Glancing down at my phone, I instantly press the call button. The message simply says:

Adam hasn't come home from work yet and I'm frantic. He was supposed to be spending the day helping a mate dig out some footings for an extension, but I have no idea where. What should I do???

'Ivy?'

'Oh, Jess! I've been texting everyone I can think of for the last hour and a half, trying to ever so casually check whether they've seen Adam. I'm running out of options and I'm not sure whether I should call the police.'

I close my eyes for a second, trying to picture Adam and some of his old haunts from his single days. If he's spent the day with one of his long-time friends, I know where I'd look for him first off.

'How about the rugby club?'

'But he hasn't played in a long time and doesn't see any of that crowd anymore,' Ivy replies, dismissively.

'No, but where better to go if he wanted to prop up the bar and grab a few beers. Especially if he's looking for work contacts too; a lot of his old mates will still frequent the social club. Maybe they'll pass the word around that he's back in business.'

'It's worth a shot. I'll jump in the car and check it out. Speak soon and thanks, Jess. I'm sure he's fine but—'

'You'll feel much better when you know where he is, Ivy. Go on, don't hang around, and drive carefully.'

The thought of sitting around anxiously waiting to hear from Ivy is unbearable, so instead I call Cappy. When he answers, the sound of the TV in the background is so loud that I can hardly hear him.

'Jess? Hang on a minute.' There's a rustling sound and seconds later silence, as he turns it off. 'That's better. How are you and Lola doing? It's all good, I hope?'

'It is, Cappy. Lola is changing with every passing day. She's really beginning to come out of her shell.'

'And how about you?'

'I've found a local handyman in need of some regular work and we've just struck a deal. My friend Erica can vouch for him too, so I'm feeling pretty good about that. I just wanted to check I haven't missed the deadline to get work started on the outbuildings. I've trawled through the folders on my laptop but there's so many documents in there it could take forever.'

An anxious 'Hmm…' echoes down the line. 'The hard copies are in that red box file I left with you. It's mainly the planning stuff in there. I'm pretty sure I kept photocopies if you can give me a few minutes to rummage.'

He talks as he walks, and I grin to myself, imagining him climbing the stairs and going into his study, which is in the spare bedroom. It's all pristine because the little house he bought was a new build.

'Let me see…' he mutters to himself and then there's a loud bonking sound as he puts the phone down on a hard surface.

'Cappy, put it on speakerphone,' I yell, repeating it twice before I can hear his voice again.

'That's better. Now, um…' the sound of him leafing through the documents is interspersed with little comments. 'It's not that one and that's not the final one either, that wasn't approved… ah, here you go!'

I realise I'm holding my breath. I haven't seen the red box file since I moved in and that probably means it's up in the attic, which isn't my favourite place to root around.

'Goodness, talk about up to the wire. The three-year period in which to start the work is up in the middle of August. For one awful moment there I thought it might have been July.'

I collapse back against the chair, relief flooding out of me. 'Thank goodness for that!'

'I'm just delighted to hear where you're at, my girl. And you sound happy.'

'I am… I mean, we are. Anyway, how are you doing? Mum tells me you have a new hobby.'

He gives another sombre, 'Hmm,' then a disgruntled sigh. 'I did it just to get her off my back. She thinks I'm spending too much time on my own. So now, two evenings a week I sit around a table in a pokey little room at the community centre with my mate, Dave, and a bunch of other old codgers playing cards. They call it God's waiting room.'

I let out an explosive gasp. 'Cappy, that is so not you!'

'I know,' he moans, 'but anything for a quiet life.'

'Aside from that, what else do you do to keep occupied?' He isn't a man used to sitting around twiddling his thumbs, that's for sure.

'Oh, I'm still a member of the local ramblers' club and I do a bit of voluntary work in one of the charity shops in Stroud. I miss gardening though, although I call in occasionally to give your dad a hand. This plastic grass the developers laid out the back might look tidy, but it isn't the same. Still, the borders are blooming, but an hour once a week dead-heading and it's done.' He sounds miffed.

'Why don't you come and stay with me and Lola for a few days? You can potter to your heart's content, and we'd love to see you.'

With Penti Growan booked more or less back-to-back and only the one spare bedroom in The Farmhouse now, if he accompanies Mum and Dad on future visits I'm going to have to think about alternatives. I'm beginning to regret having turned the fourth bedroom into an en suite for the master; even though with the luxurious rolltop bath it has become my little sanctuary.

'I don't want to get in the way,' he mutters.

'You wouldn't. Anyway, I have a problem and, to be honest, I could really do with your input.'

'You can ring any time, Jess, you know that.'

'Yes, but… well, this guy I've found is a general builder and naturally he's expecting me to sit down with him to talk through the plans. It's your project and when he starts asking questions I'm not sure I'll have the answers.' I screw up my face, hoping that Cappy doesn't make light of it.

'That's understandable, Jess. I had a good architect, and I took him along to every meeting I had at the planning offices. It was all new to me too, at the time,' he replies, encouragingly.

'He saved an almost derelict cottage and brought it back to life. Aside from doing the usual odd jobs here and there, he's also helped out on a few garage and loft conversions, apparently.'

'I see. It sounds like you feel comfortable with him, Jess, and that's important. You've enough on your plate to juggle being hands-on, looking after Lola and keeping a control on the finances. How's business?'

'Good. Keith keeps things running smoothly and Vyvyan's mailing list saw a surge of bookings when Penti Growan went online. She keeps asking when the last of the cottages will be ready and I simply laugh and say *in the fullness of time.*' At least she never prompts me about Renweneth Manor. That's off her radar, thankfully, because I think I'd need to win the lottery before I could pull off Grandad's original vision.

'It's a lot of pressure on you, Jess. I said to your parents that maybe you should consider selling off Renweneth Manor to make your life a little easier.'

My heart skips a beat. It's the reason my grandparents bought the farm in the first place, accepting that one day it would be the culmination of their dream. It's time to, ever-so-subtly, change the subject.

'The good news is that I think you know the guy, as he also drives for the builders' merchants. His name is Riley – Riley Warren?'

'Ah, Riley! Now there's a man with determination. If he says he'll do something, you can count on him. He's a good man, is Riley,' Cappy informs me. 'Maybe I will take a trip down, just for a few days. Tell Riley that if there's time, I'll buy him a pint in The Trawlerman's Catch.'

Result! 'Does that mean you'll talk us through the plans in detail?' Hope leaps in my chest, because this is huge. Not only is Cappy suddenly sounding a whole lot perkier, the fact that I'm also coming into this having had no prior input is a disadvantage. Employing someone to do the work is fine, but in effect I'm not just paying the bills, I'm also the project manager.

'Anything to help. I miss my two favourite girls and Lola reminds me what life is all about – the good things still to come. It'll also be nice to catch up with a few old friends if there's time.'

What a surprise turnaround. Mum will be delighted to hear that I've managed to talk Cappy into coming to stay. This place means everything to our family as a whole. There are so many good memories we can cling to but it's my job to keep them coming and he's a big part of that.

My phone beeps and I see that Ivy is calling.

'I must go as I have an incoming call. Thanks, Cappy. I'll feel a lot happier after you, me and Riley get our heads together. Let me know when you can get down here and I'll tell Lola. Sending love and hugs!'

As we disconnect and Ivy's voice fills my ear, at least she sounds calmer, although her tone is hushed. 'I found Adam. You were right, he'd been propping up the bar and had a few too many. I was on my way there when I got the call. His old coach took pity on him and drove Adam back to his house to sober him up a little before calling me. Guys certainly stick together.'

'Thank goodness for that!'

'Adam can't stop apologising, but after several strong cups of coffee he's now ravenous. It looks like we're going to be at coach's house another hour at least, as they're talking about old times while his wife is frying sausages would you believe!' Ivy sounds understandably exasperated and I can't even begin to imagine what's been going through her mind.

'A sausage sandwich will soon soak up that alcohol. How are you doing, though?'

'Cross and not in the mood for comfort food, that's for sure. But at least he's safe and I'm grateful for that.'

'It's what friends do, Ivy, and Adam's a great guy. He's always doing favours for other people. I bet coach Bevan is no exception. Hopefully Adam will conk out as soon as you get home and I'm sure he'll be mortified when he wakes up in the morning.'

'If he isn't, then I'll be enlightening him. Thanks for calming me down, Jess. You were on a call when I rang, problems?'

'No, quite the reverse. I've just talked Cappy into come to stay for a little while.'

'You have? Wow, now that's unexpected.'

I smile to myself rather smugly. 'He's coming because I asked for his help. Anyway, get back to your man and I'll be thinking of you tomorrow. Stay positive, Ivy, this is a temporary blip and Adam will sort himself out.'

What an evening it's been, but I know that when my head

hits that pillow it won't take me long to drift off. I'm feeling absolutely shattered. A part of me is on a high, but the other part is crushed to think of my two best friends having to rethink their lives. I've been in the exact same position and all I can say is that there is no magic wand. What lifts my spirits is that if they stick together they'll get through it. I envy them that, because what still catches me unawares is when I wake in the middle of the night, in a cold sweat. Knowing that if I mess things up there's no one to blame but me is a vulnerable position to be in.

7

Facing the Inevitable

'Mum, Dad is going to ask you if I can spend the first week of the summer holidays with him. He told me not to mention it to you yet, but can I? Can I, Mum? Pleeeeeease.'

Tuesday was going so well, and I almost got through the entire day without any drama. Lola has only just come off the phone after a long chat with her dad; this was the last thing I was expecting. Now my stomach is in knots but I continue washing the dishes as if it's no big deal.

I knew Ben would eventually get settled properly and that this day would come. However, that's what... five weeks away and I've only just succeeded in getting Lola settled into her own bedroom here. What if going back to Stroud gets her thinking about our old life and unsettles her all over again?

'That's lovely, Lola, but uh... let's wait and see. The timing might not be good as Cappy is planning on coming to stay with us for a little break. You wouldn't want to miss spending time with him, would you?'

Her eyes are still bright and shiny, but I can see she's torn. Cappy thinks the world of Lola and he spoils her rotten. They've always had a very special relationship and he calls her his sparkly girl. He's right, because Lola does sparkle.

'Can we ring him now and find out when he's coming?' There's an urgency in her tone and my heart sinks. When I speak to Ben I'm going to tell him straight that he has no business springing this on me like that and mentioning it to Lola before he talks to me is not acceptable.

'It's getting late, Lola, and if you want to have some reading time in bed before you go to sleep, I'll expect you in your nighty, face washed and teeth cleaned, in the next ten minutes.' I point at the kitchen clock on the wall. 'Leave it with me. If it clashes with Cappy's visit, perhaps we can arrange something a little later in the holidays.'

'Dad says his friend Naomi will be on holiday too and she said we can go bowling and take some of my friends from my old school with us.'

'You spoke to Dad's... friend?'

'Yes. Naomi said that there's this fun place with a zip line for kids and we can do that, too.'

If that was supposed to be an incentive it doesn't seem to be working because Lola is pulling a pout. 'Why the long face?'

'I thought it would be just me and Dad. I do miss my friends, Mum, but I miss him more. And I don't know Naomi.'

'It's getting late but we'll work something out. Dad probably thought it would make your visit more fun. Now, off you go. I'll be up to tuck you in shortly.'

As she reaches the door Lola stops, turning to look at me. 'Is Naomi your friend too, Mum?'

Her innocent enquiry has the effect of someone ripping a plaster off an open wound that hasn't yet healed and a sharp breath catches in my throat. 'Oh... um... she works with Dad, so I've only met her once.'

Lola stands there chewing her lip. 'We have a new friend, too, and Dad doesn't know Riley, so I guess it's okay.' And with that she disappears, leaving me leaning against the kitchen sink for support. Is she really disappointed at the thought of not having her dad all to herself, or is she worried about my reaction? The last thing I want is for her to feel conflicted; it doesn't matter what Ben or I want, this is about helping Lola to adjust to the new norm.

My head starts to ache. I'm not emotionally equipped to handle such a delicate conversation. Does that make me a bad parent? Or am I the fool still clinging on to the hope that if I can get Ben to come and visit on his own he'll realise he's made a huge mistake walking away from us? Damn it – why can't I just let go and be done with it?

Lola is sound asleep and after two cups of strong coffee I can't settle. I've been channel hopping with the TV remote control for the last half an hour and although it's only nine o'clock, I might as well give up and go to bed. The problem is that my head isn't in a good place tonight. There are so many things swirling around inside of it and I can't seem to shut them down.

When my mobile rings it makes me jump and my heart feels like it's trying to turn over inside my chest. A lump rises in my throat until I see who it is and relief floods through me.

'Hi, Cappy. Have you had a good day?'

'I certainly did, thanks Jess. How about you?'

Smile, Jess, it'll lift your voice I tell myself, which is easy to say and hard to do. 'It was a busy one.'

'You sound a little down tonight.'

'It's tiredness, that's all.'

'I won't keep you chatting for long, but I've dug out my copies of the documents I left with you and I thought I might as well bring them with me. Riley will need a set and there's no point in me hanging on to them. I'm more than happy to go through everything with you both. I'm excited for you, Jess, and I can't wait to head down to Cornwall.'

It sounds like he's eager to come sooner, rather than later, so I'll have no excuse to delay Ben taking Lola back to Stroud at the start of the school holidays.

'Are you still there?'

'Sorry, my head was elsewhere for a moment.'

'I don't have to come right away if it's not convenient, but just remember work has to commence before that deadline or it means reapplying for planning approval.'

'No, it's fine. Come as soon as you want. The spare room is ready and waiting.'

'What's really bothering you, Jess? A trouble shared is a trouble halved as your grandma always said. I don't judge and I don't tattle, you know that.'

'It's not that… I just feel like I'm a bad mum.' The lump in my throat brings me to a halt and I swallow hard, but it won't shift. When I go on to explain this evening's upset, I hear Cappy utter a sorrowful sigh.

'Oh, my lovely Jess.' His voice is full of empathy. 'A divorce is much like a bereavement, and I know how that feels. A loss is a loss, my love. You go through many different phases, the final one being acceptance, and you're not quite there yet.'

Inwardly I groan. I know he's right, but I wasn't sure anyone would understand. 'I didn't mean to make you sad, Cappy. I'll be fine. I always am.'

'Now that's the sort of answer that sweeps everything under the carpet and you're better than that, Jess. You're grieving for what was and what could have been. It leaves you asking *why?* Until you finally accept there is no going back, you'll never be free, Jess. It's time and you know it.'

How do you let go of love, though? 'Hope is both a good and a bad thing, isn't it? I've been fooling myself and not facing up to the facts.'

A deep breath escapes his lips and it's a harrowing sound.

'Accepting I would never see your grandma sitting next to me again, or be able to hold her hand, was the toughest challenge I've ever faced. It made me angry; she was a truly wonderful woman and yet it was as if someone up there in the ether had flicked a switch and suddenly she was gone.'

'Oh, Cappy, we all felt the same way. The shock left us reeling.'

'I know, but anger can be a soul-destroying emotion. It can suck the joy out of life and your grandma would have expected better from me.'

'No, you're wrong. You were our rock. I remember one particular day when you sat with Lola, she was in floods of tears. You said when you think of Grandma she's in a wonderful garden, full of flowers and looking down on us all with a smile on her face. That's the vision Lola holds in her head now and it got her through it.'

He expels another deep breath, this time it's one of acceptance.

'I learnt to count my blessings, Jess, and it was humbling. I have a truly wonderful family and when I'm missing my wife I sit down and think about old times. The memories come flooding back and nothing can take those away from me. That's the precious gift I was given. And now, every day I find something to be thankful for. It helps, although life will never be the same again. But my darling Maggie would be frowning if I didn't make the best of it and that includes being there for you and Lola.'

It's a sobering moment, as I know it took a lot for him to share that with me.

'I'm not sure how to explain the changes going on in our lives to Lola when I'm still feeling so fragile, Cappy. I need to be strong for her, but inside I'm falling apart.'

'I know. Have a chat with Ben. Whichever way you decide to handle things going forward, Jess, it has to be a joint decision. Otherwise, it's easy for a child to become confused if they end up getting two different versions of the same thing. Or worse, she ends up feeling guilty for wanting to spend time on her own with her dad.'

'Sometimes he just doesn't think things through. Ben has no idea how tough this last year has been. He only has himself to consider and he went behind my back.'

'Then tell him exactly that. But you'll have to listen to what he's saying, too. It won't be easy, but it'll clear the air between the two of you. Only then can you and Ben decide how best to handle the situation for Lola's sake.'

'The truth hurts, doesn't it?'

'It does, Jess. Sometimes life gets way too real, but the truly wonderful thing is that it goes on. The thought of spending some time with you and Lola has given me a little boost. I'm beginning to feel a tad redundant if I'm being honest, and it is nice to be needed.'

'Oh, Cappy... you have no idea how much we miss you, or how valuable your input will be. I'm way outside my comfort zone and just knowing you have my back means more to me right now than you can possibly understand. So, when are you coming?'

'Oh, bless you! The day after tomorrow works for me if that's okay with you.'

'Great, thank you!'

'Sleep well, Jess, and I'm glad I rang.'

'Me, too, Cappy. Me, too.' And I mean that with all my heart.

After dropping Jess off at school, I head straight home. Having texted Ben last night saying we need to talk, he was obviously concerned because he said he'd make an excuse to go into work a bit later today. However, as I accept his video call, seeing Ben's face for the first time in quite a while now, my emotions are suddenly in freefall.

'Hey, Jess. What's up?'

I don't know if I can do this, and my throat goes dry as my eyes scan his face. The way his brow crinkles when he's anxious, accentuating that little birthmark by his left eye, makes my heart squish up.

Where do I begin? Perhaps it's best not to mention Naomi's name. 'As nice a thought as it is, Lola is longing for time with *you*, not with her old school friends. You haven't been in her life on a daily basis now for well over a year. It's been a struggle for me to coax her out of the shell she retreated into. My fear is that this could unsettle her all over again.'

'It was your decision to move to Cornwall, Jess, you can hardly blame that on me.' The words slip blithely from between his lips.

My heart is pounding and my breathing is getting shallow. 'At the beginning you promised me that you'd tread carefully when it comes to introducing someone new into the equation. I expected better from you, Ben. Your daughter is looking forward to some one-to-one time. She needs to feel she's important in your life.'

'Then we'll jump in the car this Saturday and take Lola out for the day. When we drop her back to you with a smile on her face I hope you'll relax a little and trust I can handle this.'

'You're missing the point. And, in future, you talk to me first, Ben, not Lola, when it comes to making plans.'

There are a few seconds of silence before he clears his throat, and my stomach begins to churn. 'It's not the best time to tell you this, but Naomi has moved in with me.'

My eyes begin to smart and now I feel stupid for not guessing what triggered this visit. 'Oh, right.'

'We did offer to come and give you a hand a couple of weekends ago and I was going to tell you then, but you put us off. Naomi and I decided it was something we should tell you in person. You need to accept that I don't intend to spend the rest of my life on my own and Naomi may be the one.'

May be the one? There was a time when he said *I* was the one, so now he's hedging his bets. I have no idea how Lola is going to react to the news that Dad's friend is now his live-in partner.

'My parents and my best friends were here, Ben. Did you really think we could all play happy families just like that with someone they don't know?' Someone who has now replaced me in his life.

'Jess, I didn't think it through, I'm sorry —' He looks shell-shocked. 'Naomi was happy to give a hand and I thought that as your parents were going to be there, they might like to meet her.'

Is he joking? 'They miss *you*, Ben. You're welcome any time, but if you want to stay under my roof then you come on your own. Otherwise, sorry, but it's best that you find a hotel. We need to sit down together and agree what exactly to tell Lola about your new situation before she meets Naomi in person for the first time.'

'Whatever you say, Jess. What if on Saturday I call in around eleven on my own and we can talk then?'

I pause, battling to keep my tears of frustration at bay. He has no idea what it's like for me now looking after Lola 24/7, as if I'm a single parent. The worry about how she's coping rests firmly on my shoulders and there are things I need to say to Ben. Fortunately, Cappy will be here and he'll be able to keep Lola distracted while we can set some ground rules. 'That's fine.'

'I didn't mean to upset you, Jess. If Lola's happy for me and Naomi to take her out we'll make it a fun day, I promise. I know things haven't been easy for you, or between us, but I feel like I'm treading on eggshells every time we talk. I'm not trying to hurt you or make light of the fact that you're taking the lion's share of the responsibility for parenting. The dig I made about Cornwall was out of order, a knee-jerk reaction, but I'm a phone call away if you need my help with anything. It's much better for Lola living in the country, it's just that I miss having her in my life. I know you can understand that.'

The tears I'm shedding as I put down the phone are for what we've all lost. The divorce was a fracture that rocked our world, one that had felt safe and secure for a very long time. Now any tenuous thread of hope that lingered in my heart has been well and truly severed. As I swipe away my tears, I square my shoulders and pull myself together. *Onwards and upwards, Jess*, I tell myself, because what choice do I have? As Cappy said, acceptance comes from letting go of the past and, in my case, the balloon of hope I've been clinging on to has finally slipped from my grasp.

What I feel, though, isn't a sense of freedom but rather a sense of having been cast adrift and I'm disappointed with myself.

8

Home Is Where the Heart Is

The moment I hear the sound of a car pulling up alongside the small barn, I throw off my gardening gloves and hurry over to meet my long-awaited visitor.

'Cappy!' I call out, breaking into a trot.

As he climbs out of his Defender, I check it out approvingly. 'Love the new four-wheel drive, it's quite a beast.'

'It is, and it's a pleasure to drive it. Where's old Bessie? She's not in the garage, is she?'

I give him a stern look before wrapping my arms around him and planting a kiss on his cheek. 'No, she's fine. I park her just inside the gates, the other side of the wall.'

He grins down at me. 'Bit of a deterrent, even though it's obvious no one lives in Renweneth Manor, eh?'

'Well, it might make anyone nosing around stop and think for a moment. And less of the old, she's still looking good and runs like a dream. VW vans go on forever.'

He chuckles at me. 'Built to last, Jess, built to last. Best car your grandma and I ever bought and it makes me smile to know she's in good hands.'

'The kids love a little trip to and from school in her, they think she's cool. Anyway, it's good to see you looking so well and I love the shirt.'

'Thought I'd better make a bit of an effort,' he grins at me.

'But first things first. I've a bit of a surprise in the back. It's been quite a journey with a few stops along the way.'

I glance at him, puzzled. 'Oh, your back isn't playing up again, is it? I guess it's been a while since you've done such a long journey.'

'No, my back's feeling pretty good and the seats are really comfortable. But you're right, some days I don't even get in the car as I often walk down to the shops for bits and pieces. Now, this idea of mine to put a smile on Lola's face might get me into trouble, so I brought something a bit special for you, to make amends. You get the kettle on and I'll be in directly. I must say that you've done a sterling job of tidying up the fronts of the two main cottages. The wisteria is now a joy to behold, and I know that cleaning up the stonework was a labour of love. It's all looking rather lovely, Jess.'

'I'm glad you approve. Right, tea and cake will be served shortly.' As I leave him to it and head inside, I can hear him humming away to himself. It reminds me of old times, even if he is up to his tricks again. He's always been full of surprises, some good and others indulging his indomitable and ever-youthful spirit. It's what I love about him and I know if Grandma were listening she'd have a huge smile on her face right now.

I'm slicing up a homemade Victoria sandwich when Cappy eventually walks through into the kitchen carrying a large plastic box in one hand. He stops in his tracks to gaze around. 'Painting those kitchen units was a grand idea, Jess. I can hardly believe it's the same place. It's very you. Contemporary country with a cosy feel. I never did like that heavy, dark oak look. The lighter colours as I walk through make the place feel a lot bigger.'

I hear a pitiful *miaow* and stare at him, my jaw dropping.

'A kitten?'

'You once told Grandma that a cottage isn't a home without a cat sitting in the window and looking out.'

'I did, didn't I?' I smile at him, wistfully. 'I've lost count of the times I've walked into the sitting room late at night and looked straight at Bathsheba's spot on the windowsill. Sometimes I swear my eyes stray there because I see a shadow. Then I tell myself I'm being silly.'

Miaow. Miaow.

'Here you go,' Cappy puts the cat carrier down in the corner of the kitchen. 'This little one is fourteen weeks old.' He stands back, placing an envelope on the table. 'She's been spayed, had her jabs and is chipped. I've a box of bits and pieces in the car. Just a few toys, some food recommended by the vet and a glove to brush her with. I stopped a few times so she could use her litter tray. She didn't drink a lot and slept most of the time.'

I kneel down on the floor, but all I can see is a swirl of soft pale-blue blanket and a tiny little ball of grey and white fur. Two bright little eyes peer up at me but when she opens her mouth nothing comes out 'Ah, what a cutie.'

'I did right, then?' he checks.

'Lola is going to be totally besotted. As you know, I promised her that once things were a bit straighter I'd get her a kitten. It hadn't slipped my mind; I've just been rushed off my feet. There's always something to do.'

'I can see that, Jess, and the whole place is looking a heck of a lot better for it. I let things slip the last eighteen months I was here. It all got a bit too much for me.' A momentary look of sadness sweeps over Cappy's face, but he quickly composes himself. 'Anyway, kitty comes from a good home. My neighbour rehomed a friend's two-year-old cat and they had no idea she was pregnant. This was the last one of the litter and as she was also the smallest, he kept her for a couple of weeks longer than the others. I'm hoping she'll be a good mouser, as once you start clearing out those old buildings you never know what you're going to find.'

I tease open the catches on the door of the carrier and leave it open for when our new arrival decides it's safe to investigate. Grabbing a little bowl out of the cupboard, I fill it with water, setting it down in the hope it will entice her to venture out.

'Right, I'll fetch the box and the litter tray. Oh, and that little something for you. Is there room for a puppy?' Cappy is only teasing and he laughs softly to himself as he heads back to the car.

'Don't be long, or the tea will go cold,' I call out and he waves his hand in the air, giving me a salute.

It's so good to have him here and, surprisingly, I think it actually helps that everything looks so different. I paid the removal guys to stack most of the furniture Cappy left behind into one of the bedrooms in Renweneth Manor. He's not sentimental about things, only people, but I'm hoping over time to upcycle some of the pieces.

'Here you go, this is for you.'

I look up and he places a large parcel on the table next to me. He nods his head, eager for me to open it.

As I start tearing off several layers of tissue paper, I see metal twigs and I gasp. 'It's not the birds... is it?' I glance across at him as he pulls out a chair and sinks down on to it, beaming at me. 'Oh, Cappy!'

'I should have bought it that day we spotted it in your favourite... what's the place called?'

'Odds and Tods. It was too expensive to buy on a whim, but I love it and thank you so much. I haven't been able to find anything to use as a table centre and this is perfect!'

For me the kitchen is the hub of The Farmhouse; the oversized and characterful old pine table was missing one thing. Now it's complete. Each new dent and ding will add to its story.

As Cappy tucks into the cake, I pull off the rest of the paper and undo the two little packages that come with it. It's a large, narrow, rectangular box cleverly made out of metal twigs and with the two hand-sized birds placed inside of it, it's like they're peeking out from a nest inside a bush. It's simple, unusual and I fell in love with it instantly until I saw the price tag.

'Drink your tea, you can sort that out later,' he pipes up. But his eyes are sparkling as he knows he's made my day.

'One final touch and it'll be done,' I promise. Rushing upstairs, I reappear a couple of minutes later with two stems of silk olive leaves in my hand, sporting tiny aubergine-coloured fruits. I lay them at opposite ends inside the nest and Cappy can see how delighted I am as I manoeuvre it into place.

'You certainly have the touch and an eye for the unusual, Jess. Now stop fiddling, sit down and drink your tea. I want you to catch me up on your news. Did you make this cake? Another slice would go down well.'

'No, Daisy's mum, Erica, baked it when I mentioned you were coming. She said to give you her best regards and tell you that you've been missed.'

'Ah! I promise I won't leave it so long next time, Jess.'

As I transfer another piece of cake across to Cappy's plate, I reflect on how lovely it is to have some company that's nothing to do with solving a problem. In reality, I spend a lot of time here on my own. It does get lonely at times. That's ironic, given that on the other side of the trees, beyond the stone wall, there are probably fifty to sixty people in tents and caravans. Still, with lots of new visitors about to come and stay in Penti Growan opposite, Lola and I will no longer feel quite so out on a limb. And it's only going to get better and better as time goes on.

Cappy insists on fetching Lola from school, so I give the secretary a ring to let her know and finish off potting up some planters for the campsite.

As I start trundling the small trolley out into the courtyard, Keith is walking towards me, his stride purposeful.

'I'm glad I caught you before you headed out for the school run, Jess, but you're a bit late leavin', aren't you?'

'Cappy's here for a few days and he offered to collect Lola.'

His face brightens. 'Oh, tell him to drop by later and I'll give him a tour. No doubt, he'll be surprised by the changes.'

Yes, he will, that inner voice fills my head. I find Keith's reaction slightly irritating, but it would be petty of me to hold it against him. In his eyes the real boss is back and I must admit I sort of feel the same way too.

'I was just about to wheel these around. They're going either side of the park entrance. I also have a few hanging baskets to put up along the edge of the play area. Isn't this one of your days off this week?'

'Yep, but Len called me in. There's been a bit of a ruckus.' His expression is dour.

Len covers for Keith on his days off. It's mostly popping in to greet our scheduled new arrivals and show them the facilities. Also manning the mobile contact number on our signage if there's a problem, or for people who turn up on spec, hoping to get a pitch.

'Two lads, backpackers, turned up first thing this mornin' wanting to stay for a couple of nights. He said they seemed okay, but by mid-mornin' he'd already had several complaints and had been over to see them twice. He asked them politely to pick up their rubbish and keep the noise down. Then the family next to them said they were smokin' somethin' and high as kites. Len rang me and we booted them off the site.'

Usually, a little word as a reminder that it's a family campsite does the trick. 'I'm sorry you got hauled back to sort it out. Are you expecting any further trouble?'

'To be honest, they treated it like a bit of a joke until a couple of the other campers walked over to back us up.'

'When I see Len, I'll thank him for his quick action. But I did ask him not to bother you on your days off, as aside from the school runs I try to make sure I'm around in case of an emergency.'

Keith purses his lips and I notice his left eyelid starts to twitch. It's probably from the adrenalin. 'I don't think it's somethin' you should be handlin' Jess,' he replies rather dismissively. 'I've just called the station to tip them off, in case the lads decide to stay local, like.'

'I'm grateful to you, Keith, and I'm sorry it interrupted your day. Just count it as a normal workday and book another day off to compensate.'

It is good of him, but for some reason he always makes me feel as if he doesn't think I'm capable of sorting out the problems. I'd simply have called the police in front of the troublemakers and I'm pretty sure they'd have scarpered before anyone arrived.

'I'll drop by later tonight, a couple of hours after Len's last walk around. I doubt they'll come back as their presence didn't go down well. I'll leave you to it then, Jess. Do you want a hand with the trolley?'

'No, I'm fine thanks, Keith. You get off home. Give Vyvyan my best and tell her I'll be able to send over those photos she wanted soon to update the website. I thought I'd pretty things up a bit first.'

'Fine. Tell Cappy I'll catch up with him over a pint. It's good to have him back. I'll um... leave you to your flower-arranging.'

I'm sure he doesn't mean to sound condescending and maybe I'm being unduly sensitive. Our weekly conversations when we walk around the site are pretty much the same, rather stilted. If he's having an off day, it's hard to get anything out of him and sometimes I feel like I'm intruding. He's a puzzle, for sure.

Three runs with the trolley and I'm happy. The blast of colour makes a huge difference and I stop to take a few photos. Judging by how long it's taking Cappy and Lola to get back, they've taken a detour and have gone to get ice cream in Polreweek, which gives me an extra hour.

I drop by to check kitty, who is sound asleep and doesn't seem to have ventured out, before I finish off today's task. When the guests staying in Penti Growan return from their trek across the moor, there will be an abundance of colour either side of the front door.

It's funny, but as Cappy's reaction sinks in I do feel proud about what I've achieved. I tend to look around and all I see is the huge amount of work still to be done. He noticed a vast improvement and I was touched to see how pleased he was. He lost sight of the dream after Grandma died, but I'm determined to see it through because now it's my dream too.

By early evening the youngest member of our family will still only venture outside of the carrier when we're peeping through the crack in the door. I haven't been able to coax Lola out of the kitchen for more than ten minutes at a time and I join her to sit cross-legged on the floor.

'You're settled on the name Misty, then?' I check. It's perfect, as she is a little beauty. With her pale grey and white coat, and those huge Citrine-coloured eyes, she has the classic teddy-bear look of a British Shorthair.

'She seems to like it, Mum. When I reach in and talk to her she licks my hand.'

'It's almost time for bed, Lola. Cappy said he'd read you a story if you like.'

Lola turns to look at me, her forehead wrinkling up.

'What about Misty? Won't she be lonely?'

I reach out and smooth Lola's hair, scooping some straggly bits back behind her ear. 'No, she's still a baby, so she sleeps a lot of the time. Misty has her snuggle blanket, which is very important as there are so many new smells around her and it's a comfort zone.'

'Will you leave the light on for her?'

I smile at my darling daughter. 'Didn't you know that cats can see in the dark? I'll put down some fresh food and top up her water before I turn in for the night. She's using her litter tray, which is good, but it might be a few days until she's brave enough to go exploring. When she's ready for her first big adventure she'll let us know. Don't forget she had a long journey to get here and once she's used to her new home and us, you'll be able to keep her occupied with her toys.'

'It's wonderful having Cappy here, Mum, isn't it?'

'It is, Lola, and now The Farmhouse is all finished, and we have that nice guest bedroom, he can come and stay any time he likes.'

'Mum, do you think Bathsheba will mind us having a kitten in her old home?'

Goodness, I didn't think Lola even remembered her. Lola was probably four at most when Bathsheba died at the grand old age of fifteen.

'I'm sure it would make her happy, Lola, to think of you having a little furry playmate.'

Lola yawns, it's been an exciting few hours and I'll tell Cappy not to pick too long a story.

'I can't wait to tell Daisy we've decided on a name, Mum!'

'I'm sure she'll agree that it's perfect. Right, off you go. Shout down as soon as you're settled.'

Left alone to sit here for a few moments, even though Misty hasn't moved and only opened one eye as Lola whispered, 'Goodnight Misty, love you,' on her way out, I sense that something is different. The presence of an animal is as real as having another person in the room and it's just what Lola and I needed. Clever old Cappy. As he said earlier on, 'You don't get to my age without learning a few things; not many of them will be that important as it turns out, but a few of them will.'

It turns out that getting a kitten was one of them.

9

The Day I Hoped Would Never Come Is Here

After a leisurely Saturday morning family breakfast, I leave Cappy in charge as I gather everything together to do my first changeover at Penti Growan. At ten-thirty on the dot, I wave off some very happy holidaymakers who said they'll be leaving a glowing review and fully intend to come back again.

It's a great start to what could end up being a rather stressful day. Lola knows that her dad is coming to see her a bit later on. I told him to park next to Bessie at the entrance to Renweneth Manor and to come looking for me rather than heading for The Farmhouse. I'm pretty sure Lola's attention will be elsewhere, as earlier on Misty decided the world is a big place and even ventured out into the hallway. Unfortunately, Lola's screech of excitement sent Misty scurrying back to the safety of her blanket. It didn't put our brave little kitten off, though. With Lola now creeping around quietly as she follows Misty on her adventures, there's no chance at all that Lola will be idly gazing out of the windows.

My nerves are jangling as it approaches eleven o'clock. I left the door to the cottage ajar and it seems like an age until I hear a familiar voice calling up the stairs.

'Jess? Are you there?'

'I'm upstairs changing the bed,' I call out, steeling myself because I know this is going to be tough.

When Ben appears in the doorway, my heart sinks.

'Hi, Jess.' He looks as ill at ease as he sounds. 'Uh... are you doing okay?'

It's too little, too late. If he'd asked that any time at all during the past year and a bit, it might have meant something. But not today, on his first visit to Renweneth since Grandma passed away.

'I'm fine,' I reply, adamantly. 'I'm pushed for time and Lola is waiting.'

'You left her on her own?' He sounds shocked and I stop what I'm doing to glare at him.

'Of course not, she's with Cappy.' How dare he question me like that.

'I thought he wasn't coming down until the start of the school holidays?'

Why is he on the attack? It must mean he's nervous.

'There was a change of plan. If Lola is happy to stay with you for that first week, then I'm fine with it. Just as long as she calls or texts me every day, whichever is less disruptive for her.'

He leans against the door jamb, watching me as I work. Was he hoping to put me on the back foot, feeling the need to justify myself to him? That isn't happening. Not anymore.

'That's great. And what's the plan for today?'

'I don't know. You tell me.'

He wasn't expecting that. 'Oh, right... um... do you want us to tell her together? About Naomi, I mean.'

'I've given it some thought, and I think it's best if you put that to one side for now and introduce Naomi as a friend from work. That's how Lola thinks of her. She asked if Naomi was my friend, too, so the word *friend* means just that to her. I'm not sure she's quite ready to discover you're together, but we have a month to tackle that before she comes to stay with you.'

He shrugs his shoulders. 'If that's what you think is for the best, I'm happy to go along with it. So, what happens next?'

When you've loved someone for almost a decade and suddenly the person you see standing before you has changed in ways that make them unrecognisable to you, it's a shock. This isn't the Ben I know, even though that voice resonates down to the very core of me. He looks different, he's acting differently and that magnetism between us is missing.

'I'm on a tight turnaround here, so why don't you head over to The Farmhouse? Say hello to Cappy and tell Lola you've come to take her out for a surprise picnic. Just have her back by six o'clock as she was up early this morning.'

I don't know what he was expecting, but a look of relief passes over his face.

'Great. I'll give Naomi a quick call. Naturally she's stressing, and if we're going to take Lola out as we'd originally planned, I can't spring it on her. Thanks for not making a big deal out of this, Jess. It's not the way I thought things would pan out between us, but as you said, the focus is on making sure Lola is happy. See you later then.'

After nine years of marriage, his first reaction is to be concerned for poor Naomi, back at the hotel, about to stress out over having to pull a picnic lunch together. How will she cope in the middle of the night if Lola wakes up with a raging temperature?

Ben was never any help because he always slept through everything. If Naomi's relying on him when it comes to childcare, she can forget it. The night Lola was poorly with chickenpox I slept on the sofa with her on my lap, wrapped in a cotton sheet, with a fan blasting out because the poor mite was so hot but couldn't bear her skin being touched. When Ben sauntered down the following morning he was surprised to see us there, curled up together. Did he offer to stay home so I could catch up on some much-needed sleep? No. He assumed I'd call my boss and take a few days off. Which is precisely what I did.

As I pull off the pillowcases, I find myself punching the pillows back into shape a little too energetically. As angry as I'm feeling, when I hear a creak on the landing and look up to see my darling daughter appear in the doorway and promptly burst into tears, I rush over.

'What's wrong, Lola?' I kneel down next to her, wrapping her in my arms as she swipes impatiently with her sleeve at the tears trickling down her cheeks.

'I don't want to go, Mum. Misty is going to miss me and she might think I'm not coming back.'

'Oh, Lola! I'll keep popping in to check on her and in between she'll probably enjoy having a little time to wander around and explore. It'll make play time with you later even more special.'

A frown creases her forehead as I gaze up at her troubled face. 'Cappy asked Dad if he could come with us and he said yes but I don't want you to feel lonely, Mum.'

She's worried about leaving me behind and she's transferring that anxiety on to Misty.

'I have lots to keep me occupied and I'll spend some time with Misty in between.' Somehow I need to raise a smile to banish those unspoken fears. 'Now have fun and not too much ice cream, or you'll end up with brain freeze and you know how you hate that!'

Lola sniffs, making a concerted effort, presumably for my sake. Then she gives me the biggest hug, as I kiss her soft little cheek.

'I know. I had it when I went to the ice cream parlour with Cappy. But he had it, too, Mum, which made me laugh. And you're sure you'll be all right on your own?'

'I'll be just fine, I promise.'

Memories are full of silly moments that make us laugh in hindsight. I would never deny Lola access to her dad, although it's hard to hand her over as she's the main focus of my life. I'm delighted Cappy managed to invite himself along though. I can't imagine for one moment Ben extending the offer to him but I'm grateful, as it means I can relax a little knowing he'll keep a watchful eye. Do all mums feel like this the first time their child spends time in the company of their ex's new partner? The more youthful and carefree version of me, in this case, if my memory serves me well. Naomi is a few years younger than I am; there isn't a wrinkle or a worry line in sight – yet.

I watch them all head through the archway to the car parking area inside Renweneth Manor's gates; it's good to see Lola chattering away excitedly. Naturally, I want her to enjoy spending some time with her dad, it just makes me feel sad that her parents' lives have gone in two different directions.

Did Ben fall out of love with me because I'd become boring? Just a mum, trying to juggle work and family life, often a little sleep deprived and not always recognising the reflection staring back at her in the mirror. I'm feeling more alive now than I've felt for quite a long time. Maybe this was always meant to be. Who knows? I guess only time will tell because so many things are still – literally – a work in progress.

I manage to coax Misty out of her little nest with a feather on the end of a stick. She doesn't like anything that moves quickly, so I inch it slowly along the floor. Misty watches it intently from the safety of the cat carrier. Then I gently drag it back to within reaching distance and do the same thing all over again. On the fifth attempt she stretches out her paw and ten minutes later she does her first pounce, catching the feather between her front paws and snagging it.

Having succeeded, she sniffs at her food and carries on by, stopping to lap up some water from the bowl. Seconds later, she's curled up again on her blanket, her back to me, and it's snooze time.

I'm feeling a little jaded and having greeted the incomers, two guys who are here for a week before heading down to Land's End, I think some fresh air is in order.

As I'm about to swing open the front door, a loud rap on the knocker makes me jump. When I open it, it's Riley.

'You must have been poised,' he laughs. 'Cappy said to call in if I was passing.'

'Ah. His plans changed last minute, and he won't be back until about six, I'm afraid. It was a spur of the moment thing.'

I can see Riley is a little disappointed, but he gives me a fleeting smile. 'No problem, Jess. I was in the area and thought I'd call in on the off chance he was around. I should have called first to check. Sorry for barging in – you're obviously on your way out so I won't keep you.'

He stands back and I turn to lock the front door. 'I thought I'd take a walk down to the coastal path. I'm in need of some fresh air.'

When I turn back around Riley is looking rather dispirited and I feel bad turning him away. 'You're very welcome to join me if you're at a loose end.'

He opens his mouth and I'm pretty sure he's about to decline when his mood suddenly shifts. 'You know, I think a walk is precisely what I need right now. If you're sure, that is.'

'Good. I don't think I'm my own best company at the moment,' I declare, laughing at myself.

Riley gives me a slightly jaded smile. 'I know the feeling, Jess.'

I respond with an encouraging grin and we set off in silence. As the lane narrows, a signpost marks the public footpath, and he offers me his arm as I clamber over the stile next to it. The narrow swathe of moorland has a well-beaten trail which meanders around some large outcrops of rock.

'This is one of my favourite walks,' Riley confesses. 'I love the ruggedness of the terrain with that tantalising shimmer of water on the horizon.'

'Mine too, but my grandparents rarely suggested a traipse across the moor. We usually ended up driving to Penvennan Cove; or heading into Polreweek to browse the shops in the narrow alleyways. Drakestown is another favourite of mine with the tall ships.'

'There is another trail beyond that massive rock over there, but you can't see it from this vantage point. If you're heading for Penvennan Cove, it cuts across and saves a little time.' Riley indicates to our right.

We stop for a moment to simply look around and take in our surroundings. As I gaze back at the farm, the rear of both The Farmhouse and Renweneth Manor sit well in the setting, the sturdy stone wall giving privacy without obstructing the views of the sea from the first floor. The narrow strip of moorland here extends for miles in both directions. Ahead of us, as the crow flies it's a ten-minute walk over ground that gently slopes down to the clifftops.

'Right. Lead the way,' I reply, content to follow him.

The ground is stony and uneven in places and I'm glad I plumped for my stout walking boots. I just hope they don't give me blisters, as I haven't worn them in a while. On the other hand, my steel-toe-capped working boots are now well worn and comfy. However, they do bear the scars of my attempts at plastering; and the gun-metal-grey paint I used on the picket fencing and the fence panels I put up to give Penti Growan's courtyard some privacy.

I'm certainly glad I grabbed a fleece and tied it around my waist, as once we're up on the exposed headland, even with the sun overhead, the wind comes in gentle gusts and I'm more than grateful to cover my arms.

'Who doesn't love the smell of the sea?' I remark, wistfully. 'It's wonderful to get a whiff of the salty air sometimes when I'm working outside but out here it's another thing entirely.'

'How do you feel about taking a leisurely ramble down to Penvennan Cove to grab something to eat and a drink? It's about a five-mile round trek. There's a nice little pub there.'

'That sounds good to me. Cappy and Lola won't be back until sixish, as her dad is taking them on a picnic. Gosh, I hope they're not going to the cove.' I grimace, trying to imagine how awful it would be to bump into them.

'Ah… they might jump to the wrong conclusion. It's fine, at

least you know the way now. Just say when you're ready to turn back.'

'It's not that, and I am hungry. We've been divorced for a little over a year now. The problem for me is that today is the first time my daughter is meeting my ex's girlfriend.'

The cliff path is now in sight and as we walk side by side, Riley turns to look at me.

'I can totally empathise with what you're going through. It's an emotional rollercoaster, for sure.'

'That's a great analogy, Riley. I haven't quite got my head around the happy, blended family situation yet and it might take me a while to adjust. The new lady in my husband's... darn it... I keep doing that. I mean, my *ex's* life, is little more than a stranger to me and yet she's about to become a new *friend* to Lola.'

'That's a situation to steer clear of, but it's not a problem,' he grins at me. 'I have the perfect solution.'

'You do?'

'Yes. Trust me when I say your paths won't cross.'

'Then let's do this.'

The tenseness I was feeling in my shoulders and jaw is already easing and as we maintain a steady pace, there's time to notice the little things. At one point a slow worm darts across the path in front of us. I haven't seen one since I was a child and Cappy picked it up to let me touch it. This is just what I needed today.

I get Riley chatting about the work he did on his own cottage and the awful conditions in which he lived for the first few months after he arrived in Cornwall. He doesn't mention his family, or his son, in that context and I'm guessing he prefers not to dwell on what is, obviously, still a stressful situation. That's something with which I can most certainly empathise.

An intermittent stream of people, many of them with dogs in tow, pass in both directions. Most smile and exchange a little pleasantry. It would be lovely if there's time while Cappy is here to fit it in a walk with Lola; it would be a great way to spend an afternoon. While there is quite a drop in places, the path itself winds around the coast like a ribbon, following the natural lie of the land. On sections where the path narrows due to large rocky outcrops rising to our right, it's more of a climb. It certainly stretches the calf muscles, and we stop to lean on the sturdy metal handrails.

'Now that's what I call a view,' Riley remarks, letting out a long, slow breath.

I pull a scrunchy from the pocket of my backpack, then struggle to capture my flailing hair and draw it back into a ponytail.

'The breeze is refreshing,' Riley remarks, watching me and smiling.

'Yes; that's better, at least I can see it properly now. Just look at the water. It's like liquid silver.' Grabbing my sunglasses, I am relieved to put them on as the glare bouncing off the water is almost blinding.

Riley lowers his peaked cap. 'I'm thirsty, I don't know about you?'

'Hmm, definitely.'

'Once we get to the top of this section, it's all downhill and there's a fork in the path. Taking a right turn leads away from the cliff edge, but if we take a left, we can walk down through a little forest of trees.'

'The cove is closer than I thought. I've only ever driven there before.'

'If you don't mind hanging around here, I'll head down to the café and pick up a few things.'

I didn't think anyone could understand how I'm feeling right now. It's not that I'm hiding, I just can't face the thought of maybe bumping into Ben, Lola, Naomi and Cappy. My reaction to what's happening feels alien even to me. However, Riley doesn't appear to think it's at all odd. It's one of those occasions when only someone who has been through it themselves can see that logic goes out the window. 'Appreciated, thanks Riley.'

'It's no trouble at all, Jess.' His parting smile is both warm and supportive.

Left alone with my thoughts, I decide I can forgive myself a little paranoia, today of all days. It's the first of many to come and, hopefully, it will get easier.

10

A New Me is Finally Emerging

I'm perched on an enormous moss-covered rock eating a traditional Cornish pasty from Pascoe's Café and Bakery. I'd forgotten just how good they are.

'This is certainly putting a halt to the rumblings in my stomach. It feels like a long time since breakfast.'

Riley nods in agreement. He takes a swig from his bottle of water before dipping a hand into the carrier bag next to him.

'I don't suppose you fancy a cold beer?'

'Ooh, now that would go down really well, thanks.'

I watch as he pulls his keys from his pocket and takes off the bottle caps with something hanging from the fob. Whatever it is, it's bright pink.

'That's a nifty idea!'

'There's a bit of a story behind this,' he muses, and I raise my eyebrows at him curiously.

'You can't stop there.'

As I dust the crumbs off my fleece, he laughs softly.

'I was at Heathrow airport, about to fly off with some mates for a week in the sun. As you do, I emptied out my pockets into the plastic tray and walked through the scanner. But on the other side two guys came up to me and took me off to a side table where one of the officials was going through the tray. I learnt the hard way that carrying a Swiss Army knife on your keyring isn't the best idea.'

I burst out laughing. 'Surely they realised you're no terrorist?'

'Hmm… they weren't amused when I explained that it hadn't even occurred to me it was illegal and, naturally, they confiscated it. I thought this was a great replacement, though. No sharp points in sight and pretty darned useful, as it turns out.' With that, he holds up what turns out to be a pink flamingo with a conveniently pointed beak.

It's great to see him chuckling away and anyone who can laugh at themselves is fine by me. When he produces a waxy paper bag and opens it to reveal two saffron buns, my eyes light up.

'Dessert?' he offers.

'Oh, go on then. Seriously, I have no willpower when it comes to food.'

We eat in silence for a while, watching a ship far off on the horizon and a few smaller boats cross the expansive vista between the leafy trees and shrubs partially framing the view.

'Have you always been a… handyman?' I ask. 'Although, you're more of a general builder really, aren't you?'

'I started out as a carpenter and joiner making bespoke kitchen cabinets, but I've always been open to tackling anything DIY. Working on my own cottage there was no time pressure, as I had to earn the cash to buy the materials I needed as I went along.'

I can only admire Riley's determination. It makes me realise what a fortunate position I'm in. 'It must have been hard to figure out where to begin.'

'I started at the top and worked down. The roof was leaking like a sieve and all the guttering needed replacing. At first, a few friends with some handy skills would drive down for the weekend and give me a hand. They thought it sounded like fun, until they got here. That's how I picked up a lot of tricks of the trade, but it gave the term *roughing it* a whole new definition. My life had changed in ways I couldn't even get my head around and suddenly the people I used to know seemed to drift away.

Most of my friends were in long-term relationships anyway and socialising tends to be a couples thing.'

We lapse into an awkward silence. I genuinely thought it was a safe question and I certainly wasn't expecting such an honest response. When I glance at my watch, Riley takes it as a hint and grabs the empty bottles, popping them into the carrier bag.

'Right, let's make our way back.' He stands, taking one last lingering look out to sea. 'If only all days could be like this. It's hard to think of anything negative when you see a view like that, isn't it?'

'Being in nature and playing music...' I reflect.

'What's that?'

'When life gives me a knock, it's the two things I turn to that help to turn my mood around. Nothing lasts forever, even if it feels like that when you're going through it. But this little interlude has reminded me of that. It's been lovely, Riley, and I've appreciated your company.'

'Same here, Jess. And I'm looking forward to us sitting down together with Cappy to go through the plans in more detail. It's an exciting project for me and it's come at just the right time.'

For us both, it seems. I'm now firmly convinced that Riley isn't the sort of man who would intentionally let anyone down. He's a man of his word.

Waiting for Cappy and Lola to return, I end up sitting on the floor in the kitchen while Misty trots around looking much more at ease. Having tried to tempt her with every toy in the box, the only thing that she keeps going back to is a cardboard tube from the middle of a toilet roll. She's not quite sure what it is and creeps up to bat it with her paw, then runs away as if expecting it to follow her.

Ivy's been on my mind, so I decide to give her a quick call.

'Sorry, Jess, I've been meaning to ring you. I'm just locking up.' She sounds tired.

Checking the clock on the wall, I see that it's almost half-past five. 'It's a bit late for you, it must have been a busy day.'

'Oh, it was, we shut at five as usual but I've had not one, but *two*, electricians here for the last couple of hours.'

'Really?'

'One guy finally managed to fix the alarm. Well, fingers crossed, but I suppose only time will tell. The other one was here to talk about some rewiring work.'

'That's brilliant news. I guess whatever you said to your landlord really sunk in.'

'I've asked for five extra sockets in the kitchen and he's going to upgrade the main distribution board. It'll mean closing the shop for half a day as, annoyingly, they won't do it on a Sunday, but things are going in the right direction.'

'How's Adam doing?'

'Better than he was. Word is out that he's setting up on his own again and he is getting a few little jobs here and there just from the general chatter. In between he's working for a flat daily rate for one of the big developers, laying pavers on a huge new residential development. It's not ideal, but he needs to keep busy. He's having some business cards printed up and we'll be passing them out like crazy. I'm going to have a pile on the counter here at the café.'

She sounds a lot more positive than the last time we talked.

'It's frustrating for him, but I'm sure that it's the same in Gloucestershire as it is down here, a good builder is in demand.'

'I know,' she sighs, aware that it takes time to build a client base. 'We're hoping it won't be long before he gets those word-of-mouth recommendations, as that's the best sort of advertising and it's free.'

'It's how I found my builder. Cappy is here for a few days and I'm getting excited. We're going to sit down and really get a handle on what needs to be done.'

'You mentioned there was a deadline. Is that the reason you're eager to make a start?'

'Only in part,' I divulge. 'I'm home alone – well, that's not quite true – waiting for Cappy and Lola to return. Ben's here for the weekend with his now live-in partner, Naomi. They spent the entire afternoon together.'

'OMG!' Ivy sounds horrified. 'Who's there with you then?'

'Misty, the kitten Cappy brought with him as a surprise for Lola.'

'Aww…' Ivy's voice immediately softens. 'But seriously Jess, you sound way too calm about this. What's going on?'

Letting out a short, sharp, breath I gather my courage together. 'Ben never is going to come back to me, Ivy. I think you knew that all along.'

'When Ben started making excuses to bow out of our get-togethers I did wonder whether Adam or I had unwittingly said something to upset him. Then I wondered whether it was just a phase the two of you were going through, it happens to us all. After that there was only one conclusion left…'

'I know, but it's only just beginning to feel real. Today has been tough because I don't know Naomi, and the truth is that I don't really want to get to know her. However, she'll be spending time with Lola so I'm going to have to put my feelings to one side for the sake of my daughter. Today, somehow, Cappy managed to tag along. Ben wasn't expecting him to be here, but knowing he was keeping an eye got me through it.' Together with Riley's company, for which I was extremely grateful, I reflect.

'I'd love to have seen the look on Ben's face. I mean, no one can say *no* to Cappy, can they? He's such a great old guy.'

'I'll be honest, Ivy, I would have ended up being a nervous wreck just handing Lola over and yes, I will quiz Cappy out of earshot of Lola when they get back. It's weird, because we didn't have a master plan and it's pure coincidence he was here.'

'Ooh, a chill just ran down my back, Jess. That's freaky. It's like someone is watching over you.'

'I thought the exact same thing! Perhaps Grandma had something to do with it,' I muse, only half-joking. Grandad always said there's no such thing as a coincidence. And when two occur at the same time – Cappy being here and me giving in to Ben's request at the last-minute – it makes me stop and think.

'Either way, you got through the first hurdle, Jess, and I'm proud of you. It's a day we've avoided talking about, isn't it?'

'We have, and you know me so well. Sometimes I need to mull things over for a while, and only then am I ready to face what's coming.'

Ivy's tone suddenly changes. 'There's something else, though. I can tell. You sound much more upbeat. You can't leave me hanging, Jess.'

Now is not the time to mention Riley's name in any context. 'I think I'm ready to push forward with the plan. Oh, I think I heard someone at the door, sorry, I'd better go and check. Take care, Ivy. Love to you both, mwah!'

'Lola didn't have very much to say, Cappy, I know she was tired and wanted to spend some time with Misty before bed, but I was expecting her to rabbit away as she usually does.'

He looks across the sitting room at me, a frown creasing his brow.

'It was okay, Jess. Naomi was nervous and because of that Ben was rather anxious at times. In all honesty, I'm glad I was there to add a bit of banter when there were awkward moments.'

'Like?'

'Naturally, Ben's used to holding Lola's hand, but Naomi wasn't sure how she fitted in. I engaged her in conversation and the two of us tended to walk behind Ben and Lola to give them some time together. You're right, she is young – not just in age. At twenty-four, if the only person you've had responsibility for is yourself, suddenly having someone else's child come into your life is a big ask.'

I grab my wine glass off the coffee table between us and take a big swig. The last thing I was expecting was for Cappy to feel sympathetic towards Ben's new partner and I'm confused.

'Don't look at me like I'm a traitor, Jess, because I'm not. Ben made Lola the focus of the afternoon, and rightly so, but he hasn't yet got his head around how to include Naomi without upsetting his darling daughter.'

I shake my head, trying to push my emotional turmoil to one side. 'Give it to me straight, Cappy. How do we get this to work and, more importantly, can I trust that Lola is in safe hands?'

He tilts his head back, considering his response, and my stomach begins to churn.

'Of course she's safe. Ben dotes on Lola, and you know that, Jess.' His tone is one that won't countenance any dispute. 'The difficulty is that Ben and Naomi have to find a balance. In my opinion, he should step back and let her and Lola have a little bonding time together.'

My expression hardens. 'Bonding time?'

'Come on, Jess. Like it, or not, Naomi isn't going anywhere, and Lola misses her dad. You got this, Jess, if... and I stress that if... you don't see her as a threat. She's never going to replace you and that's a fact, but by keeping things friendly I wouldn't be surprised if she reached out to you for advice. She doesn't have any experience at all with children and you can't blame her for that.'

'Great, that's just what I wanted to hear!' The words explode from my lips and when I see the look on Cappy's face, I'm horrified that I couldn't disguise my sarcasm. 'Sorry, I didn't know what to expect today. A part of me wanted my girl to come back buzzing with excitement and a part of me—'

'Would have felt wounded if she had,' he continues. 'Why do you think I invited myself along, Jess? Ben couldn't refuse my offer, but as it turned out he was jolly glad I was there. Lola spent some much-needed time with her dad, and I was able to reassure Naomi that no one expected anything from her. In time she'll get to know Lola and it will become easier, but Ben is the parent and that's an entirely different role.'

'And Naomi took that on board?'

'With much relief, Jess. It allowed her to relax and give Ben and Lola some space.'

'But he wants Lola to go and stay with them. How will that work?'

Grandad gives me a pointed look. 'I'm sure some of Lola's friends at school are in a similar situation. Relationships don't work out for all sorts of reasons and that's life, I'm afraid. You need to set your emotions aside, so that Lola doesn't feel guilty about accepting Naomi as her dad's new partner.'

In my heart I know Cappy is right.

'So, what should I do now?'

'When you're ready, text Ben and say Lola had a great time, which is true. Don't question Lola about anything, treat it as if it's the new norm, which it is, Jess. Why not casually suggest that Ben gives your phone number to Naomi ahead of that first trip back to Stroud? Say she can call you anytime if she has any questions or concerns.'

Ever practical, Cappy has managed to put things into perspective for me, much to my shame.

'Sorry I'm so emotional. This wasn't how I imagined my life playing out.'

'Jess, you can't look back, only forward. Make a friend of Naomi and if she has a problem with anything to do with Lola, she'll talk to you before she talks to Ben. That's in everyone's best interests, isn't it?'

I've learnt that kids are more resilient than we give them credit for, mainly because they're constantly learning new things. It's only as you get older that change becomes a thing to fear because it's venturing into the unknown. 'It is and you're right, Cappy.'

'With what you're doing here, Jess, you're showing your daughter that life is what you make it. You can either give in and feel sorry for yourself or get motivated and make the best of life's opportunities. In my opinion, she couldn't have a better role model, but be the one with the cool head sitting in the driving seat, not the person hiding under the duvet covers.'

I roll my eyes. 'Grandad! I'm pretty sure that last sentence was a line from a film I watched recently.'

His eyes sparkle as I look across at him. 'But it was one worth repeating, wasn't it?'

11

It's Time to Work Those Muscles

After an enjoyable Sunday morning lie-in, I'm now up to my elbows in dishes. Having cooked a full roast dinner with all the trimmings in Cappy's honour, in some ways it feels like Christmas in June. During lunch he tells a string of jokes and most of them I know by heart. There's a lot of laughter and memories of the old days come flooding back.

Lola is still enthralled with her present and hasn't strayed far from Misty's side, but this afternoon, for some odd reason, she's talked Cappy into making her a tent for her bedroom.

'But you have a princess bed, Lola,' I'd pointed out when she raised the subject.

'Yes, but this is for Misty. Somewhere we can snuggle and she'll feel safe.'

Just like the drapes around Lola's bed, which turned it into her little sanctuary. I leave them to it, wanting to finish clearing up the kitchen as quickly as possible. Riley is coming around early evening so we can pore over the plans and no doubt we'll both be questioning Cappy about the technical stuff.

The problem I have is that when it comes to budgets, I work with spreadsheets. Cappy's rough estimate of costs are all hand-written and need updating. He pulled this together probably four years ago, in advance of submitting his final set of revised plans. Obviously prices have risen over time but not all the figures have breakdowns, so I'm thinking maybe there are a few pages missing. In the end I realise this was only ever a very rough estimate, probably to help him weigh up whether it was, in fact, a dream that he'd never be able to see through. I'm going around in circles, when all that concerns me is making a start and focusing on one building at a time.

Trying to ignore the ominous sound of sawing and the shrieks of laughter coming from upstairs, I focus instead on the cash situation. Working out precisely how much I can safely transfer over into the building fund, while keeping enough in the bank to cover the overheads, requires my full attention. On paper we're as good as fully booked throughout the entire summer season, but it would be foolhardy to count that as income until the money is in the bank. I'm hoping that, by the end of the summer, there will be enough put aside to extend the project into the back end of the year without any issues.

'Mum, do you have any old bed sheets?' Lola calls down the stairs.

Putting the PC into sleep mode, I call up: 'I'm sure I do. Give me a couple of minutes and I'll see what's in the linen cupboard.'

Naturally, that ends up turning into a couple of hours. One bed sheet isn't large enough to cover the widest part of the robust-looking teepee. Having sewn two of them together, we now have to work out the correct angle to make the cone.

'Why did they make teepees such an awkward shape?' Lola puzzles as we struggle to pin the fabric around the poles.

Cappy tries his best to keep a straight face. 'They're easy to build and quick to put up if you're on the move, Lola. And the hole at the top meant that when it was cold, or they were hungry, they could light a fire. The smoke is funnelled upwards as it is with a chimney.'

She catches her lip between her teeth, deep in thought.

'But isn't that dangerous?'

Both Cappy and I start laughing, as he ruffles her hair.

'Yes, and I'm not suggesting that's what we do, light a fire inside it. But remember that the original teepees were really big, so big that it was safe. If they didn't have heat, they couldn't survive the often harsh winters.'

'In the pictures we looked at in school some of the teepees had drawings on them.'

I did wonder what she was up to when she was whispering away to Cappy just before lunch. So, this was all Lola's idea.

'I believe they did sometimes. Probably animals or plants.'

It's obvious what's coming next.

'Mum, can we draw a pattern on the outside once you've sewn it together?'

'It's almost teatime, Lola. Let's focus on getting this to fit first. Maybe we can think about decorating it tomorrow after school.'

'Okay, Mum.'

'Lola, why don't we leave Mummy to it and head downstairs to make tea?'

I give him a grateful smile. At this rate I'm going to be here all night.

Stepping into the kitchen, I find Cappy and Riley head down, deep in conversation.

'Hi Riley, thanks for coming. I'm sorry it took so long to settle Lola down and I'm glad you made a start. What have I missed?'

'Only me asking lots of trivial questions,' Riley declares. 'I found an access point when I put in that outside tap for you, Jess, and it was obvious the pipework was all new, but I wasn't sure which way it ran.'

'No question is ever trivial, Riley. It's all about the detail,' Cappy continues. I pull out a chair and join them. 'You'll remember the massive trenches going around the courtyard, Jess, and across into the main field.'

'The mud bath?'

Cappy and I exchange a knowing smile. 'The mud bath. The wettest autumn for years, they said. Anyway, all of the services are in the same trench, which runs parallel to the French drain in the courtyard. We had that constructed at the same time to take the surface water away and stop it puddling in front of the old workshop.'

'The plumbing should be straightforward enough and when the time comes I know a good electrician, unless Jess already has someone in mind?' Riley offers.

They both turn to look at me, but I'm way out of my depth here. 'Can we just um... backtrack a little? I'm assuming what you just said is good news, as Riley is smiling.'

'Sorry, Jess. Basically, the new services – water, sewerage and electricity – are ready to feed into the buildings.'

'That's a real bonus, Jess,' Riley confirms. 'It must have cost a fair bit re-laying the cobbled areas, Cappy.'

'It did, but it was worth it to get the infrastructure set up ready to go.'

It's obvious that Cappy feels Riley is up to the job and I feel bad now having quizzed Erica about him.

'Right, let's talk about building regulations next, then,' I reply. 'It's all new to me, so don't leave anything out.'

It could be a late one, but the enthusiasm around the table is tangible.

'Cappy, why do you have to go home? Why can't you stay a bit longer?' Lola's bottom lip wavers as Cappy puts his suitcase down next to the front door. His week here has flown by. It's been nice having some of his old friends stopping by to say hello, but I feel bad he didn't get to the pub after all.

The toot of a car horn prompts a sudden flurry of activity, as Erica kindly offered to do the school run today.

'Lola, grab your school bag and I'll get your water bottle.'

Cappy swings open the front door, walking over to say hello to Erica and Daisy.

Lola slinks down the stairs miserably and I gaze up at her feeling much the same way. 'Come on, let's not send Cappy off feeling sad and—'

'Mum!' she squeals, pointing and I turn around to see Misty trotting over the doorstep.

We both spring into action. 'Cappy! Cappy! Catch Misty!'

Unfortunately, the raised voices, the sound of a car engine idling and then three people heading straight for her makes her zigzag over towards the small barn.

We all stop, realising we're making it worse.

'Leave this to me, Mum,' Lola says quite confidently as she slips off her backpack and disappears inside.

Seconds later she reappears with Misty in her arms. 'You don't want Cappy to go either, do you, Misty?' she coos.

'Lola, come on. Give Misty to me and say goodbye. We've had a lovely time and we don't want to make Cappy sad, so turn that frown into a smile. If you don't hurry up you and Daisy will be late for school.' I turn and call over my shoulder, 'Sorry, Erica – Lola's just coming.'

As Lola gently places Misty in my hands, it's not just the kitten's heart that is thudding away. Cappy stoops to give Lola a hug and she throws her arms around him, ominously looking like she doesn't intend to let go.

'Hey, I'll be back, and soon, Lola, I promise. Riley and Mummy are going to be really busy around here, so I'll expect you to take good care of Misty and make sure she doesn't get into trouble. This little minx won't want to miss out on the fun, so you'll need to keep a constant eye on her.'

'Don't worry. Misty loves her tent and Mum said we can put her nest inside so she can sleep in my room. I love you, Cappy.'

I hand Misty to him, and hurry Lola over to the car as Daisy swings open the rear door.

'Thank you, Daisy. And thanks, Erica, for offering to do the school runs through to Friday. It's a bit crazy here this morning with Cappy leaving and the building work starting today. I'm a bit all over the place.'

'No problem, Jess. Are you using Riley?'

'I am. He's going to be here for the next five consecutive days so we can make a solid start. Then he's working for the builders' merchants for two days before he'll be back.'

'In that case,' she lowers her voice, indicating for me to come closer. 'Would it help if Lola came for a sleepover on Saturday night? I could collect her first thing and bring her back after lunch on Sunday if you like.'

Both girls are straining their ears to listen. They sit bolt upright, leaning forward in anticipation.

'I don't think I'm going to be very popular if I say no,' I grin at her. 'That would be perfect as I'm taking on the role of labourer. I can only hope I'm up to it.'

'Oh, I'm sure you'll do just fine. Come on girls, I'll put some music on and we can have a singalong.' Erica gives me a knowing look. I put my hand over my heart, my eyes full of gratitude from one mum to another.

We wave them off just as Misty decides to wriggle out of the nook of Cappy's arm. I quickly stoop down, both hands open, and catch her just in time.

'You little minx! You can't wait to explore, can you? It's a bit soon yet.'

'Misty's going to be a lively little one,' Cappy remarks as we turn to go back inside. I place her on the stairs, as it'll keep her occupied for a while. Each step is only just about within her reach and going up is like climbing a mountain. Coming down is hilarious and she bounces well.

'That's just what we need, it's way too quiet when we're

on our own. We're certainly going to miss you, Cappy. It feels so right your being back here. And now with the work about to start...' my words tail off into an uneasy silence.

'When you need my input, you only have to say. You'll crack on with it and I'm leaving you in good hands with Riley. And I meant what I said to Lola, I hope to be back very soon if you'll have me.'

He steps forward, wrapping me in his arms and, in truth, I don't want him to go. 'Any time, Cappy. Any time at all. That spare room is yours; Mum and Dad can always bring their campervan when they visit.'

He does a belly laugh. 'Oh, Jess... you've got it all figured out, haven't you?'

'Not quite. Admittedly, I'll keep a close eye on the cash flow, so I don't get myself into trouble. And I'm happy to roll up my sleeves to help Riley and learn a few useful things along the way. But if he comes to me with questions I don't have the technical ability to answer—'

'Then you'll give me a ring and I can always jump in the car and head down. My time is my own, Jess, and it's good to feel useful again.'

The way he said 'again' is poignant. A part of me can't help wondering whether he regrets moving back to Gloucestershire, even though it's only a short walk to my parents' house.

'If I'm being totally honest, I don't think I can do this without your input. Travel safe, Cappy, and thank you... for everything. Don't forget to text me when you get home.'

As his car disappears from view, I hurry back to The Farmhouse but before I reach the door, I hear a vehicle turn into the courtyard. Glancing over my shoulder, I watch as Riley brings his old white van to a halt in front of the small barn. Swinging open the door he climbs out, his face beaming.

'Morning, Jess. I just passed Cappy and gave him a wave. Sorry I'm a bit later than planned. I drove over to Polreweek to borrow a woodchipper off a mate of mine. He owes me a favour and it saves hiring one.'

Riley has no idea how relieved I am to see him, not just because this is day one on the next stage of the journey, but sometimes I miss having people around me. It's a mental boost, knowing I have a full and productive day ahead of me no matter what I end up doing, and it's a real tonic.

'That's great, Riley, and much appreciated, thank you. I'll grab some gloves and you can put me to work.'

He's already opening up the rear doors of the van and pulling out what looks like a folded tarpaulin. Eager to make a start, I stride away purposefully. With Misty asleep in the teepee, I'll make a quick coffee to keep my builder happy and then I'm ready to get stuck in.

'Hi, darling. I'm just checking in to see how it went today,' Mum asks, her voice full of enthusiasm.

'It was brilliant. We managed to totally expose the far end of the row of outbuildings where it butts up to the small barn.'

'Was it as bad as you'd feared?' She sounds hesitant.

'Considering no one has been in there since Cappy had the first set of plans drawn up what... well over five years ago now, it was obviously dank and smelly. There's some damage to the stonework on the back corner, where Riley had to use a pickaxe to get out the roots of the Virginia creeper. However, the walls are so thick he said it's easy enough to repair and there were no visible cracks inside. The good news is that now we can see along the entire roofline, Riley was more than happy. There are a couple of ridge tiles that are crumbling but he says it's a quick fix.'

'You sound happy, Jess, and Dad will be thrilled to hear you've made a good start.'

'Looking across now from The Farmhouse, it's not hard to envisage the end result. After a jet wash and a bit of repointing here and there, it's going to look like a beautiful row of old cottages, instead of a collection of neglected buildings.'

'It's exciting to see your hard work finally paying off.'

'Next time you come down I'll show you the plans. Cappy went through them in detail with me and Riley last Sunday.'

'I popped in to see him earlier on and heard all about your new addition to the family,' Mum declares, sounding amused. 'You didn't mind?'

'No, not at all, although it was a total surprise. Misty spent several hours today sitting on the window seat in Lola's bedroom watching us work.'

'And how is our girl?'

'Lola is doing really well, Mum. She was a bit mopey when she got back from school because Cappy wasn't here, but when Misty came hurtling downstairs to greet her she soon perked up. She's the same when you and Dad go back home.'

'But when we do get together we make the most of it, don't we?'

'We do, and I guess once the work is all done and I'm a lady of leisure, every visit will be just family time.'

'That's not you though, is it, Jess? You take after your dad. Just when things are ticking over nicely he comes up with another plan to turn things upside down.'

'That sounds ominous. How are you both doing?'

'Up to our eyes in soil. Dad has decided to dig up the lawned area, the other side of the apple trees. He's just ordered a second greenhouse.' Mum's tone indicates it's a level of disruption she could do without.

'You know he loves a project and with two greenhouses to maintain it'll keep him out of mischief,' I laugh.

'Hmm... it's the only spot in the garden that gets the sun all day. It's my favourite place to sit and read. Admittedly, he's leaving a small patch of grass to placate me, but he'll be in and out, and back and forth all the time.'

'What you need is a little place of your own where you can sit undisturbed. Something with glass doors you can open if it's sunny and close if it's raining.'

'A reading nook? What a great idea. Like a small office. If it faced up the garden I suppose he wouldn't disturb me as much. Now that's worth considering, Jess.'

'Oh, I'm full of good ideas. The problem is turning them into reality,' I reflect.

Mum chuckles. 'Well, your dad has time on his hands. I just wish he paid as much attention to the house as he does to his precious garden, then I'd be over the moon. I'm about to start repainting our bedroom to freshen it up. After seeing the transformation you've achieved at the farm, I've decided I prefer the lighter colours. Oh well, I suppose I'd better go and make your dad a cup of tea. He'll no doubt want a hand to wheelbarrow the turf he's digging up over to the compost heap.'

It's hard not to laugh, as Mum is equally as bad as Dad. Fortunately, they each have their own domain and it works... most of the time. As she rings off, I reflect that at least I don't have that age old problem of give and take. When it comes to decisions about the farm, I'm in the hot seat, so let's hope I get it right first time.

It's been a satisfying day and suddenly the drawings we pored over at the weekend are making a lot more sense. Today, I've used a reciprocating saw to cut through some two-inch thick vines and a wood chipping machine to turn it into mulch. Then I trolleyed bag after bag of the stuff to lay it on the decorative borders at the front of the campsite. No wonder my muscles are aching. Even though it's only nine o'clock, the thought of sliding between crisp, cotton sheets is a temptation I can no longer resist. Being free and single isn't necessarily the key to doing what you want when you want. But it's only thinking about Lola's future that keeps me motivated to go forward. She truly is my inspiration.

12

Day Two and It's Eviction Time

I've spent all morning filling the back of Riley's van ready for yet another tip run. It would have been a huge bonus to find something that was left over from the days the bakery here supplied everyone within walking distance. Having carried piles of old, rotting wood and a few bits of metal that Riley can't recycle, I wander through to see what he's doing in the next room. There's a step down as this half of the building is at a slightly lower level.

'That's all done. What's next?'

'You could take a look upstairs. I think it's mainly wooden crates. There might be a few worth salvaging. The odd bit of woodworm we can treat if you can find some that are intact. I haven't had time to take a close look, though. Just be careful there aren't any rusty nails.'

Riley has been working flat out lifting some beautiful old flagstones we're hoping to recycle. Sweat is dripping off his forehead from the exertion, as he has to lift them on to the sack trucks one by one and stack them outside.

'I could give you a hand with that, you know. I'm stronger than I look. I might not be able to lift a dead weight, but if I stand them upright I can walk them across the floor.'

He straightens, mopping his brow with his sleeve. 'I'm good, really. By the end of the day, I want to have all of these shifted and at the rate you're going, we'll have both buildings emptied.'

'I thought it was all one building. That's how it appears on the plans.'

'No. Originally the bakery was half the size and that's why the floor levels are different.'

I can see that he doesn't really want to stop and chat, but it's almost lunchtime and I'm hungry.

'I'll make some sandwiches and a cold drink. Say, twenty minutes and make your way over to the cottage? I need to check on Misty, anyway.'

He looks at me, holding up his hands and glancing down at his clothes. Adam is mired in a layer of grime that covers the heavy flagstones. 'Maybe we could eat outside? I'd hate to trample this through your hallway and into the kitchen.'

My clothes will probably dust off quite easily, so I nod my head. 'I'll give you a shout when it's ready.'

What is obvious to me, is that Riley isn't used to having an assistant. He's either worked alone, or as a contractor happy to be given a specific job and left to get on with it. I don't want to be a nuisance to him, but the man has to eat. It's not good to go all day fuelled solely by mugs of coffee.

Misty is now trotting around like she owns the place and even when I put down her fresh food, she comes to sniff it then runs off into the sitting room. She's discovered Bathsheba's old favourite spot on the windowsill, and I think she likes to see what's going on.

It makes me feel awkward that Riley doesn't feel comfortable coming inside, as if he might inconvenience me. Anything but, because I value his skills and there's nothing wrong with a bit of dust and dirt. A quick mop through at the end of the day freshens up the flagstones and the floorboards I spent hours sanding and waxing. That's the joy of living in a charmingly rustic old building. Nothing is ever pristine; it simply looks well-loved, which is how a home should feel. Besides, he's good company.

I carry everything over to the lawn in front of Renweneth Manor. They don't make cast iron tables and chairs as solid as these anymore. This set didn't come off a production line, it was hand forged. It was here long before my grandparents bought the farm and, with a fresh coat of paint, it adds to the ambience of the garden.

I give Riley a prompt, saying there's soap and a towel in the downstairs cloakroom and informing him that lunch is ready and waiting underneath the oak trees.

As I sit waiting for him to join me, all I can see is the high stone wall with a glimpse through the wrought iron gate of the archway into the main courtyard. From this angle I can just see the new fencing I put up alongside Penti Growan. It's so private here and with the towering oak trees, it has a very different feel to the view from The Farmhouse.

Riley comes striding towards me, a key dangling from his fingers. 'I brushed myself off before I went inside and I locked up afterwards,' he says, handing them to me before taking a seat. 'I hope you don't leave it open during the day. Anyone could walk in, particularly if you're in the small barn, or over here.'

'Thanks, and I usually remember, but you're right. It's easy to be lulled into a false sense of security. Anyway, tuck in.'

I covered the tray with a tea towel, and I lift it, handing Riley a plate.

'You don't have to cater for me, you know. I rarely eat lunch.'

I raise an eyebrow, staring back at him. 'When you're working this hard you need fuel.'

And he is hungry, because he fills his plate and begins eating with relish. After a few seconds he grins at me. 'Most homeowners think builders live on doughnuts and biscuits.'

I shake my head, as I pour us both a large glass of Lola's

favourite cranberry and orange summer drink. When Riley takes a sip he looks pleasantly surprised.

'This is very refreshing, thank you, Jess. It's not soda water, though. You've put something else in there.'

'The secret ingredient is ginger ale. The ice takes the fizz out of it.'

'Hmm... I like it.'

We eat in companionable silence, Riley quite happy to look around. It doesn't take any persuasion at all to get him to refill his plate and I'm glad he's beginning to feel more relaxed.

'Lola is going to stay at her friend's house this weekend, so I'm free all day tomorrow, Saturday and up until lunchtime on Sunday.'

He looks at me studiously. 'If we can keep up the pace, I'd like to be in a position to get the building inspector in on Monday morning. I won't be here, of course, but it's just to check he's happy with how far down we're going before we lay the damp-proof membrane.'

My eyes widen. 'It's as simple as making a call?'

'Yep. I submitted the form and I'll call him on my way into work. Just leave him to it and he'll tell you if there's anything he's not happy with.'

'And after that?'

'I'll be back bright and early Wednesday morning. If all goes well, will you be up for some cementing if I place an order?'

'Why not? I've made a few cakes in my time and iced them, too. How hard can it be?'

To which Riley bursts out laughing. 'It's all about levelling, so you could be a dab hand. As long as the mix is right, you can't really go far wrong, but we'll need to work fast.'

'What's the plan for this afternoon?'

'If you can finish emptying out the upstairs and leave me to lift the final flagstones, we can start pulling down the ceilings. I want to get all the mess out the way before we start digging out the bakery floor to lower it to the same level as the former greengrocer's shop.'

I drain the last dregs from my glass. 'Right. Let's do this!'

I think my scream could probably be heard for miles around as I fly down the stairs, two at a time.

'What's up?'

I bump into Riley as he sprints towards the bottom of the rickety staircase.

'Something ran along the floor!' I exclaim, my heart pounding in my chest.

Before he has a chance to respond, I push past him and run out into the sunshine. My heart is leaping in my chest and not in a good way.

'Yuck!' I shudder, despite the fact that I'm hot and bothered.

'It's okay. I don't think it was a rat, probably a mouse,' he assures me a few minutes later. Great. That's fine then. 'I found the nest but it's empty. If they weren't already on the run with the noise we've been making, your scream did the trick and they've gone in search of a new home.'

He carries the last bundle of crates in his arms and my eyes are darting everywhere, half-expecting a mouse to run up his arm and wondering what on earth I'd do.

'Is there any chance of a coffee?' he ventures, hesitantly.

I expel a long, slow breath, trying to get my erratic breathing back under control. 'Coming up,' and, like the mouse, I scuttle away to safety.

As I cross the courtyard carrying a loaded tray, I'm surprised to see Vyvyan walking towards me.

'Hey, Jess. It looks like work has begun in earnest,' she notes, watching Riley as he struggles to push in a couple of pieces of wood so he can shut the van doors.

'It's full so I'm just going to do a run to the tip. Hi, Vyvyan,' he calls out. 'I'll grab a coffee a bit later, Jess.'

I glance at the tray and back at Vyvyan. 'I don't suppose you have time to stop?'

Her face lights up. 'Whenever there's cake it's a yes from me.'

She follows me around to the rear of The Farmhouse. There's a nice shady spot in the corner and we sit at the little bistro table and chairs I rescued from the small barn. Having given them a quick sanding down, three cans of white spray paint later I was pleased with my find.

'This is all looking lovely. A lot has changed since I was last here. You've certainly been hard at work, Jess.' Her eyes take in the scarf wrapped around my hair.

'I'm covered in dust, but that's par for the course these days. How do you take your coffee?'

'Milk, no sugar, thanks. Did you make that cake?'

'No. Daisy's Mum, Erica, made it. She keeps saying I need fattening up and every time I see her she insists on giving me something fresh out the oven. Here you go. Help yourself to a fork.'

'This feels rather civilised,' Vyvyan states, smiling. 'Afternoon tea at Renweneth Farm!'

'Not quite as posh as I'd like,' I grin back at her. 'One day maybe, who knows? How are things going with you?' I slip a forkful of cake into my mouth, savouring it. I needed the sugar, I was beginning to run out of steam.

'Good. The website is incredibly busy.'

'Thank goodness for that,' I reply. 'I thought for one moment there was a problem.'

One glance at her face tells me that something isn't quite right.

'Jess, this is about Keith. I didn't tell him I was going to drop by to see you, so if he does spot us talking I'll say I was just checking you're happy with the photos I uploaded to the website.

I picked out the best ones but do take a look and say if you want any of them swapped out. Personally, I think they look great.'

'I will, and thanks. What's up with Keith?'

'It's about Len. They've had a bit of a falling-out.'

'Over what?'

'You mentioned to Len that if he has a problem to give you a call. Keith sees that as... I know this sounds silly, but if something goes wrong he thinks it's his job to sort it out.'

My face falls. 'Oh, I see. I just thought that on his days off...'

'I know you meant well, but Cappy left Keith to it and that's what he's used to. When Len received the second complaint about the two young guys the other day, he wasn't sure quite what to do. He rang Keith out of courtesy to let him know he was about to call you. Keith got into a bit of strop and told him not to do anything until he arrived.'

'I see. And they ended up escorting the troublemakers off site.'

'Yes, but Len wasn't happy because now he's conflicted. I can see both sides to this. Len felt that Keith was undermining your instructions, which he was. But Keith feels it's his place to be on call for things like that. Now there's an atmosphere between them.'

'Oh dear, I've really put my foot in it, haven't I? I was only trying to avoid Len calling Keith in on his precious days off for something trivial, when I'm literally on the doorstep.'

'The problem is that Len was right, but in that particular situation it did take two of them to make sure things didn't spiral out of control.'

'I get the drift. What do you suggest I do to put things right?'

'It's entirely up to you, but you could have a word with Len when he's covering next week. Just reassure him he did the right thing letting Keith know and you're happy with how they dealt with it.' Vyvyan raises her eyebrows, letting out a sigh. 'That way, no one is in the wrong.'

I put down my fork and lean back in the chair. 'Maybe I'll also tell Len that it's not easy for me to break off now that I'm tied up with the building work and to go through Keith in future. Do you think that would ease the tension between them?'

She looks relieved. 'I think that's wise. It's true anyway, as you're obviously getting very hands-on.'

As I start laughing a piece of something falls out of my headscarf, bouncing off my leg and disappearing out of sight among the grassy stalks at my feet. 'Gosh, I hope that was a leaf, or a bit of wood. I just stumbled across a mouse, and I hate to think what's fallen off the large bits of wood I've been lifting up over my head as I've been throwing them in the back of the van.'

'Yuck!' Vyvyan groans and we both instinctively find ourselves taking a moment to glance around the garden. Then she gives a satisfied little sigh 'I think we're safe. And thanks for understanding, Jess. Keith is a bit of a moody bugger at times, but he means well. He knows you have your hands full and he's more than happy to take whatever pressure he can away from you.'

'To be honest, I couldn't cope if I didn't have all three of you on the team.'

And I mean that with all sincerity.

'Mum, when are we going to decorate the teepee?'

I gaze across at Lola who is lying on the sofa and, I thought, totally engrossed in the film she's been watching for the last half an hour.

'I need to get some special paint. Why don't you draw the design you'd like on a piece of paper and colour it in so we can work out what to get?'

Lola sits there chewing her lip, deep in thought. 'Can Daisy help us?'

'Of course she can. You're staying at Daisy's this weekend, but we'll work out when she can come for a sleepover here. We can take the cover off the teepee and lay it out on the floor in the small barn so it's easier to paint.'

'Oh, Mum, that would be great. Aren't you going to be really busy, though?' Her forehead puckers up and I wonder what's going through her mind.

'Yes, but there will be times when Riley won't need my help. And we'll still get our quality time together, Lola.'

'If Dad was here, would he be doing what you're doing?'

'Perhaps. He'd want to help, for sure.'

'But you don't want Dad to help now?'

That's a tough question to answer. 'Dad lives and works a long way away, Lola.'

'You could ask him to come and stay.'

I close my laptop and put it down on the coffee table, walking over to snuggle up next to my darling daughter. Sometimes being a mum is more important than balancing budgets.

'When we came to Cornwall, I told you that this was our adventure, Lola. Yours and mine. Dad is busy settling into his new home in Stroud. Soon, you'll be able to go and stay with him for short breaks, because he really misses you.'

'But he doesn't miss you?'

'Remember when we talked about the divorce and I told you that it's very sad, but sometimes married people change. It's no one's fault when it happens, but if two people are happier apart than they are together it's the right thing to do. Dad isn't a part of our life here, but all that matters is that we both love you, Lola. Nothing will ever change that.'

'It is sad, Mum. And I wish I could help you more.'

'You're busy at school and when you come home Misty really looks forward to spending time with you. Remember, the school holidays are coming up and I'm sure that if we ask Riley there are lots of little tasks you'll enjoy doing.'

'Really?'

'Yep. We just need to get the horrible messy bits done and then we'll have a blank canvas.'

'Like painting a picture,' she laughs. 'I know how to use a paintbrush, Mum, don't I?'

'You do, Lola.'

'Mum, who's going to live in the farm shop when it's finished?'

'That's something I can't answer. It will probably be rented out to a local business.'

'We'll have a real shop? On our doorstep?' Her eyes light up.

'Yes.'

'Will it sell sweets and ice cream?'

'Maybe. If you were camping in the fields, what would you want to buy to make your stay more enjoyable?'

Lola's face crumples up, turning her sunny smile into one of intense concentration.

'Biscuits. Definitely cake. Bread for toast in the morning and... pizza.'

'Well, it's going to be a little while until we know, but it's exciting, isn't it?'

'Maybe Cappy could rent it, Mum, and I could help him serve the customers when I'm not at school.'

Only in a child's mind could those dots be connected. In truth, I haven't given much thought to what happens when it's finished as that still seems a long way off. However, with a large delivery of insulation, plasterboard and some pretty hefty replacement timbers due tomorrow, maybe I do need to get my head around what type of business would best serve the campsite sooner rather than later.

'I surprised a little mouse this morning when I was clearing out some old wood, Lola. There was a nest so there was probably a family of them. If you go into the small barn don't be surprised if you see one of them running around. They won't hurt you, but they like to hide behind things and might make you jump. You won't be scared, will you?'

'Will it try to run up my arm, Mum?'

'I think it's more likely to run away from you, as it'll be scared. You'll look like a giant to a tiny mouse.'

'Poor mouse. Cappy said he thinks Misty will chase the mice away. That's not very kind, is it?'

Maybe it's time to get Misty a collar with a little bell on it to warn her prey that she's around. I don't mind evicting mice, but I don't think Lola is ready for the dead mouse on the doorstep thing. Or even worse, a bird. Let's hope that when the time comes, I can handle it without letting myself down in front of Lola.

13

The Rosy Vision is a Little Blurred
Around the Edges

After a stop–start Friday directing delivery men and making sure the building materials were stacked in the small barn according to a little plan Riley drew up for me, I ended the day a little disappointed with what I achieved. I did what I could when it came to helping Riley dig down to reduce the floor level in the farm shop and laying some of the hardcore, but I was glad of the excuse to keep breaking off.

I've finally managed to find a cleaner to handle the Saturday morning changeovers at Penti Growan, which is one pressure less to contend with.

It's seven o'clock when I hear Riley's van pull up outside and I quickly fill the mug I'd prepared with hot water and head straight out to say good morning. He's unloading tools and I clear my throat as I don't want to make him jump.

'Hi, Riley. Another early start?'

'I don't do lie-ins and you're paying me by the day, remember. I want you to get your money's worth.'

My eyes casually sweep over his face; there's always a smile bubbling just below the surface. It's nice having him around.

'I'm about to make breakfast for Lola, would you like to join us?'

'That's a kind thought but I rarely eat anything this early. The coffee will hit the spot, though.'

'I'll be late starting this morning as I want to spend a couple of hours with Lola before Erica and Daisy arrive for the sleepover. After that I'm all yours.'

As I hand Riley the mug and our eyes meet, he gives me a mischievous look. I realise that didn't sound quite right. Feeling a little flustered, I mumble, 'See you in a bit,' and hurry back to The Farmhouse.

This is all new to me, not least being a builder's mate. I don't want Riley to think I'm taking advantage of him by not pulling my weight. And that's a subject I intend to tackle later on today. Anyway, Lola and I are about to make a batch of pancakes with crispy bacon and maple syrup. During the week we keep breakfast simple, but weekends are leisurely and today is no different.

Trudging across the courtyard in my work boots, I raise a smug little smile when I see that the breakfast tray I took out to Riley is on top of a stack of flagstones. Beneath the foil I covered it with, it looks to me like the plate is empty.

He's nowhere in sight, so I head inside and can hear him moving around upstairs.

'I'm back,' I call out.

'I'll be right down. I'm just checking a few measurements.'

With the floor now level and the compacted hardcore covered with sand, the flow between what was formerly two buildings is more practical. As Riley descends the stairs I glance up at him.

'No more creaks,' I declare, with surprise.

'It didn't take long to fix them. A few of the treads were loose and needed a bit of extra support underneath, but it's solid now. Just take care if you go upstairs, as I had to take out the bottom step. Once the damp-proof membrane and the insulation is laid, the concrete will bring the floor up and we should be spot on for levels. This staircase will be a great feature with a bit of sanding back.'

'That's a bonus. What's the plan for today?'

'I'll be drilling some holes in preparation for the plumbing work. Given the thickness of the walls it's going to be noisy, dusty and I'll be attacking it from both sides, hoping to meet in the middle. I wondered whether you'd like me to take off the front door and carry it into the small barn so you can work on it?'

I take that to mean he'd rather I wasn't around to get in his way. Is it because I ask too many questions? I wonder. Or maybe he's a man who prefers his own company when the task in hand is a bit of a challenge.

'That works for me. I'll help you carry it through.'

'It's fine, just go on ahead and set up the trestles if you like. It might take me a few minutes to get it off the hinges. I'll replace them when we put it back on, as they're rather battered.'

I can tell that his mind is elsewhere; he just wants to get on with it, which is fair enough.

It turns out to be a cathartic morning for me, sanding and then oiling the door with a lint-free rag to preserve it, as I did with Penti Growan. I think it's important that this side of the courtyard has a consistent look. The further into this renovation we get, things that hadn't even occurred to me before are now buzzing around inside my head.

Apart from breaking off to make a couple of cups of coffee and to hand the keys over when the new holidaymakers arrive, I don't stop to chat to Riley. The drill is too loud to talk over and the fact he continues means it's not a good time for him to down tools.

However, at midday he comes in search of me. He walks into the small barn, drinking thirstily from a litre bottle of water.

'It's nice and cool in here,' he observes, walking over to inspect the door. 'That's coming up a treat.'

'I thought so, too. I'm ready for a break, how about you? I

have some homemade pasties defrosting ready to warm up for a quick lunch before we get back to it.'

'That works for me. Afterwards, we'll turn this door over and with a bit of luck we should be able to get it back on by the end of the day.'

'That's the target, then.'

He grins at me. 'I feel guilty. I'm notoriously bad about thinking ahead when it comes to food. I usually eat in the evening or grab a sandwich when I'm filling up with petrol. As I've said before, please don't feel obliged to cater for me, Jess. I'm really not expecting it.'

'It's not a problem, Riley. It's as easy to make something for two, as it is for one.'

'If you're sure you don't mind I'm not going to complain. Let me just clear up the mess I've made first.'

'Let's say twenty-five minutes in the orchard?' I propose, and he seems happy enough with that.

'It works for me.'

While I'm prepping lunch, I give Vyvyan a call, putting her on speakerphone.

'Hi Jess, how's it going?'

'Good. Hectic, though. I just wanted to let you know that I gave Len a call last night. I thought it was better to nip this little problem in the bud as quickly as possible. He sounded relieved when I said my focus was going to be elsewhere for a while and everything should go through Keith.'

'That's much appreciated, Jess. You know that Keith would never let you down. The two of them work well together, but that will have put Len's mind at ease.'

'I didn't mean to upset the status quo and I'm grateful to you for raising it. Actually, while I have you on the line, there's a question I wanted to ask. At some point I'm going to need to look for a tenant for the farm shop. I have no idea at the moment exactly when it will be ready, but I'm guessing we could be looking at early autumn. The thing is, is it something we could advertise on the website to see if there's any interest?'

'My past experience in the commercial rental market is that you'd find a tenant a lot quicker if you went to one of the agencies. I'll tell you what, let me ask around and we can have a chat once I know what sort of fees you'd be looking at.'

'You are an angel, Vyvyan. I wouldn't know where to start.'

'It's not a problem. I'll do some research. Before you go, are you sure you don't want to book Penti Growan out for the Christmas and New Year period? I've had several emails asking to be put on a reserve list in case there's a cancellation.'

'Sorry, I've reserved it for family as I want our second Christmas here to be rather special.'

I hear a soft, 'Ahh,' echoing down the line. 'I'd feel the same way if I lived at Renweneth Farm. It's going to be amazing when all the work is done, Jess. It will be a little oasis on the edge of the moor.'

That's the dream.

With Misty fed and sprawled out halfway up the stairs, gently snoring away, I carry lunch through the archway and into the orchard. It's lighter and brighter here, without the heavy cover overhead from the oak trees in front of the manor.

Riley tapped on the door to use the cloakroom a while ago and then disappeared. As I take the path around to the side it's a surprise to see him seated at the cast iron table, his arms crossed and his head back, relaxing. He's wearing sunglasses and I wonder if he's asleep, but the second he spots me he jumps up to relieve me of the tray.

'The pasties smell great,' he remarks, placing the tray down.

I whip off the tea towel and he grins back at me.

'I'm going to miss this when the job's done.'

'Oh, don't worry. The way things are looking, we'll be able to go straight into the work on the cottage the other side, if you're up for it.'

As I'm about to settle myself down he pulls out a chair for me. 'Thank you, Riley.'

'It pays to keep the boss happy,' he says, giving me a little salute. 'I'm glad this is working out; for both of us.'

'Me, too. Now let's eat, because I'm ravenous.'

Riley doesn't need any prompting at all and immediately begins tucking in. It doesn't take him long until he's sitting back, downing a small bottle of sparkling elderflower pressé. It fascinates me watching him, and the more he relaxes in my company, the easier it is for us to just sit and chat.

'Are you happy with the way things are going, Jess?' he checks.

'It's satisfying seeing the plans coming to life, Riley. I try to imagine what it's all going to look like when the courtyard complex is completed.'

'Different, that's for sure.'

'It's one thing looking at some drawings, another to witness it actually taking shape. It's a bit of a relief, actually.'

'I think given how hands-on you are, *witnessing* isn't exactly the right word. You're not having second thoughts, though, are you?'

'No. We're out on a limb here and while that's lovely for a relaxing, back-to-nature break, it has its drawbacks. Some holidaymakers are content to stay local and with some great walks around here, there's no need to jump in the car until they need a few basic items.'

Riley looks at me, nodding his head in agreement. 'In its day, it was a thriving little settlement for a reason.'

'You seem to know a lot about the history of this area, Riley. Were your family originally from around here?'

He pauses, placing the empty bottle he's been cradling in his hands back on to the table. 'No, I came here as a virtual stranger to this part of Cornwall.'

'The setting is beautiful, isn't it? Was that what attracted you to the area?'

'Not really. My life had become impossibly complicated; it almost pushed me over the edge. I had this crazy idea of finding a remote cottage somewhere with the aim of eventually living off the land.'

'The simple life, eh?'

'Pretty naive, as it turns out. The upside is that when you live in an isolated spot, second-hand books are a cheap source of entertainment for those long winter evenings.'

I'm pretty sure that light-hearted air of amusement is solely for my benefit, and I can't imagine how tough it must have been. I think of the renovations to the farm shop and having to live and work in it. That takes guts.

'You have some books on this area?' I ask, moving on quickly.

'I do. I'll try to remember to bring over a couple that mention Renweneth Farm. Originally, they had sheep and rights to let them graze on the open moorland. However, heavy grazing eliminated a lot of the common heathland species the sheep thrived on, leaving mat grass and heath rush, which are relatively unpalatable to them.'

'That makes sense, as you can't graze that many animals on two fields,' I reflect.

'Every little cottage on the moor grazed as many animals as they could afford to buy, too. When free grazing was no longer a commercially viable option for this place, it became a sort of permanent farmer's market. The stone outbuildings were probably used as accommodation for traders coming from further down country. Having the bakery here attracted local people within walking distance, because it's quite a trek into Polreweek.'

'It's like turning back the clock for the farm, in that case. A part of me loves the idea of lots of folk coming and going, but...' I stop mid-sentence, unable to put my reservations into words.

Riley studies my face.

'Plans are just that, if something needs changing you can always sit down with the planning officer.'

'I will admit that I didn't think twice about taking on the farm because it felt like a lifeline at the time. It's only now I'm able to sit back and see the bigger picture.'

Riley begins to load up the tray and it's time to get back to work.

'You make a great pasty, thanks for that,' he says, as our eyes meet. 'I'll carry this back to The Farmhouse, shout when you're ready to turn that door over.'

'My pleasure, Riley. I'll just check in with Erica and have a quick chat with the girls.'

He must have been keeping an eye out for me, because when I walk into the small barn a short while later he suddenly appears.

'One side down, one to go. You're winning,' he says, as we flip over the heavy piece of oak.

'Thanks, Riley.'

'No problem.'

I watch him turn and walk away. 'Are you in a rush to get home today?' I call after him.

He turns, furrowing his brow. 'No. Why?'

'If you're not doing anything, would you like to join me for dinner? Nothing fancy, just pasta and a salad. I'd rather like to ask your opinion about something.'

'Sure, although the state I'm in, I'd best go home first to change. I'm covered in stone dust.' Riley stands in the doorway, patting the legs of his trousers with his hands and sending a cloud of tiny particles up into the air. He sneezes twice.

'That's a pity, it's quite a drive there and back.'

'Okay. How about I head over to the campsite shower block? I've my usual set of spare clothes in the van.'

'You're more than welcome to use the shower in The Farmhouse,' I offer.

'No, I wouldn't want to traipse a trail of debris through your lovely clean home,' he grins at me artfully. 'Not when I'm getting another free meal.'

As I watch him walk away, he starts humming to himself. Over his shoulder I spot my newest holidaymakers letting themselves into Penti Growan. They've obviously been shopping and have quite a haul. There are some lovely shops in Polreweek and just outside of town, on the retail park, is a wonderful interior design outlet. If I'm not mistaken those carrier bags look familiar, as I've shopped there myself on numerous occasions.

I do like having people around, but how will I feel when there's a constant stream of visitors traipsing back and forth on a regular basis? The rosy picture in my head might not match the reality and my concern is getting the mix right. I suddenly have a vision of a newspaper stand leaning against the wall next to this door that I'm painstakingly bringing back to life. The image makes my heart sink. Maybe a convenience store isn't quite right, not in this setting. It's time for a bit of a rethink.

14

A Totally Different Perspective

I hear the front door click shut. 'It's only me,' Riley calls out.
'I'm in the kitchen,' I reply.

As he wanders through to join me, he gives an amused chuckle. 'I really must expand the range of my mobile wardrobe.'

From where I'm standing, the other side of the island, Riley looks more than presentable to me. He's a good-looking guy, whose job gives him a free workout. His curly hair is still damp, but he's dust free and there are only a few creases in his T-shirt. I think his spare wardrobe is growing as I haven't seen this one before and it looks new.

'Considering you've been crawling around on a dirty floor and drilling holes most of the day, it's a real transformation,' I reassure him.

'I do own some tidy clothes, honestly. I just don't carry them around with me.' He glances down at his feet where I see the tidy pair of trainers he's wearing are devoid of shoelaces.

'It's a work van,' I point out, 'not a mobile home.'

'True. Is there anything I can do to help?'

'You could sort the drinks. There's beer and wine in the fridge. Glasses are in that cupboard over there, the tall one.'

'What are you having?'

'Wine for me, please. You'll find a corkscrew and a bottle opener in the drawer.'

'I'm used to wine with a screw top, so I think I'll join you. It's been a while since I pulled a cork.'

'It's French. When I was a teen my parents were considering buying a holiday home in France and we spent two weeks looking at properties. I was so disappointed when they changed their mind and bought their first campervan instead. I fantasised about them buying a chateau and spending my summers there.'

'The idea is sometimes a lot more charming than the reality. Some of those wonderful old properties need to be totally gutted. I often wonder how many people buy something on a whim and live to regret it, unaware of what they're taking on.'

'Quite a few I suspect. At least my situation is a little different,' I admit, slicing up a chunk of cucumber before tossing it into the salad bowl. 'I knew exactly what I was taking on and I was more than ready to roll up my sleeves to dive in.' There's a loud pop as Riley extracts the cork and I watch him as he holds the bottle up to read the label.

'*Flavours of green apple and Mirabelle plum, with herbal and floral undertones. Great choice.*'

I laugh. 'It's not a really expensive wine, but it's very drinkable and perfect with pasta. It's a vineyard I've visited a couple of times when holidaying in the Loire Valley. A wine merchant in Polreweek sells it by the case.'

I walk over to give the chicken breasts one last turn now that they're browning nicely in the pan and it's time to tip the linguini into a bubbling pan of water.

'Right, three minutes and I'll be dishing up.'

As I grab two pasta bowls, Riley pours the wine and carries it over to the table.

'Take a seat and relax. That was a punishing day for you.'

'Oh, I've tackled a lot worse than that. It's a similar construction to my own cottage. The problem with walls that thick is everything takes a lot longer than you think.'

Adding a little cream to the frying pan and a slosh of white wine to loosen the golden residue from cooking the chicken, a quick stir and I leave it to thicken while I drain the pasta. The final touch is a sprinkling of tarragon and it's done. When I set a bowl down in front of Riley, he looks up at me appreciatively.

'It smells really good, Jess, thank you.'

'There's lots more pasta if you want it,' I add. 'I'm used to cooking for three and old habits die hard. You'd think I'd have learnt by now but when I cook I don't always engage my brain.'

He gives me a sobering look. 'For me it's the problem of not falling into the trap of living on omelettes, or beans on toast, just because it's quick and easy. Takeaways are usually cold before I get them home and I don't own a microwave.'

'Me neither, and I don't own a dishwasher. I decided an extra cupboard was much more useful. Let's toast to always finding that happy medium,' I reply, holding up my glass.

Riley's eyes light up as we exchange an empathetic glance. 'Life is full of surprises, isn't it? The trick to surviving them is to treat each one as an opportunity.'

'I'll second that. Now let's eat while we can. Misty will wake up soon expecting Lola to be here to play with her, so I hope you like cats. Unless you fancy doing the dishes?'

That raises a huge smile. 'There's no such thing as a free supper,' Riley mocks. 'I like to think I'm multi-skilled and I can do either.'

He's fun to have around and just what I needed this evening. When Lola rang an hour ago to say goodnight, they were about to settle down to watch a film before bed. I felt she was actually more concerned about me, rather than the other way around.

Riley and I are both ravenous and my mind wanders as we eat. It's sad to think that he has a son he rarely sees. It must be painful to accept and I guess he's decided there's no point in dwelling on it. Not all splits are amicable. And yet he felt comfortable mentioning it to Lola. I can't imagine what that must be like, not being a part of your child's life. Then I groan inwardly, I was supposed to text Ben to let him know Lola is still up for her first visit at the start of the school holidays. Then it occurs to me that I haven't thought about him at all recently. Cappy was right and acceptance is the final stage.

'Are you up for a wander around Renweneth Manor before we tackle dessert? I'm at a bit of a crossroads when it comes to what I'm going to do with it.'

'Are you kidding? I've always wanted to take a look around.' Riley looks down at Misty, apologetically. 'Sorry girl, playtime is over.'

'Here you go, Misty,' I place her food bowl on the floor next to the carrier she hardly uses now. She comes trotting over, tail in the air. 'See, food wins every time.'

Riley finds my remark funny as he jumps to his feet.

I walk past the table, grabbing my wine glass and draining the last drop. 'I'm going for a refill, how about you?'

'I'm driving, so I'd better not.'

'That's a shame. Look, I have a spare room, Riley. You're going to be back here first thing tomorrow morning, anyway.'

He seems surprised by my offer, but it's not a big deal to me. The next couple of months this is going to be like his second home, anyway.

'There are times when backing on to a moor is a little unsettling,' I continue. 'It's still strange for me to be here all alone.'

'That's only natural, Jess. Besides, the thought of not having to do the drive is rather appealing. Usually when I sleep on the job, I lie out in the back of the van on an inflatable mattress, but I don't carry it when I'm carting rubble to and from the tip.'

'I wouldn't let you do that, anyway. Not after the work you've put in this week.'

'It's been non-stop, but I like to get stuck in. Don't feel you have to make yourself available every day I'm here, Jess. You've got a lot of other stuff going on.'

'I meant what I said, Riley, I fully intend to be hands-on. Even though I haven't done a tenth of what you've done, I think we both deserve an evening chilling out. In which case, I'll top up our glasses and grab the keys.'

Leaving Misty curled up on the sitting room windowsill watching as we traverse the courtyard, I'm surprised when Riley mentions that he's never been inside the manor before. 'I assumed that as you knew my grandparents, Cappy would have shown you around.'

'The occasion never arose and I didn't like to ask, so I'm excited to see inside.'

We follow the flagstone path between the two oak trees, walking past a long border of lavender that is full of bees busy gathering pollen. The smell is evocative, reminding me of summer holidays Lola, Ben and I spent here, wandering around this garden with Grandma. It makes my heart ache as I think about her. Never in my wildest dreams did I envisage the day when I'd be the one running the farm and making the decisions. This wasn't how it was supposed to be.

Maybe I'm too emotionally attached to this place. I do believe that Renweneth Manor is the quintessential country house that many people would describe off the top of their heads if asked. A long, rectangular building with chimney stacks at both ends. But it's the symmetry and proportions that give it that romantic, country elegance.

At ground level the original, wide solid oak door sits grandly in the centre of the building with an impressive window either side of it. The door itself is almost as wide as it is tall. I don't have to stoop walking through it, but Riley will certainly have to if he doesn't want to hit his head.

The entrance is protected by what Grandma called *a farmer's porch*. Two solid stone walls support the grey slate roof over the top. The front is open to the elements, but either side the worn wooden benches make my heart heave a heavy sigh. I love this building and can imagine the farmer and his family sitting here to prise off their muddy boots before heading inside to eat.

At first floor level there are three windows and what I see is perfection, I don't see the problems – only oodles of character and the charm.

When I turn to look at Riley he's deep in thought.

'The stonework is in pretty good condition from the outside. Pity about the windows, most of them are beyond repair by the look of it. I believe Cappy had some work done to the roof a while back, which I'm guessing means it's got water damage inside. When I sorted that blocked gutter for you I had a bird's eye view from the ladder and the repairs looked pretty extensive to me.'

I gaze upwards, never really having taken the time to stand back to appraise it with a critical eye, as Riley is doing now. It's so easy to get caught up in the charm of the place and what it could be.

'Are you talking about the two large areas where there isn't much moss?'

Riley nods his head. 'Yep. The builder used reclaimed slate tiles, so it's a good job. Brand new ones never really blend in as it takes years for them to weather in. If the old moss was cleaned off, no one would probably be able to tell it wasn't all original.'

'Sadly, the damage inside is pretty extensive because it was leaking for a long time before my grandparents bought the farm.'

Riley holds my glass as I fiddle with the heavy iron key. The lock works well, but there's a knack to getting it to turn. 'Ah, that's it. I've given it a squirt of oil but it's still sticking.'

'It probably needs taking apart. A bit of filing here and there should have it working like new. I'll take a look at it. It's a half-hour job, that's all.'

'I think you have enough on your plate, don't you?' I muse. 'Besides, Cappy and my parents think I'm better off selling this place.'

'Surely not. It's a beautiful old building. I mean, picturesque old manor houses like this one are a real gem. If you imagined yourself in a chateau, this is the next best thing, surely?'

Riley follows me inside, handing me back my glass. 'Having a dream and affording it are two very different things, I'm afraid. If I do sell, then the long-term future of the farm is assured.'

He stares at me, furrowing his brow. 'There's a but coming and I think I know what it is.'

I can feel my cheeks colouring up. Ben never really understood what was important to me, so I doubt Riley has any idea what's going on inside my head. There are times when even I doubt myself, as common sense tells me that selling is absolutely the right way to go. Well, it did until I found Riley.

'You do?' My laugh is genial, as I don't want to sound dismissive.

'How frank do you want me to be?'

'Let rip. Everyone in my family has an opinion on what I should do. However, if you think this is financial jeopardy, I'm better off knowing that now.'

'Right, then let the tour commence.'

Wandering from room to room, I let Riley lead the way. It's grim viewing. It smells musty and decayed. The effects of the water damage are plain to see in places and I can't remember it being quite as bad as it looks now. I guess for the first time I'm seeing it in the cold light of day, without my wistful imagination kicking in.

In two of the rooms, a part of the original ceilings collapsed a long time ago, but Grandma had it all cleared out. Now there are little heaps of grey dust and debris beneath each hole again. However, it's still full of beautiful features ready to be restored and I watch Riley as his eyes seem to home in on every little detail.

From the main staircase in the entrance hallway, to the sitting room and the second reception room, then on into the huge kitchen. It's captivating and the potential to turn this into both a business, and a home, is enormous. Beyond that, what Cappy refers to as the boot room, is where the dogs would have slept and it even has a flower sink.

'This would be perfect for a downstairs cloakroom and if it was partitioned off, a separate utility room.' Riley talks as we walk, pointing out little things that even I haven't noticed.

He's intrigued by the narrow back stairs that lead up into the fifth bedroom, it doesn't have any access to the rest of the first floor.

'I'm guessing this would have been the housekeeper's room,' Riley comments before poking his head around a turn in the stairs.

'Probably, and from there it leads up into the attic. Grandma said this house once belonged to a well-respected family who ended up employing a number of local people.'

Riley doesn't seem surprised. 'Farmers are notoriously hard-working, their wives too, but having a cook and a housekeeper wasn't just a status symbol, it was a necessity unless they had daughters. Sons would work on the land or tend the sheep and at its peak Renweneth Farm would have been quite something. A constant hive of activity.'

'Oh, how I'd love to see a photo of it in its heyday.'

Riley's mind is elsewhere. 'You could have two sizeable ensuite bedrooms up there,' he says, craning his neck. 'If you had dormer windows put in at the back the views would be spectacular that high up. It's a question I should have asked before, but this place isn't listed... is it?'

'No.'

'Then you're lucky. The broad criteria are age and rarity, architectural interest and close historical associations. You find manor houses like this all over Cornwall, but if you put it up for sale you'll have no problem at all getting a buyer given the location. Someone with bags of money wanting a picturesque second home for entertaining at weekends will snap it up.'

'And if I don't?'

He grimaces. 'When it comes to this sort of renovation there's little point in setting a budget. As you begin tearing out the insides who knows what horrors you're going to find. You pull down a ceiling thinking it will take a couple of days, only to discover that the joists supporting the floor above are rotten. It could potentially be one horror story after another, and it would be wrong of me not to give you the worst-case scenario. Having been through it myself, admittedly on a smaller scale, it seemed like one blow after another. That's not what you wanted to hear, and I fully understand that because it's an exciting project. It's something you'll always regret not doing if you sell it. However, if you take the risk and go with your heart, the budget could spiral out of control.'

As I sip my wine I'm deep in thought. 'I already knew the answer, but I had to ask the question, you know… just in case. I think we'll give the attic a miss tonight as the light is going and I have a homemade apple pie waiting.'

'You have time to cook apple pies?' His eyes widen.

'No, but Daisy's mum does, and hers is way better than mine, anyway!' I concede.

Maybe it's the wine, or the effects of unwinding after what has been a decidedly intense couple of days. However, after a traditional dessert with clotted cream ice cream, Riley and I sit opposite each other in the sitting room of The Farmhouse in a mellow mood.

'I feel like I've put my foot in it, Jess,' Riley confesses.

'That's not true. It's just that everyone is coming at it from a different angle. Cappy doesn't want me to hold on to his original dream because he thinks it's too much work for me to take on. Mum and Dad worry about the finances. On the other hand, you did exactly what I'd hoped you'd do.'

He looks at me with a puzzled expression on his face. 'Which was?'

'Confirmed what my head was saying, but you also spoke from the heart.'

The laugh he returns sounds a tad jaded for Riley, which surprises me. 'It's easy enough to see the potential when you're not the one footing the bill. If you don't end up selling it, whatever budget you have in mind, I'd say double it at the very least.'

As I sip my coffee, I nestle back a little further into the sofa. 'If this was your decision, what would you do?'

'I don't know, Jess. What I will say is that it's easy to see that you're emotionally invested in the manor. This is your chance to have your dream home, and whatever happens the other side of that dividing stone wall in the courtyard, living in The Farmhouse puts you on the wrong side of it.'

With Riley working his other job for the next two days and Lola at school, I can't settle to anything. Top of my list for today was to jet wash some old stone planters. As I work I'm thinking about Riley's feedback, which was spot on. What hadn't occurred to me was if I do sell Renweneth Manor, what if I end up not feeling the same about The Farmhouse? A big part of what I love most about this place will be lost to me.

By lunchtime my head is buzzing and I need to break my chain of thought, so I text Ivy.

Morning, how are things with you and Adam? Did you have a good weekend? 😊

Seconds later my phone rings.

'You've been ominously quiet the last couple of days. Is everything okay?' Ivy is good at totally ignoring what I say and sensing when something is up.

'Yes... I've just been busy. Riley was here and Lola had a sleepover with Daisy. It was productive, but today I'm feeling shattered, and this morning I have a stonking headache. I was going to call you yesterday, but I thought it might be difficult to talk with Adam around. Is he bouncing back?'

'He's still a bit up and down, Jess. He managed to get some work on Saturday but yesterday he cancelled his sports package on TV. I said he didn't need to, that we'll manage, but he's on a bit of a guilt trip. His mum suggested I go with the flow. She said he's not the sort of person to wallow for long and she's right. But I'm proud of him for making a stand.'

'I know you are, and rightly so. He'll soon be back on his feet again and no more conniving bosses to battle with.'

'Anyway, it's exciting to hear that things are going well at your end. And Lola wasn't around so you had the cottage to yourself, but Riley was working? Shouldn't you be grabbing some down time when you can to socialise, instead of spending it being a builder's mate?' Ivy doesn't sound too impressed.

'Riley needs the extra income and I appreciate every day he can give me. I can socialise all I want when the bulk of the work is out the way.'

There's an ominous silence. 'Unless you had an entertaining time with Riley, I mean… you know, when the working day was over.'

'Ivy! Chatting after a hard day's work can't possibly be considered to be *entertaining* someone. Seriously, my main topics of conversation these days aren't exactly scintillating. One thing we do have in common, though, is a shedload of problems.'

'Well, it obviously hasn't put him off as he's still turning up!'

'He has another job driving for a builders' merchant a couple of days a week. That gives me time to catch up with some of the other tasks I'm falling behind on.'

'Jess, all work and no play doesn't reflect a healthy lifestyle, does it? When Lola is at Daisy's house you need to be able to take at least some time off to let your hair down.'

'I'd rather just concentrate on keeping my handyman/builder happy for now.'

'Oh, Jess! Don't get me wrong, Riley seems like a genuinely nice guy and the day he appeared out of the blue and helped to shift the chippings in the rain said a lot about him. But, my lovely friend, you don't have the spare capacity to get caught up in someone else's drama. You've enough to battle with, as it is.'

I know Ivy means well, but she's wrong.

'Tell me what you're thinking,' Ivy cajoles. 'I know you; this is not a good sign. Last time we spoke I felt you'd come to a decision about something, Jess, but you're being very guarded about it.'

'Only because I'm still trying to get things to slot together here, that's all. At the end of the day, it comes down to what I can afford to do, as opposed to what I'd like to do.'

'As long as you don't let anyone talk you into doing something that doesn't feel right, you'll work it out.'

I've spent my entire life so far being sensible and where did that get me? My man deserted me for someone younger, making me feel that I'm no longer exciting to be with. Maybe that's true and it's because I've lost my spontaneity. What if I turn that around and take a risk? There's one more opinion I need to seek out before I go any further, because going forward it's just Lola and me.

15

The True Meaning of Empowerment

'Hi, Ben. Is it convenient to talk?'

'I'm on leave today, so it's a leisurely start before a trip to the mall to buy a new rug. Are you doing all right, Jess?'

That means he's going with Naomi, as he hates shopping.

'Yes, it's all good here. I wanted to talk about Lola.'

'She's thrilled to bits that Cappy gave her a kitten.'

It's weird having no idea what Lola and her dad talk about, as usually she takes my phone up to her bedroom while they chat. I make a point of not asking her any questions afterwards but I am curious.

'Has Lola said anything about coming to stay with you?' I ask.

'I've... um... steered clear of the subject after what you said. I was going to bring it up with you again in a couple of weeks' time.'

'I was hesitant for a reason, Ben. What I didn't want was to wave her off full of smiles only to get a tearful phone call when you got to Gloucestershire because she wasn't ready. The last few weeks have really turned things around and she's much more settled. She seems to understand that while you aren't a part of our life here, that doesn't stop her being a part of your life in Gloucestershire. It's that final acceptance of the way things are between you and me. I'm just not sure how she'll handle Naomi and you living together.'

The pause grows. 'Hmm. Maybe I'll have a word with Naomi. Perhaps, for Lola's first visit, Naomi can stay with her sister and join us for trips out. I really want this to work, Jess, for all our sakes.'

'I know. Me, too.'

'You do?'

'I was angry, Ben, but looking back I was hanging on because it's easier to dismiss a problem in the hope it will go away, rather than confront it head on. We're way past that now. It's important that Lola feels we're always going to put her first, no matter what.'

'Then I'll make sure nothing gets in the way of that. Naomi understands you know, she's just not used to being around kids.' His voice softens. 'You're a great mum, Jess, always were and always will be.'

A few moments of silence hang uncomfortably in the air as I dismiss a wave of sadness that comes at me out of the blue. 'Right, I'd best get on. I'll block out that first week of the school holidays on the calendar then. Enjoy your shopping trip.'

A subtle laugh echoes down the line. 'You know I won't.'

We understand each other so well and now none of that matters anymore. I have no doubt there will be times when we don't agree on something as Lola grows up, but it's our job as parents to put our egos to one side and focus on our girl. For now, this is a positive step forward and I mustn't lose sight of that.

A sharp tap on the door reminds me that I'm expecting a very important visitor and I hurry to answer it.

'Good morning. Mrs Griffiths? I'm Pete Miller, from the building control team.' The man flashes an identity card under my nose.

'Yes. Hello. Riley said to expect a visit. Shall I show you around?'

'Oh, I've already poked my head in and taken a look. I'll text Riley and let him know it's fine. Renweneth Farm has had a bit of a facelift since my last visit. It's good to see. I understand that you're Gabe's granddaughter?'

I'm rather taken aback as I wasn't expecting a fly-by visit. If he didn't have an official-looking clipboard in his hands, Pete Miller looks like he could be selling replacement windows.

'Yes, I am.'

'Give him my best next time you talk to him, won't you?' he replies, leaving me standing here speechless as he walks back to his car.

'Onwards and upwards,' I half-whisper to myself before I realise that Misty is halfway across the courtyard and heading straight for the small barn. Watch out mice, I'm not sure how much longer we're going to be able to keep her indoors and I doubt you'll outrun Misty.

As I race after her, I know she's going to love having Daisy here tonight and while the girls are painting the teepee cover, I'll take Misty with us so she can have a little nose around the small barn at leisure. It's not ideal having a sleepover on a Monday night, but I promised Erica I wouldn't let them stay up too late. I'm doing the school runs today and tomorrow, which suits Erica as her mum has a hospital check-up today and physiotherapy tomorrow. She'll have more than enough running around to do as it is.

Still, I have a few hours now to catch up on some housework and make a few meals for the freezer. From Wednesday onwards it will be all go once Riley returns and I'm excited about the thought of laying a concrete floor. How sad am I?

'Mum, please, please, *please* can we play in the treehouse for a bit before we go to bed?' Lola pleads and Daisy's eyes light up.

'You know the door is sticking and I haven't had a chance to look at it.'

There's nothing worse than seeing their eyes sparkle and then their faces immediately fall.

'I'll tell you what, you take Misty back to the cottage while I grab some tools.'

They start squealing and poor Misty runs for cover. 'Keep the noise down,' I caution the girls, 'or you'll never catch her!'

As they try to coax her out from behind one of the piles of insulation waiting to be laid on the farm shop floor, I grab a rubber mallet and a small plane. I'm quite proud of myself considering that before we moved here the only things I'd wielded when it came to DIY was a paintbrush and a roller.

Daisy manages to scoop Misty up in her arms and amid a lot of laughter and words of gentle reassurance, I escort them across the courtyard. I wait while they settle her down and when they reappear it strikes me how little Lola uses her iPad now. It's good to see kids getting excited about playing outside.

As we wander around to the orchard, we chat as we walk.

'What's the best thing about Renweneth Farm, girls?' I ask.

'The treehouse,' they both reply in unison, giggling.

'Anything else?'

'The garden is very pretty,' Daisy adds.

'How about you, Lola?'

'I remember when Great-grandma planted the roses by the arch and I helped her,' she says, proudly. 'The chippings and the flower borders are nice in our garden Mum, but I love the grass and the oak trees. And the orchard is great fun.'

The girls hang around as I climb the little ladder, perching on one of the lower limbs of the tree while I try to coax the door to the treehouse open. Below me I listen to the back-and-forth chatter between the girls.

'I wish my garden was like this,' Daisy comments, as she twirls around several times before sinking down on to the soft grass. 'It's nice to have trees, isn't it?'

'I love trees. We didn't have any in the garden of our other house,' Lola informs her.

A few gentle taps free the stuck door and I adjust my position so I can plane a sliver or two off the top corner. 'Nearly fixed, girls!'

A loud 'Woo-hoo!' filters up through the mass of leaves and I watch as both girls lie out on the grass, staring up at the sky.

'Mum, are you and Riley going to work on Renweneth Manor next?'

'No, darling. Once the farm shop is ready, we'll be working on the cottage next to it. After that the small barn is going to be turned into an indoor market.'

'That's a shame.' She sounds genuinely disappointed.

'Why?'

'Great-grandma said that one day I could have a bedroom in the attic overlooking the garden.'

That stops me in my tracks. 'She did?'

'Yep. She took me up and showed me it. It's the one on the left. Not the one where the water poured through the roof.'

'Where she stored the boxes of apples?' I gaze down at her bright little face to see that she's in earnest.

'That's why I chose it, because it smells nice.'

Daisy rolls over on to her tummy, to look at Lola.

'That's cool having rooms in the attic. Are there spiders?'

'Probably, as we never go in there now. But Mum shooed them all out of The Farmhouse and made it nice again, so she'll do the same with the manor. It's going to be our forever home,' she announces.

There's a brief pause as I wonder how on earth I'm going to respond to that when Lola calls up to me. 'We gave a lot of the apples away last summer, Mum, and then we cooked the rest. Can we store some too, this year?'

'Sure, we can. Maybe Daisy can help us when they're ready to be picked and take some back for her mum,' I reply breezily, but this conversation has thrown me.

As I sit back to test the door, it no longer sticks. 'There you go. It's working.'

'Was it broken?' Daisy asks, curious.

'No, this branch here has grown and was pressing against the side of the treehouse. It'll stick again, but I can always fix it.'

'Your mum is clever, Lola.'

'I know,' my daughter replies and then, to my amusement, adds, 'but your mum makes better cakes!' To which I burst out laughing, even though it's true.

I climb down, content to wander and do a bit of deadheading among the rose bushes and a pale pink clematis that shimmers with colour. As calming as it is, my thoughts are still racing ahead of me. My intention was to mention to Lola the prospect of selling the manor to get her reaction and now I'm glad I didn't get that far. I think she might have been horrified. Images of Grandma fill my head, the memories coming fast and furious. I can see her walking around the garden doing exactly what I'm doing now. My hand is now stuffed full of old flower heads and to avoid dropping petals everywhere, I make a pocket by folding back the bottom hem of my top. She used to say to Lola and me, 'Come on girls, who needs a bucket? Let's get as many as we can and then we'll empty them straight on to the compost heap.'

The problem is that children have long memories when it comes to promises made. And Lola is right, we should store some apples this summer because it does make the attic rooms smell nice. Is that why I didn't want to take Riley up there the other day, because it was Grandma's favourite room? One memory too far for me, maybe? He was right, though. If dormer windows were added at the back, the views would far outstrip those from The Farmhouse. Is it a dream too far though, to even consider breathing life back into this old manor house?

I've been concerned that even if I can get my head around fixing it up, Lola is so happy in her new bedroom that it never occurred to me that from day one she only ever saw it as our temporary home. Three generations of females with the same dream... that's way too much of a coincidence. Now that feels like fate giving me a nudge and saying *stop thinking about it and just do it*. As Grandma always said, 'the bravest leap is a leap of faith in one's own abilities' and I think I finally understand what that means. I might not be able to finance it now, but as the farm's income increases anything is possible as long as I don't get ahead of myself.

I'd be lying if I didn't acknowledge the little thrill that courses through me as I hear Riley's van pull into the courtyard. He texted first thing to say he'd be a little late and Lola was disappointed he hadn't arrived by the time Erica and Daisy dropped by to pick her up.

Lola had a little moan, saying she always misses the exciting things. I laughed and said that I'm not sure a lorry load of concrete can be described as *exciting*, but it's a first for us and I understood her reluctance to leave.

Riley offered to pick up a mate whose help he's enlisted today, as he warned me we're going to have to work fast when the lorry gets here. And there's a lot to do before it arrives at eleven o'clock. As I head over to say hello and get my instructions, I find the two of them inside the farm shop, deep in conversation.

'Hi guys.'

Riley turns around, giving me a welcoming smile. 'Steve, this is Jess. The boss lady.'

'Hi, missus. Nice to meet you.'

I thought Riley was muscular, but Steve makes Riley look wiry. He's wearing a black, sleeveless vest and a pair of ripped jeans, so he's come ready to labour, but it's hard not to stare at his bulging arm muscles. This guy clearly lifts weights, and heavy ones at that.

'Your help today is much appreciated, Steve.'

We shake hands and he tips his head in acknowledgement.

'Right. The first job is to get the damp-proof membrane laid. It's in the small barn, Steve. If you need a hand, shout.'

Steve disappears and I look at Riley, trying not to look too eager. After all, it's just a floor.

'It's a shame I missed Lola.'

That's a nice thing to say, as he didn't need to.

'I think it's just as well, as she didn't really want to go to school and miss the fun.'

'Fun?' he dismisses, jokingly. 'Maybe I'll take a few photos and show them to her at the end of the day.'

It's funny, but I have missed Riley's presence. 'Did you have a busy couple of days?'

'Same old, same old. I spend a fair bit of time driving back and forth to the depot, so for me it's a bit of a rest.'

Considering Riley hasn't had a day off in over a week, it doesn't dampen his spirits, or his motivation.

Steve appears with a massive roll of blue, impenetrable-looking membrane. He carries it on his shoulder and the only problem is getting his wide torso and the long roll through the doorway. This is going to be one interesting day

'How did it go?' Mum asks tentatively. 'Does the farm shop have a new floor?'

'It does,' I reply, proudly.

'Thank goodness! I've been thinking about you off and on all day, Jess. I couldn't wait to give you a ring. Your dad and I were concerned it would be too much for the two of you.'

'Oh, we had some help. A mate of Riley's and boy, did he work hard. Laying the membrane was fiddly even with the three of us because of the sheer size of it. But when the lorry arrived to pump in the concrete it was nothing at all like icing a cake, I can tell you.'

Mum laughs. 'Icing a cake?'

'I know. That's the analogy I used when I assured Riley I was more than happy to have a go. But when you are wading around in wellington boots, ankle deep in gooey concrete and trying to level it with a rake as the pipe is shooting it out, it's punishing on the arm muscles. And the legs. Honestly, Mum, when this stage of the project is finished I'm going to be a good few pounds lighter and a whole of a lot fitter than I've ever been.'

She tuts. 'Is money that tight, that you have to throw yourself into doing the hard stuff, Jess? Can't you employ this mate of Riley's, too?'

'I'm enjoying being a part of it, Mum. I'm sure we'll have other help along the way and other trades. It's not solely about the money, and I need you to understand that.'

'But don't you have enough to deal with, Jess?'

This conversation is well overdue but it's awkward. 'I understand it's difficult for you both being so far away. You can't call in and check that we're okay, but we are. I have all the help I need for now. Things are running smoothly and each month we're seeing a massive increase in profit compared to last year. I'm really excited about what's to come. So is Lola.'

'You do sound upbeat.'

'Look, please don't mention this to Cappy, as I want him to hear it from me first.' I pause, wondering how best to break the news as I didn't intend saying anything just yet. But I figure it's best to get it out of the way.

'That sounds ominous, Jess. What's going on?'

I clear my throat, nervously. 'I'm not going to sell the manor, Mum. Once the farm shop and the cottage next door to it have been brought back to life, and the small barn has been turned into a market hall, Renweneth Manor will be the final project.'

I wait while it sinks in. 'Jess, it's wonderful to hear you sounding so positive. Since the day you arrived at the farm you've made a lot of significant changes and it was only a matter of time before it really started to pay off. But listen to what you're saying, that's a huge commitment on top of everything else.'

'And when it gets to that point I'll be more than ready and have a sizeable budget to cover at least the first phase in tackling the manor house.'

Mum sighs. 'I'm wasting my breath trying to convince you to slow down a little, aren't I?'

'Sorry, but yes, you are.'

'Cappy came back from his stay with you buzzing with excitement and he can't wait to get back down there to see for himself what's going on. How he'll feel about it when you tell him you're not selling the manor, Jess, I don't know. If you're doing this simply to keep your grandparents' original dream alive, things have moved on, lovely. You could have a nice chunk of capital behind you that would take away any financial worries for the future.'

Mum is wrong, I'm doing it for me… and Lola.

'The truth is that I'd rather have Renweneth Manor than money sitting in the bank, Mum. Ploughing the profits back into the business, as I'm doing, increases the farm's future income anyway. That's our security.' I don't want to upset her but the decision is mine.

'I'm sorry. I'm not doubting your abilities, Jess, please don't think that for one moment. However, it's time to face facts. The farm was very much a work-in-progress when you took it over and your dad and I are concerned that you're trying to press forward too quickly. It's not only about the possibility of overstretching yourself financially, but as your team grows that's an additional pressure. What experience do you have when it comes to managing staff?'

It seems my parents think I'm getting in way over my head and that's a bitter blow. 'It was at Ben's insistence that I didn't go back to work full-time after Lola was born. He was under pressure at work and I couldn't count on him for any help whatsoever. Considering what I was juggling – working part-time, shopping, cooking and keeping the house clean… and having to bolster Ben's confidence on a daily basis when I was sleep deprived – I think it more than equipped me for what's ahead.' That came out sounding a little bitter, which isn't the case at all. I did it gladly and was grateful to have that bonding time with Lola, as Ben was trying to build a better future for us all. But I was a young, inexperienced mum; I had so much to learn and a husband who was often too stressed to listen to my problems. And yet I kept going, even on days when I just wanted to climb back into bed and pull the covers over my head.

'But it's all work, work, work, Jess. You can't sustain that sort of pressure for months on end without it affecting your health and that's a real cause for concern.'

I sort of get it, given the situation. Not only have Lola and I been uprooted from what was a very stable and normal lifestyle, everything I'm doing here is an enormous learning curve. But so was getting married and having a baby by the time I was twenty-one years old. I had no idea how tough it would be at times and, looking back, Ben never really pulled his weight. I put everyone else first, and my needs and aspirations at work were an afterthought.

'I know you're only thinking of what's best for Lola and me. I don't mean to sound ungrateful, but this is filling that big gaping hole that opened up in my life when Ben left me. If it stops being fun for either Lola, or me, then I'll ease back. But this last week I only thought about him once, Mum, and that was in the context of arranging Lola's first stay with him at his new house.'

Mum does a sharp intake of breath, which catches in her throat. 'Oh, Jess! Why do I get the feeling that you're listening but not taking any of what I'm saying on board?'

'It's not up for discussion, Mum, and you need to accept that,' I state, firmly.

'I'm sorry you feel that way, Jess,' she snaps back at me. 'Anyway, I must go. Please give our love to Lola.' With that, the line goes dead. Mum has never put the phone down on me before as she's not usually one to get angry.

I'm left feeling totally gutted, although I stand by what I said. What hurt the most, though, is that I rarely talk about my feelings for Ben. Opening up to Mum about what was a huge step for me last week was totally lost on her. And yet it had been an empowering realisation. I know how to balance a budget and new skills I can learn along the way, but taking back control of my heart seemed, for a while, like a total impossibility.

As Riley told Steve, I'm the boss lady. The thing is, I don't have a problem with that, or with making decisions, and failure is not an option.

JULY

16

The End Is in Sight

It's been nearly a month since we were celebrating the laying of the floor in the farm shop and now we're on the final leg of the transformation. We're hoping that this weekend is going to be the last big push.

I had intended to get Riley to check whether Steve was free, but when I was talking to Ivy she said Adam would love to come and give a hand, and she was up for wielding a paintbrush. Any excuse, she said, to get away and I didn't have the heart to say no.

In return for a not-so-relaxing weekend away, I'm rewarding them by supporting Erica's new business venture. She'll be delivering some hearty, home-cooked meals as I've had no time at all to bake, let alone batch cook for the freezer.

When Ivy texted to confirm they were on the road at five this morning, a little fizz of excitement bubbled up inside of me. A new, and let's be honest, exciting life comes at a cost and I miss the people I love being able to simply drop by for a chat. The upside is that when they do get to visit it makes it a very special couple of days.

Misty is curled up on my lap, as the last forty-eight hours have been very confusing for her. My cleaner, Hendra, kindly offered to come and stay overnight on Thursday while Lola and I headed to Mum and Dad's. It was time to make peace with my mum. About a week after that awful phone conversation,

I'd called to clear the air and we ended up apologising to each other. But things are still a little strained between us. As soon as we were face to face, though, we hugged each other and the tears began to fall. Thankfully, Dad steered Lola outside for a stroll around the garden so that Mum and I could pull ourselves together. I was emotional anyway, anxious about handing Lola over to Ben the following day.

And now I'm back home and it's just Misty and me, and she's moping around. Every little sound makes her raise her head, ears perked as if she's expecting Lola to come barrelling through the door. Then her hopes are dashed and her little face looks crestfallen.

Beep, beep!

As I very gently scoop Misty up in my hands and lay her down on the sofa next to me, she gives a sad little whimper. I make a comforting shushing sound and she half-opens one eye, but it's barely more than a slit as she's exhausted from keeping watch.

Racing to open the front door, the sight of Ivy and Adam as they get out of their car is a real tonic.

'Look at this,' Adam calls out, pointing in the direction of the farm shop.

'I know,' I reply, hurrying over to them.

Ivy is staring at me. 'What?'

'And look at *you*!'

'Oh,' I brush off her comment as we hug. 'Long hair isn't practical when you're constantly covered in dust and debris.'

'It really suits you, Jess. What I'd give to have naturally curly hair with a gloss like that. You look wonderful!'

'I don't know about that, but after catching sight of myself in the mirror the other day I decided I had to do something. It didn't even look like me!'

Ivy stands back and Adam steps forward wrapping his arms around me and lifting me ever so slightly off my feet. 'Ivy's right, Jess, you look good and happy. And trim!'

'Thanks, Adam. It's all the manual work,' I grin at him. 'How are you doing?'

He rolls his eyes and as Ivy walks around the car to open the boot, he places a finger against his lips.

'Good. And looking forward to giving a hand.' His expression is one of caution and it's obvious there's a bit of an atmosphere between the two of them.

'Are you saying that a change is as good as a rest?' I reply, playfully.

'You feed me better down here than Ivy does at home,' he jokes, but I can see the tension reflected in his eyes.

'I can hear every word you're saying, you know!' Ivy calls out. 'And this case is too heavy for me to lift.'

'That's because you don't understand what travelling light means.' But even as Adam joins in with the banter I can tell Ivy's upset with him.

'Come on inside. We'll get you settled and then I thought I'd rustle up some bacon sandwiches while you sit and have a coffee.'

'Right, you ladies get busy in the kitchen,' Adam states, 'and I'll carry this lot inside.'

Ivy slings a bag over her shoulder and walks towards me with a potted plant in her hand.

'This is for you, Jess. It's a succulent; an aloe vera plant. There's a little booklet with it. You can peel the leaves and use the gel to revitalise your skin and it makes a wonderful cooling eye mask.'

'Um... thank you, Ivy. I must have really looked tired last time you were here,' I muse, as I take it from her.

She bursts out laughing. 'Ooh... I wasn't dropping hints and anyway, today your skin is glowing. It must be all that fresh air.'

'The result of my weekly pamper session,' I confess. 'It was time I started taking a little time out for me.'

Adam strides over to catch up with us. 'Don't take it the wrong way Jess, Ivy is always giving me things to try,' he chuckles.

Ivy turns to stare at him over her shoulder. 'Don't knock it. I made your migraine go away with peppermint oil and acupressure, didn't I?'

'You did, Ivy,' he replies, sounding genuinely apologetic. 'I'm not dissing it because I know it works.'

'Right, guys, come on inside.' Oh dear, this isn't the best start to what I'd hoped would be a fun weekend that would help them both to relax.

Sitting around the table talking, I can't help feeling that Adam is putting on a brave face when he tells me all about his new business venture.

'It might take a couple of months to get to the stage where I'm not scratching around for work on the odd day here and there, but at least the phone is ringing again.' Adam glances at Ivy, but his eyes don't linger for long.

After splashing out on the wedding of their dreams eighteen months ago, ever since Ivy and Adam have been saving up to put a deposit down on a house of their own. If they suddenly find themselves struggling to make ends meet, they'll be eating into their nest egg and I know Adam will feel like they're going backwards.

'How long is Lola staying at Ben's house?' Adam asks, swiftly changing the subject.

'He's driving her back next Friday. It's going to be the longest week of my life,' I declare.

Ivy makes a pouty face. 'Aww... she'll be just fine. He'll do the typical divorced dad thing, no doubt, and spend the entire time spoiling her!'

'Ivy,' Adam says, quite sharply, and she glances at him, puzzled.

'What? Let's not pretend Ben is going to be any different, Adam. My ex-brother-in-law is another prime example. It's the guilt. Admittedly, it's not always the mums who get custody, but the main parent is the one who keeps the routine, and the discipline, going. Isn't it, Jess? The other parent gets to do the fun stuff and then hand them back.'

Ivy is cross because she feels it's all Ben's fault, anyway. I wish I could say the same thing hasn't gone through my mind many times over, but it has.

'To be honest, Ben didn't even consider having Lola to stay until he got his new place sorted out.'

Ivy flings both hands in the air. 'My point exactly. Look at the chaos you've had going on here and yet you've managed.'

My dear friend is angry on my behalf, but the reality isn't as simple as that.

'Yes, but I wasn't ready to let Lola out of my sight... not until I felt she could handle being so far away from me without having one of her meltdowns. Sometimes her emotions overwhelm her and, as you know, we've had a few of those. She's going to text every day, so if she does ring I'll know she's feeling homesick, and I'll deal with it.'

Ivy sighs. 'Life changes aren't easy for adults to cope with, let alone little ones.'

'A part of the reason why I said I'd drop Lola off,' I admit, 'was to impress upon her that she has family close by. As Thursday was an inset day, we took a leisurely drive up to Stroud and stayed overnight with Mum and Dad. Then we spent yesterday morning with Cappy. If she gets upset, they've both offered to drive her back no matter what time of the day, or night, if need be.'

'Ben's lucky you're such a great mum, Jess,' Ivy reflects, her tone softening. 'You make it easy for him. But then, you always did – he just didn't appreciate that.'

Ivy doesn't usually rant on about things and even Adam is surprised by her forceful remarks. I've always done the lion's share of the parenting anyway because, in fairness to Ben, he was further up the ladder than me career-wise. After Lola was born, right up until she started pre-school, I only worked part-time.

That meant everything to me and it was only possible because Ben was prepared to work overtime.

'Right,' Adam says, pushing back on his chair and making his way over to the sink with his empty plate and mug. 'That hit the spot, thanks Jess. I'm going to change into my work clothes and then we can get started.'

He glances at Ivy, a little frown creasing his brow, but he quickly turns it into a half-smile. 'I'd offer to do the dishes, but you know how clumsy I am.'

Unexpectedly, Ivy walks over to throw her arms around Adam's neck. 'Sorry I'm grouchy, babe.' She gazes up at him, and it's a tender moment.

As I drag my eyes away from them, I begin clearing the table.

Ivy turns to look at me. 'Jess, I'll clear this lot up and then I'll go and change too. Don't wait for me, you go on ahead and show Adam where to start. I'll join you shortly.'

'Ivy doesn't seem quite her usual, bubbly self, Adam. If the two of you need some time together relaxing instead of—'

Adam shakes his head. 'No. To be honest we needed to get away. On the trip down I made the mistake of saying I regretted walking out on my job over my principles. Ivy went off on one and gave me a lecture about how important it is to stand up for what you believe.'

I turn to look at him and he rolls his eyes.

'Oh. I see. She'll calm down.'

'I know, but I meant it, Jess. We're both self-employed, but at least my income was fairly stable. It isn't now. I'm only getting some of the jobs I'm taking on because I'm undercutting other peoples' rates. I feel I've let Ivy down.'

'That's just it, Adam, you haven't. Doing the right thing is more important to Ivy than anything else.'

'I disappointed her when I said that, then? Even though it means our plans for the future are on hold right now.'

'Yes. Plans are just that; they're subject to change and that's something Ivy will take in her stride. Taking a stand on something you believe is right means something to her and she's proud of you for doing just that.'

Ivy has a genuinely good heart. She's one of those people who believe in sending out good karma and she treats others as she'd like them to treat her. But it doesn't always work out for the best. Before she met and fell in love with Adam, her previous boyfriend of five years had an affair. She found out when his best mate told her what was going on behind her back because he thought it was wrong. Ivy was horrified and it took her a while to trust someone again; fortunately, that someone was Adam.

Adam's sigh as I lead him into the farm shop touches my heart. 'All I want to do is give Ivy the security I promised when I encouraged her to start up her own business, Jess.'

'Then tell her exactly how you feel so she knows it's not that you regret your decision, what you regret is the fallout. You'll get back on your feet and Ivy knows and accepts that.'

'Thanks, Jess. I miss our little chats. I'm hoping that a couple of days away from it all will be like a restart for us. We're both so wound up and it's hard to relax. Anyway, let's hope it's all upwards from here. Wow – look at this beautiful row of stone buildings!' Adam emits a low whistle. 'The first two are the bakery and the third one is going to be another rental cottage?'

'Yes. Now we've removed the overgrown mass of greenery at the far end, you can see the entire thing in all its glory.'

'The third side of the square is coming alive.'

'I know, and I can't wait to move on to the small barn. Riley was right to insist we clear everything back at the start.'

'Ivy said you've been working alongside Riley.' Adam gives me a sideways glance. 'I hope he realises your aim is to make him redundant once you've honed your new skills.'

I give a self-deprecating chuckle, as Ivy steps through the door looking ready for work in a pair of old jeans and a T-shirt that says *Born to be wild and free*.

'What's funny?' Her voice is bright and she's definitely looking perkier.

'Adam thinks I'm trying to turn myself into a builder and dispense with Riley's services.'

She looks at me, questioningly. 'Talking about Riley, I thought he was going to be here this weekend?'

'He was. He's been on site since last Wednesday. As I was driving home yesterday, he texted to say he had a family emergency and had to dash off. He said it might take a couple of days to sort out.'

'Poor guy. In which case, the sooner we get started, the better. What's first on the list, Jess?' Adam asks, keen to make a start.

'If you're content to tackle the tiling in the kitchen upstairs, everything you need is in the small barn. There are some boxes of lime green tiles next to the tile cutting machine. I thought maybe Ivy and I could start painting the walls down here.'

'Perfect. I'll be in and out, but I'll try not to get in your way,' Adam replies, stopping to steal a quick kiss from Ivy on his way out the door. Nothing is going to come between these two for long and Ivy isn't one to dwell on the negative.

'Right, what colour are we using?' Ivy checks.

'White. I want to keep the space as bright and flexible as possible until I have a tenant.'

'Can we have a quick look around first?'

I slap my hand to my forehead. 'Of course! I forget this is the first time you've been inside here. Let's start upstairs. After you,' I indicate proudly towards the wooden staircase situated behind the impressive, solid oak countertop. 'I spent hours sanding and staining the wood. Riley managed to fix the creaking treads and they're good as new.'

'It's a lovely feature, Jess. I love the beams overhead, too. And leaving some of the walls in the natural stone finish adds that wonderful rustic touch.'

'It just seemed a shame to plasterboard everything.'

Ivy makes her way across the landing and I follow her into

the room on the far left. 'This is the smallest of the two but it's still a good size.'

Ivy heads straight over to the window to stare out across the courtyard. 'Gosh, I'd happily move in here. It's still going to be a shop, though, isn't it?'

'Yes.'

She gazes around at the newly refinished oak floorboards. 'It really is a blank canvas, and much bigger than I thought.'

'It was originally two cottages, but they were knocked through at both ground and first floor levels.' She follows me back to the top of the stairs. 'The first door leads into a large kitchen.'

'It's gorgeous and everything is so pristine,' Ivy mutters, wistfully.

'We'll probably end up putting in a partition. I expect we'll need to fit it out with racking for stock, that sort of thing. There's no point doing that until I know how the space is going to be used. That wall over there is just plasterboard and on the other side of it I went with Riley's suggestion. He installed two separate cloakrooms. He said if I ever want to turn it into a cottage, then one of them could be converted into a shower room.'

'The whole of the downstairs will be retail then, and up here there's plenty of space for both storage and an office.' Ivy seems impressed as she wanders around.

'That's the plan.'

'How many bedrooms will there be in the second cottage?'

'Two doubles. It's not quite as big as this. The bathroom in there is going to be cosy, but we'll still be able to squeeze in a bath and a shower.'

'It's all so lovely, Jess, and full of character. I love those multipaned windows. And it's so the right thing to keep it light and bright. It's going to be handy being able to walk over here when you run out of anything.'

'I guess it will.'

'Is it all right to come up?' Adam calls out.

'Yes, we're only nosing around,' Ivy replies, brightly. 'I'm just imagining myself moving in here… to live,' she laughs.

We stand back to let Adam pass.

'Are we laying these horizontally or vertically, Jess?' He carries what is a really heavy box as if it's light as a feather.

I turn to look at Ivy. 'What do you think?'

She makes Adam hold up a tile against the kitchen wall and we agree that horizontal works best. It's a real boost for me today having them here and I genuinely hope it turns out to be a tonic for them, too.

After two-plus hours of almost non-stop painting, it's time for elevenses. Adam is in the small barn with the tile cutter going and Ivy and I saunter over to The Farmhouse just as Erica pulls up in the car.

'Hi Jess. How's it going?'

'Good, thanks, Erica. I don't think I had a chance to introduce you to my friends when they were here before. You were dropping off some cakes you'd made if I remember correctly. This is Ivy and her husband, Adam, is the one making all the noise in the small barn.'

'It's nice to meet you Ivy. I assumed it was Riley. Tell him there's a Victoria sponge sandwich to go with his coffee.'

'He's not here this weekend.'

'Oh, that's unusual. He all but lives here these days.' She grins at me. I can see Ivy tuning in with great interest.

'Riley has family stuff to do deal with up north. Can we give you a hand?'

'If you don't mind.'

Ivy follows me around to the rear of the car and Erica hands us both a box.

'I need to rejig the boot, as the casserole is at the back. I'll just be a moment,' she confirms.

'When I open the front door watch out for Misty,' I warn

Ivy. 'She's a little minx and good at getting out. I don't want her running off to the small barn with the tiling machine up and running.'

'So, Riley virtually lives here,' Ivy remarks, as she follows me into the kitchen. 'Has he stayed overnight?'

She sidles up next to me, placing the box she's carrying alongside mine on the island as I start unpacking it.

'If I stack these up can you put them into the fridge for me, please?' I ask, keeping my head down.

'Jess, look me in the face and answer the question.'

Of course, that makes me laugh and her jaw drops. 'He has!' she blurts out, her eyes widening as Erica walks through the door.

'Here you go. One chicken and red wine casserole. There's an instruction sheet in the second box with the oven temperatures and timing on it for this, and the side dishes. There's a cold starter ready to plate up and an Eden cake for dessert.'

'Ooh, that's sounds interesting.' Ivy's face lights up. 'I've never heard of that before.'

'It's lemon and poppyseed sponge soaked in rose gin syrup and coated with buttercream,' Erica enlightens us both.

'Sounds yummy!'

'Um... what else,' Erica pauses to think. 'Oh, yes, the cake for Riley and I put in some Cornish fairings too.'

Seriously, Erica, you aren't doing me any favours bringing up Riley's name all the time.

'This is amazing, thank you so much, Erica. It's handy knowing I can order in when I'm up to my eyes in it.'

'This is a takeaway meal service?' Ivy asks, sounding impressed.

'Yes. Well, that's the idea if I can cook up enough business,' Erica laughs.

'Nice one. Go you, Erica.'

'Well, with a little girl the same age as Lola and my mother suffering from crippling arthritis, this allows me to do something that I enjoy while working around my other commitments.'

'And it's a boon. You're going to do really well, Erica, and don't forget to give me some of your business cards to put in the rental cottage.'

'Oh, yes. I will. I think you're all sorted. Sorry to dash off but I have another delivery to make and it's the other side of Polreweek. I hope you all have a great weekend. I'll see myself out, Jess.'

As Ivy struggles to fit everything into the fridge, she's not about to let our previous conversation drop.

'You know, Jess, it's about time you had a little flirtatious fun. I don't know why you can't just admit it. I mean, married and having a baby by the age of twenty-one, then juggling motherhood and work. And now getting divorced and taking on the farm. It's time to celebrate being single. Unless you already have your eye on someone. Maybe that's the reason for the fetching new hairstyle.'

'I'm having fun, just not the sort that you're implying. Okay, I do enjoy having a little company from time to time but holding hands over drinks in the pub is not for me.'

'That weekend we were all here and Riley turned up to help, I swear I saw a little glint in your eye, Jess. It looked like you were checking him out as he worked. He's dependable, obviously, looking at what you've achieved with the farm shop. From the little he did say when we all had lunch together, he also understands the complications that arise following a break-up. Two lonely people thrown together—'

'You can stop right there, Ivy,' I state, giving her a pointed stare. It's not a topic I want to get into right now because there's nothing to say. 'Passing quickly on, poor Adam is still reeling, so I hope you'll forgive him if he says something wrong. He really doesn't mean to upset you.'

'I know. But he has never, ever let me down and it makes me angry to think he feels that way. He's been my rock through thick and thin, Jess. I hate it when he blames himself for something that wasn't his fault. In my eyes he would have been less of a man if he hadn't walked away.'

It's obvious she's simply feeling frustrated on his behalf and it's a relief to know there's nothing more serious going on between them. 'If he'd simply backed down I don't think he would have continued to work there for much longer anyway,' I reflect. 'From the little things he'd mentioned to me it was obvious he was unhappy about the way it was going.'

'It will put a dent in our savings, but on the upside my landlord is finally beginning to listen to me. Now the alarm has been replaced and with the extra sockets he had installed, it's business as usual. I've decided now is not the time to press for an upgraded kitchen, as he'll obviously hike up the rent. However, seeing Erica has given me an idea. Let's have this coffee break and then I can mull over a few things as I wield the roller.'

'Only you, my lovely friend, only you!'

Most other people would want to sit down quietly to think, but not Ivy. She's a doer.

17

What a Night That Turned Out to Be!

After several texts back and forth with Lola throughout the afternoon, I can finally relax. Ben took her shopping in town, and she was able to spend some of her pocket money. They had lunch and then went to the park. There's no mention of Naomi and I'm glad he had the sense to understand that at least her first day there was all about bonding.

Tonight, I'm going to let my hair down. It's been a long day, but we've had a few laughs and, thankfully, this evening my two best friends are in a much better place emotionally than they were when they arrived this morning.

'You must pass on our compliments to your excellent chef, Jess,' Adam states, wiping his mouth on a paper napkin. 'This casserole is delicious; I don't suppose there are any leftovers?'

'There are, and some more roast potatoes, too. Why don't you help yourself?'

Adam is up and out of his chair before I finish speaking and Ivy catches my eye as we watch him and smile.

'I can't thank you two enough for what you've done today,' I state, letting out a sigh of satisfaction as I settle back in my seat.

'Well, after a meal like this the question is when can we come again?' Adam jokes.

'Seriously, guys it means a lot. Not just for getting stuck in, but for your company. Lola is obviously on my mind and although

I'm feeling more relaxed knowing she's had a good day, it would have been a long, lonely evening.'

Adam returns to the table, sinking back down on to his seat. 'The problem here is that you're a bit out of the way. It's not easy to make new friends, is it? I mean obviously you mix with people at the school, but the holidaymakers come and go.' Is Adam's mind heading in the same direction as Ivy's? I wonder.

'It's companionship I miss, but I'm not looking for a man to step into my life if that's what you mean.'

'Would it really be a bad thing, I mean if it happened?' Adam questions, before popping a forkful of food into his mouth.

I swirl the wine around in the bowl of my glass as I give it some thought.

'I freely admit that, for a long time, having Ben by my side made me feel complete. Now I've accepted there is no going back, the only thing I really miss is having someone to talk to at the end of the day when Lola's in bed. It's actually nice to be able to focus on her and the farm, and just do my own thing. What I do find annoying, is that everyone is worried I'm working too hard and doing too much. Is it because I'm a woman on her own?'

Adam looks up, pulling a face. 'Did I just unwittingly put my foot in it again?'

Ivy and I burst out laughing. 'No,' she reassures him. 'It's my fault, entirely. I said to Jess she should have some fun for a change. It sounds like Riley is in the same boat, from what he said that day he joined us shovelling chippings in the rain. I just thought... there are all sorts of friendships and they're both free agents.'

'Yes. Not love birds, though,' I enforce, adamantly. But the thoughts going through my head are conflicted. Riley hasn't been in touch. Naturally, it's none of my business and why would he? It's obvious that we're very comfortable around each other and I like to think of him as a friend, not just someone I hire. But am

I kidding myself, because I'm sitting around the dinner table with friends thinking of Riley and wishing he were here?

'Did you mention there's a dessert?' Adam prompts, pushing his plate away.

Ivy stares at him, then raises her eyes to the heavens. 'Adam! The conversation was just starting to get interesting and all you can think about is food.'

'There's absolutely nothing to see here guys, as the saying goes, so let's move along, shall we?' They both look at me and shake their heads, as if I'm a lost cause.

However, it means a lot that Ivy and Adam, whom I regard as family, are here tonight as the thought of being home alone is unimaginable. Just then something touches my foot and I look down to see Misty looking up at me, as if to say, 'What about me? I'm here.'

'Come on, let's get you some fresh food,' I say, as I scoop her up. 'Then I'll get the coffee going.'

With the tiling and the painting completed by mid-morning, I encourage my guests to go for a stroll along the cliff path. I can't stray too far in case Lola gets in touch and the signal is so patchy it's not worth the risk. Besides, two is company, three is a crowd when it comes to a couple badly in need of some quality time together.

My mission while they're gone is to open the patio doors at the rear and sit outside with a book. I put Misty's snuggle blanket on the patio and her water bowl next to it, along with a little pile of treats. My biggest fear is that because she's so desperate to explore, whenever she escapes we naturally chase after her. What that does it to encourage her to run as fast as her little legs can carry her and she's growing by the day. I'd hate for Misty to head towards the five-bar gate and run straight out into the road. Luckily, she's wary of loud noises, so that's why she tends to run in the opposite direction.

My phone pings several times in quick succession and Lola is sending me some photos. Someone else is taking them, as she's sitting in what I assume is Ben's new garden, on a colourful rug with two of her old school friends. My heart skips a beat. She looks happy, though, and I let out a long, slow breath. *That's all that matters in the long run*, I tell myself. The fact that she's holding her own and not feeling anxious is a major step forward.

'Jess?' The sound of Riley's voice seems to appear out of nowhere and I sit bolt upright. When he strolls around the side of The Farmhouse he has Misty in his arms. 'Look who I found about to set off on a tour of the estate!'

My heart feels like it's about to leap out of my chest. Is it the sight of Riley, or the fact I didn't even know Misty had gone walkabout? The answer is that I can't be sure, but seeing both of them together takes my breath away for a brief moment.

'Hi Riley, thanks for spotting her. Was she running?'

'No,' he smiles. 'Just nosing around in the shrubs at the front.' He leans forward to put her down next to me, but I stand and indicate for us to go inside.

'I'm ready for a cold drink. Can I get you something?'

Misty trots over to her bowl as I pull the patio doors shut.

'A soft drink would be great, thanks. It was a long drive. I saw Adam's car parked up in front of the small barn and assumed you were all around the back sunning yourselves.'

I bat my eyelashes at him. 'If that's meant to make me feel guilty, you wait until you see what we managed to get done.'

Riley's grin is artful and for the first time as our eyes meet, there's an intensity between us that hasn't been there before. Or has it and I just haven't noticed? Is that why Ivy was grilling me? He's glad to be back and it's obvious I'm pleased to see him, as I can't stop smiling. I turn my back, busying myself filling two large glasses from the jug of apple and raspberry fizz I made earlier.

This weekend has been great, but it wasn't the same without

Riley here. He's become a part of this adventure. Should the fact that he didn't go straight home tell me something?

'I—'

'I—'

Riley gives a dismissive little laugh when we start speaking at the same time, shaking his head to himself. 'Sorry, Jess. You go first.'

'Oh, I was just going to ask if you managed to… get things sorted?'

I hand him a glass and we sit opposite each other at the kitchen table.

'Just about. It was a bit stressful, that's all. I thought I'd better show my face and let you know I'll be back bright and early on Wednesday morning.'

We sip our drinks in silence and it's agonisingly awkward. 'Ivy and Adam are doing the cliff walk before we have lunch and they set off home.'

Riley studies my face in earnest. 'I just wanted to check that you were okay. You know, as Lola is um… well, I'll leave you to it then.' With that, he downs his glass in one and pushes back on his seat.

My eyes follow him as he carries the glass over to the sink. This is the smartest I've ever seen Riley and it's not the Mr Fix It I'm used to. Usually, he has a bit of a stubbly beard going on, but today he's clean-shaven. He's wearing a pair of grey trousers and a pale-grey check shirt with his sleeves rolled up to the elbow, and I even catch a waft of aftershave as he walks around. It's aromatic, with a hint of smokiness.

Before I get a chance to reply, Ivy and Adam come bustling through the door.

'Riley!' Adam steps through into the kitchen and immediately goes to shake Riley's hand. 'Great job you've done on that first outbuilding, mate. And in record time.'

'Thanks, Adam. I gather Jess has had you and Ivy rolling up your sleeves.'

'She has,' Ivy chimes in. 'The final finishes are always the most fun, aren't they? Are you staying for a while?'

Before I know it, Adam is taking Riley over to inspect his tiling and Ivy can hardly wait for them to be the other side of the front door.

'Riley certainly cleans up well. He was looking a little distracted. Did you say something to upset him, Jess?'

'No, why on earth would I do that?'

'You're sure there's nothing romantic going on between the two of you?'

'Absolutely not.' I reply, dismissively. What's unsettling, though, is that I've never felt flustered in front of Riley before, but I did this time. And he felt the exact same way because I saw it reflected in his eyes. If ever there was an *ah-ha* moment, that was it.

I guess we're both more used to seeing each other in dirty jeans and T-shirts, often covered in dust and debris. Having had a little time to myself this morning, I thought it was important to make the effort for my guests. I want to send them off having had a relaxing lunch out on the patio. Now I have a dilemma. Do I walk over and ask Riley if he'd like to join us, or do I take that as a given?

Come on, Jess, why are you overthinking this? My inner voice pipes up. *It's just a friendly lunch, not a quiet meal for two, and he'll stay if he wants to.*

'It wasn't that funny!' I declare, sounding miffed as Ivy and Adam start laughing.

I glance at Riley, and he holds up his hands defensively. 'Sorry, Jess. That just sort of slipped out.'

Ivy continues to giggle. 'How long was it before you discovered your keys had fallen out of your pocket?'

'Not that long,' I reply, begrudgingly.

'Long enough for them to disappear beneath the surface of

the concrete though, if the three of you had to go rooting around to find them,' Adam points out with great amusement.

'Admittedly it was a bit of a panic to find them. It was a hot day, and the cement was starting to dry out.' In truth I'd felt awful. We fished them out from a section Steve had already tamped down to get out any air bubbles and was perfectly level. Sweat was literally dripping off our faces at that point and suddenly we had to redo a whole section.

'A rookie mistake, it could happen to anyone,' Riley comes to my rescue. 'But even with Steve's help, it took all three of us working flat out to get the floor laid before it started to become unworkable. Give Jess her due, she didn't complain once and it was stiflingly hot in there. It's the first time that I've laid concrete where the boss was alongside me raking it out.'

'See, Jess, we're not laughing at you, we're laughing *with* you.' Ivy grins at me, loving the banter going around the table.

'That's okay then,' I retort, narrowing my eyes. 'I won't mention Riley's little problem as that might make me sound petty.' My lips twitch as I struggle to keep a straight face.

Ivy and Adam turn to look at Riley and he pulls a face. 'Um, which *little problem* are you referring to, Jess?'

'There's been more than one?' Ivy joins in, looking intrigued.

Now it's my turn to pull his leg. 'Only one that I've witnessed, but I've heard a few curses here and there when I've been out of sight. I'm talking about the day I walked in to find Riley scratching his head. I'm talking about the turn in the stairs.'

'Now that's unfair,' he comes back at me. 'It was at the end of a long and tiring day, and I knew I hadn't made a mistake. I always measure twice and cut once.'

The look that passes between us is light-hearted. 'Riley was standing there with a carefully cut triangular piece of wood in his hands, puzzling over why it wouldn't fit.'

'True,' Riley takes over. 'But in fairness to me, I was simply rechecking my measurements and I would have worked it out eventually.'

'Yes, well, when I told him he was holding it the wrong way round, he rolled his eyes at me. How long he'd been there trying to figure out what was wrong, I have no idea, but let's just say his patience was wearing thin.'

'Classic one, mate,' Adam roars. 'We've all been there. I remember being on a job once and, no word of a lie, one of the guys installed a window frame the wrong way round. The beading to keep the glass in place was on the outside. When I pointed out a thief could prise it off and take out the pane, I saw a look of panic flash over his face. I'm pretty sure it wasn't the first time he'd done that, but it was the last.'

Riley shakes his head, seemingly not at all surprised to hear it. 'Is there plenty of work in your neck of the woods, Adam?'

'There is, but I've just gone from subcontracting, to setting up on my own again. It takes a while for word to get around and I'm taking anything I can get, including some site work. Have you always been in the building trade, Riley?'

I start clearing the plates and Ivy gets up to give me a hand, but I'm all ears.

'No. For a few years I was a partner in a small joinery company, we were just getting into making and installing custom built home offices. After a falling-out, we decided to end our business arrangement. Moving to Cornwall and buying an almost derelict cottage meant I had to learn a few new skills in double quick time. Since then, I've done a bit of work for a few of the larger building companies in the area in between some private jobs.'

'It's a market that has certainly exploded with more and more people working from home; it's a pity about the timing from your point of view. I'm in a similar position, so I know what it's like to feel you're going backwards for a while.'

I, too, am curious about why Riley would walk away from a business with such huge potential.

Ivy is busy slicing up Erica's fluffy Victoria sandwich while I wash the dishes, and I'm not sure she's listening. I'm trying to make as little noise as possible, to catch what's being said.

'I went through a rough patch and had to start over again. It's the sort of thing you hear and wonder how anyone can have been so stupid not to see the inevitable consequences of some really bad decisions. But that's life; you make mistakes and you pay the price.'

'It's lucky for Jess, though. When she gets her teeth into something she's not one to hang around, she goes for it. Having a builder who knows what he's doing is half the battle. The trouble is, coming here and seeing what's been done, Ivy now has cottage envy. I'm afraid once our finances are back on track we'll be looking at a small two-bed property on a housing estate at best, if we're lucky.'

Ivy walks over to the table, plates in hand. 'Who wouldn't envy this sort of lifestyle?' she questions. 'Most people can only dream about it.'

'Yes, but a rural location means very little is on your doorstep and it's quite a car ride just to get the weekly shop, Ivy. Imagine having maybe a thirty-to-forty-minute-plus journey to work. That makes it a long day. And Riley will no doubt agree that with travel time and petrol costs to factor in, as a self-employed builder sometimes a job simply isn't worth doing.'

Riley nods his head in agreement. 'Often, I make more as a casual driver for the builders' merchants than I do taking on some of the smaller jobs. There's a ceiling to what a customer is prepared to pay, regardless of how far away they are. And even with bigger jobs, if you're hanging around waiting for materials they've ordered to be delivered, some customers see that as time you're not on the clock. That's why small builders often have more than one job going at a time. No one wants to pay to see you sitting around waiting, even when it's not your fault.'

'What was it like renovating your cottage?' Ivy asks, genuinely curious.

Riley emits a soft groan at the memories. 'Roughing it was tough at times, I can't deny, but it paid off in the end. It's worth a fair bit now. Even if you have to live in a caravan for a while, as long as the price reflects the condition and you can afford to do the work, it's worth considering.'

'There you go, Adam. When the time is right I'm sure somewhere in Gloucestershire there's a lovely little place just waiting for some TLC.'

'Tender loving care? With our budget as it stands, if it has a roof and four walls we'd be lucky.'

'I knew you'd come around,' Ivy retorts.

I'm not sure Adam is totally on board with her new vision, but I really hope before too long they'll be in a position to start looking for a place of their own. Both Ivy and I turn thirty next year. The irony is that as teenagers, I saw myself as a career woman, content to put marriage and kids on the back burner until I'd made my mark. Ivy was the one who imagined herself happily married with at least two children and a dog by now. It's becoming increasingly important to her to be able to put down some roots sooner, rather than later, and I think that's what is eating away at Adam.

Now I'm troubled, because for Ivy I feel this weekend just added to that sense of longing to realise the future she's always envisaged. One that, sadly, didn't include wasting five long years on Mr Wrong.

18

A Whole New Set of Rules

'I feel like I kind of barged in on you and your guests today, Jess. That wasn't my intention.'

Having waved Ivy and Adam goodbye, it's obvious that Riley has something he wants to say to me, but I didn't think that was going to be it.

'Look, let's head back inside and have a proper chat, shall we?'

'That sounds ominous. Are you firing me? I will admit that Adam did a great job of the tiling. I couldn't have done any better myself.'

I can see that he's only half-joking. 'No. Of course not. The last thing Ivy needs now is for me to entice Adam down here, leaving her home alone. Money isn't everything, it's just frustrating for them. They were so close to having enough to start looking for a place.'

We amble into the kitchen, side-stepping Misty, and Riley offers to make us a drink while I give her a fresh pouch of food.

'Tea, coffee?' he enquires and I shake my head.

'Wine for me, please. There's beer as well. Adam loves Proper Job from the brewery in St Austell.'

'I'm good with wine. Small… medium… large?' He looks at me, his face brightening as he grabs a bottle from the fridge. 'Don't tell me, I can read your thoughts. I'll make it a large one. Right, what's going on, boss? I know I've missed two full days on the job, but you guys nailed it without me. Until you have a tenant and know whether you need that extra partition put up, it's job done.'

I wasn't expecting that, and I peer up at him for a second, as I put Misty's bowl on the floor. 'Twice now you've referred to me as the boss.'

'Well, you are.'

'You're the one teaching me, Riley and there are times,' I clear my throat nervously, 'when I know I probably hold you back a little.'

His face falls. 'Oh, Jess. I was only joking around when I mentioned you having dropped your keys. I thought Adam and Ivy needed a bit of light-hearted banter. I didn't mean to offend you. I only dropped by to let you know I'm back. I feel bad for crashing your lunch party.'

He deftly ejects the cork and hands me a very large glass of wine, looking extremely apologetic.

'I didn't take it the wrong way, Riley, and I'm glad you did… stay, that is. Adam appreciated your little chat, but it made me realise that our arrangement needs a little adjusting.'

'I think I'd better sit down for this,' he gulps, as he puts the wine bottle back in the fridge and takes a seat.

I remain standing, leaning against the island countertop. 'Finding a good builder who can afford to focus on one job at a time is rare. Listening in on your conversation with Adam was an eye opener, Riley.'

'Jess, please sit down. You're making me nervous.'

'Why?'

He stares down at the untouched drink in front of him. 'It's been an emotional couple of days for me and somehow I found myself driving here, instead of going straight home.'

His body language is heart-rending. He looks like someone desperately in need of a hug.

'I overheard you telling Adam that you'd made some bad decisions. Is this to do with your son?'

Riley tilts his head back and a sigh escapes his lips. 'Ollie is asthmatic, and he had quite a severe attack. On Friday night, Fiona and I slept on chairs next to his hospital bed. They released him late yesterday and he was fine this morning when I set off. It obviously sent her into a panic because we were told that with childhood asthma they tend to grow out of it. It turns out Ollie had an upper respiratory tract infection and that's why he went downhill so quickly.'

'Oh, Riley. Why did you hurry back? Family always comes first!'

He gives a disparaging laugh. 'I haven't been a real part of their lives now since Fiona and I split up, a little over four years ago. That's when I came to Cornwall.'

'All contact ended, just like that?'

'No. I visited once a month at first, but as time went on Fiona said it was unsettling for Ollie and I understood that. Eventually, Fiona suggested I call him instead, but making conversation wasn't easy with a four-year-old and the silences were agonising. The calls grew shorter and shorter, then Fiona would say Ollie was too tired to talk, or he had a friend over and was playing. I knew it was because he didn't want to speak to me. Why would he? I wasn't a meaningful part of his life anymore.'

'It's not the same over the phone. Kids either chatter away and you can't get a word in edgeways, or it's hard work trying to get them to say anything at all,' I acknowledge. 'You need to be face to face.'

'He was changing so quickly that I lost touch with his interests and what was going on in his little world. Hence, it's unusual for Ollie to ask for me but I think Fiona needed a little support too. I was more than happy to be there for them both. It's the longest the three of us have been together in one room ever, I think.

'When he was little, Fiona and I took it in turns to stay up with him through the night when he was unwell. A simple cold was always a real problem, and it was heart-breaking seeing him struggling to breathe. We had a nebuliser, so we'd switch it on then read to him to take his mind off it. Sometimes it was the only way to keep him calm. After a few hours of wearing the mask it would eventually allow him to sink into a peaceful sleep. The worst time was always between three and five o'clock in the morning, for some reason.'

I can't even begin to imagine what an awful experience that must have been for them all. Just thinking about it tears at my heart.

'Oh, Riley. I don't know what to say to comfort you, because that's a horrible situation to be in. Wanting to be there for your son and not feeling welcome.'

He emits a long, drawn-out sigh. 'There are two sides to every story, Jess. Maybe I'm getting what I deserve. Anyway, that's enough of my troubles for one evening.'

I've never been the sort of woman to have a one-night stand. I met and married Ben when I was so young that, looking back, I was laughably naive. Because that's all I know, not much has changed. I wouldn't do well trying to find a new love of my life through an online app, because I don't know how to play the game.

Tonight, though, I found myself snuggled up in bed with Riley's arms wrapped around me and I have absolutely no regrets. When two people cling together, safe in the knowledge that they both know exactly what it's like to have one's world implode, it's comforting to know that someone understands what that does to you.

Lying with my head against Riley's chest, I could sense his pain. Ben had this *what doesn't kill you, makes you stronger* mentality and for a long time I admired that. Until the day he sat me down and told me I would always be his best friend, but he was no longer in love with me. Just like that. Looking back on what was one of the most traumatic moments of my life, I feel foolish now.

I'd known something was wrong, but it was easier to ignore the fact that the passion we once felt for each other had become a distant memory. I figured that every relationship has its ups and downs and convinced myself that it was just a phase we were going through.

Riley's problems, like mine, haven't simply evaporated; they've left a trail of emotional baggage, regret and a sense of failure. Riley hit the point early in the evening when he just wanted to switch off and I'm pretty sure it was because he'd suddenly hit a wall. Getting a call to say his son was in hospital must have scared him witless. Lack of sleep and an excess of nervous energy had exhausted him. But the fact that he sought me out meant something to me.

What I saw when he turned up this afternoon was a man who didn't want to be alone, and he knew I can connect with that. We feel safe in each other's company because we understand a feeling of emptiness and disappointment, that usually comes out of nowhere. It leaves you reeling until it passes, and it dawns on you that you're just running on empty. What took us both by surprise was that there was this innate sense of trust between us and a startling, and intense, level of passion. The connection between us that has been quietly growing in the background, even though we've both been trying hard to resist it. It's only natural to fear getting hurt a second time around, isn't it?

'Sorry, Jess. You should have woken me. What time is it?'

Riley appears in the doorway to the kitchen, wearing just his trousers and rubbing his eyes.

'It's just gone eight o'clock. You were shattered, Riley.'

He stands there, awkwardly.

'Is it okay if I use your shower?'

I chuckle to myself; we had sex last night, so I think using my shower can hardly be construed as taking a liberty.

'Of course. I didn't know whether or not to wake you. I'm not sure what time you start work at the builders' merchants.'

He stares down at his feet, seemingly surprised to see he's not wearing socks.

'I... uh, texted my boss late on Friday to say I won't be able to cover this week. I wasn't sure when I'd get back.'

'Well, that's something. You sound a little hazy this morning.'

'Is there any chance I could have a really strong coffee? I've got a cracking headache and that will probably sort me out.'

'Grab that shower first. There are some spare towels on the rack next to the bath. Help yourself and don't rush. In the meantime, I'll put the kettle on.'

He looks hanging and I'm not surprised. Physically he's strong, but mentally the last few days have taken a toll on him.

The sound of the shower running in the bathroom overhead seems to go on forever. I can imagine him standing there, just letting the water flow over his body as he pulls himself together to face another day. I've been there, too. No matter how much it hurts waking up to a reality that still makes no sense, life goes on.

When he finally presents himself, fully dressed and looking at least half alive, he's apologetic.

'Jess, I'm so sorry about last night. I mean... not sorry about what happened between us, that was... wonderful... but for falling asleep on you.'

He can't even look me in the eye.

'Riley, stop babbling and sit down. Are you hungry?'

'Thanks, but no thanks. Just coffee please. Black, no sugar. After the second mug, my brain should start functioning normally again. Well, as normal as it gets for me.'

The only way he can cope is to laugh at himself and hope I'll laugh with him.

'Here you go. Just sit and enjoy it.'

The atmosphere between us is hesitant, so many things unsaid, unasked, but he's too fragile right now.

My phone pings. It's Lola sending me a photo of her breakfast plate with a smiley face. Pancakes and strawberries, her favourite. I'm lucky that while Ben left most things to me, he knows our girl and I can relax. My fingers get busy.

Delicious! Hope you slept well. Sending a good morning hug and a miaow from Misty. Love you! xx 🐱🐈

Riley watches me with interest. 'Lola?' he asks and I incline my head.

'Yes. She's doing okay.'

'It rips your heart in two to let go, doesn't it? I mean, putting them in someone else's hands and stepping back, even for a while.'

I pour hot water into my mug and carry it over to sit next to Riley.

'She'll be fine with Ben, but I don't really know his new girlfriend. I think she's staying with her sister at the moment though. Lola's fine texting, but if she insists on calling me, it'll be another story. It will mean she's feeling homesick, and I don't want anything to spoil this bonding time with her dad. I've always been there to sort out the problems and now he's taking on both roles for a short while, he's understandably nervous.'

I watch as Riley reaches out to grab a coaster for his mug, fiddling with it absentmindedly. I wonder whether he's even heard a word I've said. After a few moments he takes a tentative sip of coffee and then turns to face me, cradling the mug in his hands even though it's still really hot. It's as if he's trying to rouse himself out of the funk he's in.

'After last night I feel I should tell you the rest of my story.'

It was just one night; he doesn't owe me anything. 'You don't have to, Riley. Unless it helps to talk about it.' I'm still trying to get my head around this latest development and the fact that I'm feeling so calm about it. It's a huge deal and yet all I want is to feel his arms around me once more.

'I wouldn't know because I never have. Maybe that's a part of my problem.' He shrugs his shoulders and I sit quietly waiting. 'Fiona and I hadn't been dating for very long when she discovered she was pregnant. We were young... you probably understand how that is, right? Things happen and you just get on with it.'

I nod, not wanting to interrupt his flow.

'Ollie burst into our lives and turned everything upside down. It was a happy time for us all, but like a lot of relationships, it wasn't destined to last. At first everything seemed fine, if a little crazy as he wasn't a good sleeper. By the time Ollie started pre-school I knew something wasn't right, so I proposed to Fiona, thinking that was the root of the problem between us. It turns out I was fooling myself. Not long afterwards she suggested we spend some time apart. I had no choice but to give her some breathing space, so I moved out temporarily.'

'That must have come as quite a shock at the time.'

He raises his eyebrows. 'It was. I'd been working long hours. My best friend, Will, and I had this carpentry business. It was going from strength to strength, and he convinced me that we should branch out into making bespoke home offices for the garden. Our workload virtually doubled overnight. We took on two guys to help us cope with the demand, but we were still working flat out. It was that which triggered the situation at home because it just made everything a hundred times worse.'

'There was no third party involved?' I ask, gently.

'No, it wasn't like that. You see... I messed up. Fiona said I'd changed. But I had to keep the house going and I was living in a small flat close to the workshop by then. She said she just wanted the old me back, the one not so obsessed with work.'

He stops, taking another large gulp of coffee, then another and another until it's empty. I take it from him and quickly brew a fresh one. When I place it in front of Riley, his forehead is no longer pinched, and I hope the caffeine is beginning to ease his headache. I slip into the seat next to him.

'Thanks, Jess. Where was I... ah, yes – losing the plot.'

I glance at him, frowning, and he gives me a look that sends a little chill coursing through my veins.

'Will and I had a big row. He said my focus was shot to pieces and accused me of not pulling my weight. That wasn't true, it simply wasn't true. I was about to lose my family because of his obsession with success at any price. I lost it, big time. I'd literally worked myself into the ground; we were both angry and a fight broke out. It took two guys to pull us apart but unfortunately one of the punches I threw broke Will's nose. There was blood everywhere and I was horrified. I couldn't believe what I'd done.'

My face probably reflects the shock I'm feeling. I just can't imagine Riley as a violent man.

'A friend told me that Will had gone to the police, and I didn't know what to do. Obviously I had to stay well away from him. My brother offered to intervene, and he got Will to agree not to press charges. In return, Will bought me out, but financially I paid a hefty price for losing my temper. Still, I walked away with enough to pay off the mortgage on our house and I told Fiona that no matter what, she and Ollie would always have that as security.'

'You didn't go back home?'

'No. Fiona said I was in no state to be around Ollie. What sort of an example was I setting him, anyway? She worked part-time and said she'd do more hours because she felt the best thing all round was if I made myself absent. It was all too much for her.'

I've been holding my breath and when I release it, the sound is pitiful even to my ears.

'Too much for you, too, Riley. You only did what you needed to do to support your family, but it pushed you over the edge. It's not a nice thing to experience, but it happens. Under normal circumstances that's not who you are.'

What a mess!

Riley shrugs his shoulders. 'Pretty pathetic, eh?'

'No. Just an unfortunate chain of events.'

'Or a catalogue of bad decisions, Jess. It's all down to me.

I sold a few personal things to scrape some money together, including a vintage car I was doing up. My brother insisted on giving me a loan, which helped me to buy a wreck of a cottage no one else wanted. That's why I had to get whatever work I could after I moved here. It was a juggling act supporting Fiona and Ollie, and just trying to survive.'

Riley sits there, a grave expression on his face.

'The fact that Ollie asked for you when he was ill and scared means you're not forgotten, Riley. He will have memories; kids don't forget happy times and I'm sure you had many together in those early years. Even if you don't get to play a bigger role in his life for the time being, as he grows up you might find he's more inclined to reach out to you. This could be a start, a real reason to reconnect.'

'I hope that's the case, Jess. I'd hate for him to be disappointed in me, thinking I don't care. I just stopped calling because I never seemed to be able to catch his interest and the silences were too painful to bear. I felt like a stranger to him. Fiona would often interrupt after a couple of minutes, saying he had homework to do, or sometimes Ollie simply wouldn't come to the phone. You can't blame the kid for that.'

It's heart-breaking to see how devastated Riley is by what happened. Only someone who cares would react in that way.

'This recent trip... it's not the first time you've dropped everything when Fiona's called, is it?'

I notice a little nervous tic above his left eyebrow as he sets his jaw before answering. 'No. She knows that I'll never ignore her if she has a problem, or if Ollie needs anything.'

'Then you're doing all that you can.'

'Maybe, but the truth is my son doesn't really know me anymore. The other pressing issue now is that my brother is getting married next year and it's time to repay that loan with interest. I'm halfway there, but I need to earn as much as I can because I couldn't have got through the last four years without his help.'

We lapse into silence for a while. Riley is a proud man and that wasn't an easy thing to share.

'There's a proposal I'd like to put to you, but after what happened last night, this feels a bit awkward.'

The eye contact between us ends up with us both laughing. 'It wasn't planned,' Riley ardently tries to reassure me.

'Oh, I'm fully aware of that. For whatever reason, we hit it off from day one, didn't we? And I don't know about you, but I have no regrets at all. I like working with you, Riley, and let's face it, there's enough here to keep you going full-time for what... a year at least, if we include the small barn. And there's potential for even more work in the future.'

'That sounds like a challenge.' His ghost of a smile makes me want to lean in and plant my lips on his. Instead, I sit quietly watching him.

'What exactly do you have in mind?' he asks, and just like that he brushes aside the things he can't fix, to focus on the things he can.

I needed to ensure I had enough money to carry us through the winter and watching every penny I spent has paid off. Cappy was right, expanding the campsite into the second field has made all the difference. I still have a little nest egg left over from the sale of the house as an emergency fund if I need to dip into it, but fingers crossed it won't come to that. If it does I know it's time to panic.

'I'm in a position to guarantee you employment five days a week at the going rate while the building work is ongoing. You can't keep working flat out seven days a week and neither can I. Besides, during the school holidays I can only work every other day during the week. Erica and I are going to take it in turns to look after both girls and keep them occupied. It works for us both, now she's trying to grow her business. Is that something you'd be interested in committing to?'

He hesitates. 'Is this because you feel sorry for me?'

'No. I just don't want to risk someone else commandeering your time.'

'That sounds good to me. I guess I'll be making a call to inform the boss at the builders' merchants that I'm no longer for hire as a lorry driver. I do appreciate it, Jess, and I won't let you down.'

That just leaves a slightly more delicate issue to raise.

'Just so we're straight. I've done the commitment thing and now I just want to keep things simple. I do get lonely, and I think we discovered last night that we both enjoy each other's company.' His eyebrows shoot up in surprise at that tongue-in-cheek remark, but he makes no comment. 'Companionship is one thing, but for me it can only be casual. Lola has enough to cope with going forward and I wouldn't want her to get the wrong impression.'

I watch as he swallows awkwardly then clears his throat. 'Right. Fine. Thanks for making that clear.'

Now he looks a little embarrassed.

'If you want to stay over for a couple of nights before Lola gets back, there are times when it's best not to be on your own, don't you think?'

Looking at him, I can't decide whether he's going to bolt for the door or start laughing. Instead, he finishes off his coffee, making me wait. I never saw myself as the sort of woman who would proposition a man, and yet here I am doing just that. The truth is that Riley has sparked something deep down inside of me and it's both scary and exhilarating at the same time.

'That works for me. But you can boot me out at any time if you change your mind, Jess. I'm out of practice… you know, at being friends—' He pauses awkwardly, but what I see reflected in his eyes is sincerity. Cappy was right, he is a good man and he's already proved that to me. Actions speak louder than words.

'Relax, Riley. When it's just you and me we're two people just getting through life as best we can and simply helping each other out.'

Gosh, as true as that is, it also sounds rather tragic in a way. Even so, he's smiling again, and I think he feels better now that I know exactly why he walked away from his old life. He relaxes back into his seat, as happy as I am that we're come to an arrangement that works for us both.

Who knows where this is going on a personal level but what's important is that we take it slowly. Loneliness is an awful thing and sometimes a hug from someone who understands is enough to keep you going. Last night, Riley needed just that. Admittedly, we went an awful lot further and I struggle to contain a wicked smile that keeps tweaking at my lips. Who doesn't need the reassurance that when the physical chemistry is right, they still have what it takes to enjoy a night of passion? We certainly had the chemistry all right, and as long as it doesn't get out of hand I'm one happy bunny, for now.

19

Work, Rest and... Play

Shortly after our little talk, Riley returns home to change his clothes and pick up a few things. On the way back he's going to call in to see his boss at the builders' merchants. He thinks they'll probably go back to using agency drivers to cover absences. However, he feels it's appropriate to add that if they're really stuck and I can spare him, he'll help them out as a special favour. I like that Riley is prepared to be flexible, especially as he managed to talk them into giving him a discount on anything he orders on my behalf.

My first task this morning is to tackle the fortnightly update of the income and expenditure spreadsheet, after a long chat with Vyvyan. My first year of making cash flow projections was loosely based on Cappy's figures. However, having doubled the size of the campsite, the second year was a bit of a finger in the air job. Admittedly, experience has taught me it's always best to err on the side of caution, but so far receipts are running at just over 20 per cent higher than I anticipated. Overheads are rising, but if it continues like this, by the end of the summer the fund for the building works could be twice the amount I hoped to have set aside.

Grandma had a saying: 'Don't spend what you haven't got', and if I didn't feel confident that I had control of the finances, I'd tread water for a while instead of pressing ahead. However, new income streams are vital if this is to become a thriving business with a long-term future. That doesn't just require investment, but the courage to believe I can pull it all together.

The only negative Vyvyan raised are the reviews knocking off one, or two, stars because of the lack of an onsite shop.

'I'm aware it's a pressing issue,' I reassure her. 'The thing is, I'm having a bit of a rethink. We'll soon be starting work on the building adjoining the farm shop and setting that up as another rental cottage. I'm concerned that a general shop might put holidaymakers off if there's a constant stream of foot traffic going back and forth. It shouldn't affect Penti Growan that much, sitting across the way on the other side of the courtyard. But what do you think?'

While the renovation work does retain that feel of a row of stone cottages, I just worry about the level of disruption.

'I can understand your dilemma, Jess. Have you considered not letting it out and employing someone to run it for you? That way you control what it sells so it's more of a quaint farm shop and less of a mini-convenience store?'

'That's an idea that didn't even cross my mind. Hmm… maybe I'll have a chat with my accountant; there might be a financial advantage in doing that. Did I mention that Riley is joining us full-time to speed up the building work?'

'No. That's great news. And the agent I talked to seemed confident that when you're ready to market the farm shop, you'd get a tenant quite quickly. Whatever you decide, when you're ready, just let me know and I'll start the ball rolling. It's a bit like the snowball effect when you grow a business. As it gathers speed it's harder and harder to slow things down.'

I utter a low moan. 'I know. How are things between Keith and Len? Any problems?'

'No. That all seems to have settled down now. A couple of shower heads needed replacing at the weekend and Keith called Len in for a couple of hours to give him a hand. With the hot weather he doesn't like to have showers out of action for long.'

Keith is an old-school type of site manager and if there's something he can fix himself he simply gets on with it.

'Pass on my thanks to Keith, Vyvyan, for sorting it out. Let him know that with Riley now formally joining the team he'll be on hand if he needs any additional help.'

'Keith will be delighted to know that. Riley is very amenable, isn't he?'

Suddenly I find myself breaking out into a smile. 'He is that. He's very handy! Thanks for the update and your input, Vyvyan. Always appreciated.'

It seems that I'm not the only one who thinks it's a good idea to have Riley join us. It's a struggle to push thoughts of last night out of my head, though, and a warm glow comes over me just thinking about him. *Come on Jess*, I tell myself, *pull yourself together. You're no lovesick teenager!*

Seconds later my phone rings and I pick it up, chuckling away to myself. 'What did we forget?'

'Jess? It's Ivy.'

'Oh, sorry, I was just speaking to Vyvyan. I was going to give you a call tonight.'

'I'm on a break and I was thinking about the weekend. It was lovely, Jess, thank you. Adam really enjoyed chatting to Riley and it helped him realise he was being a bit impatient.'

'Oh, I'm delighted to hear that. I wondered whether the timing wasn't quite right for you guys and a weekend spent relaxing at home would have been easier.'

'No, trust me. We had our little wobble on the way down and I'm sorry if there was a bit of an atmosphere at first, but a trip to Renweneth Farm is like walking into a different world. It reminded us both that just because we aren't where we'd hoped to be right now, who knows what's around the corner?'

'You said you had a new idea, something inspired by Erica, then you didn't mention it again.'

She laughs, softly. 'I was going to tell you about it but had second thoughts as I don't think Adam will approve. But I'm thinking of advertising family picnic hampers and a boxed Cotswolds Luxury High Tea. You know… tiny little sandwiches, scones, local honey and jam, Parkhurst Manor House clotted cream, that sort of thing.'

'It's a great idea but with just you, your full-timer and the two ladies who cover for your days off, won't that stretch you a bit thin?'

'Ah,' she muses, her voice full of enthusiasm. 'Spoken like a true businesswoman, which is why I couldn't wait until later to tell you about it. It will be pre-order and collect only. To begin with, anyway.'

'It sounds like a wonderful idea, Ivy. You can trial it to see what interest you get and expand it from there if it's profitable.'

'I know. The thing is, if I mention it to Adam he'll think I'm desperately casting around for a way to increase our income. That is true in one way, but if I can't venture into hot lunches because I don't have the facilities here, then this could create the extra buzz this place needs. The more people who discover us, the better. I'm proud that everything we use is locally sourced and organic where possible, so our regulars keep coming back, but this could help spread the word even further afield.'

It's good to hear her sounding so positive and maybe the weekend was a success in more ways than one. And, to my relief, the two of them left here in normal love-bird mode.

'You've nothing to lose and everything to gain.'

'Exactly! Anyway, that's enough about me. What time did Riley leave?'

The question catches me off guard and when I don't instantly answer, Ivy's shriek makes me put her on speakerphone. 'Late.'

'Late, as in this morning?' Her tone is playfully accusing.

Heck, now I'm in trouble. 'Yes.'

'Jess, you said nothing was going on between the two of you! It's not like you to tell a blatant lie, not to me, your bestie.' Now she sounds put out.

'There wasn't.'

'But?'

'Okay, so there is now. Before you say anything, I can assure you that it wasn't planned. It was as much a surprise to me as it was to Riley, for more reasons than I can count on one hand.'

It's actually a relief to get it off my chest. We've never kept secrets from each other, not when it comes to anything meaningful. Except that it's way too soon to say whether this is meaningful... that's how hearts get broken.

'But it's not going to be a one-off, I can tell. There's something in your tone that's a giveaway. You're a little bit brighter this morning. Actually, you perked up shortly after Riley appeared yesterday. Even Adam noticed it.'

'You can't mention a word of this to Adam, Ivy. I mean it. I need a builder here permanently until the work is finished, someone prepared to go at my pace so I can control the timing of the expenditure. The fact that we're both on our own and enjoy each other's company means just that. I'm not in the market for a proper relationship because I don't want the hassle. And I've made that very clear to Riley, but he's in much the same position anyway.'

Ivy splutters. 'A working relationship with *benefits* and you don't think Lola will notice that you and Riley are growing closer?'

'I don't see why she should if we're careful. Besides, I have no idea how she'll handle Ben's news when he tells her Naomi has moved in. He's going to do that about a week before her next visit.'

'Even so, it's a huge step for you, Jess. Admittedly, Riley is a good-looking guy, which obviously makes him hard to resist. You certainly fell on your feet there!' She giggles.

'Don't read too much into it, Ivy.'

'All joking aside, I'm really glad you've found someone you feel you can trust, Jess. I don't for one moment think Riley would mess you around. From what I saw yesterday he's even more fragile than you are. You're good at compartmentalising things though, I hope the same is true for him.'

'Oh, we agreed upon some ground rules. He's going to be working Monday to Friday at the farm in future.'

'And any time Lola isn't there?' She gives another annoying little giggle. 'Let's be honest... I've seen the way you drool over him and I don't blame you.'

I gasp. 'I do not! Anyway, we're playing it by ear. It'll get Riley out of a hole to have a guaranteed income for a period of time, so it's mutually convenient. Plus, I can't really work weekends as that's my main quality time with Lola. Hopefully, it will also mean that Riley can get some sort of normality back into his life and take time out to relax.'

'He did look haggard when he first arrived,' she remarks, pensively. 'I thought at first that you'd said something to upset him. I'm glad that wasn't the case. I'm just a bit surprised as this is a side of you I haven't seen before.'

'What do you mean?'

'Technically, you're sleeping with one of your employees, and yet you're fine with it.'

'Now you're making me sound like a prude! We're both consenting adults. I was the one who propositioned him and Riley doesn't seem to have a problem with it.' The moment I stop speaking I could cheerfully kick myself.

'You didn't! Oh, Jess, look out world, nothing is going to stop this woman from getting what she wants.'

'Actually, Ivy, there was a moment when I hesitated and asked myself what I was doing. I wasn't thinking of Ben, though, I was thinking of Lola and what she'd think. That's why I made it crystal clear that when she's around it's strictly business between Riley and me.'

'I would have loved to have seen the look on both of your faces when you had that conversation. I didn't think you had it in you, Jess. I hoped that at some point in the future you might stumble across someone who caught your eye and who knows where that could lead. But this is different, at least for you.'

I breathe out, contentedly. 'I've changed, Ivy. The effort I'm putting into Renweneth Farm isn't just about rising to the challenge to make me feel better about myself. Lola loves living here and if the business thrives it could be her forever home. Imagine that?'

'If I lived there I'd never want to leave,' Ivy confirms. 'Next time you invite us for a stay and Lola's away, maybe we can walk down to Penvennan Cove together. All four of us.'

'Ivy! Riley won't be working weekends in future and we're not a couple. I wouldn't want to confuse him either. Right?'

'I get the message. And I won't say a word to Adam. Promise! Have fun and I'm sure the days will fly between now and Thursday when Lola returns.' I can hear the smile in her voice and the innuendo isn't lost on me.

'Two and two make four, Ivy, stop trying to make it add up to five.'

It's probably true to say that it's rare for a meeting with one's builder to take place while meandering along a scenic coastal path, but it works for me. After what turned out to be quite an intense morning, Riley insisted on making us lunch. He came fully prepared and while I finished up crunching some numbers, he cooked up a rather delicious omelette with chipped potatoes on the side.

With even more decisions needing to be made in quick succession now, I suggested a little fresh air might help while we thrash out some of the details.

'What do you need from me, Riley, now phase one is almost complete?'

'I guess we're at a standstill with the farm shop until you have a prospective tenant. I understand your caution in wanting to keep that within your control, rather than leave it to them to complete the fitting out. Just allow for the fact that if they want a separate stock room, or to divide up what we call the office into two smaller rooms, it could be a week's work at least. There are more than enough sockets on the ground floor to accommodate chiller cabinets for soft drinks and a couple of freezer cabinets. I'm assuming you'd be expecting them to provide that.'

'Ah, I'm beginning to have second thoughts about it.'

We draw to a halt alongside a bench and sink down gratefully to enjoy the vista. It's a beautiful spot. Today it's overcast, although it's not cold, it's just grey and the sea looks dull and murky. But the gentle movement of the waves means it's a living canvas and none the less interesting for it.

'Best to have them now before you go any further,' Riley points out.

I sink back against the bench, shoving my hands in the pockets of my fleece as sitting here it is a little chilly.

'What's the problem?' Riley prompts me.

'I'm just trying to imagine a constant stream of people in and out of the courtyard carrying bread, milk and their daily newspapers.'

Riley shrugs his shoulders. 'I can't help you with that one, I'm afraid. However, I understand your reservations. You can restrict the hours they're open.'

'Hmm. I suppose I can. But any shopkeeper is going to want to make as much money as they can and in the peak season it could get a little crazy.'

I can see that Riley is surprised I'm back-peddling when I should be focused on finding a tenant.

'Okay, let's approach this from a different angle. What's the long-term plan, Jess? I don't mean this year, or next year, but say... ten years down the road.'

'I like to think that Lola will be helping me run this place and it will pay the bills and give us a comfortable living.'

'And Renweneth Manor?'

'That would be the ultimate dream, to strip it back to the bare bones and make it as beautiful inside as it is outside.'

'Then it's time to consider other options.' Riley's expression instantly changes. 'It's just an observation, but if I lived in The Farmhouse I'd want something a little more in keeping with the character of the place on my doorstep. Like a little bakery, or an ice cream shop. Something that would add to the ambience and not be too disruptive.'

I think I agree with him. 'I suppose either would add to the facilities on offer for the campers. I do want the courtyard to come alive though, rather than feeling it's totally set apart, but that still leaves me with a big problem. People see the word *farm* and assume they can get the basics – milk, butter, cheese etcetera. At the moment it's a thirty-five-minute drive into Polreweek and then the hassle of finding a parking space, which is a trial in summer.'

'Then tackle the problem in a different way.'

'How?'

'The general car park at the entrance to the campsite is hardly used, it's purely for access. No one has mentioned any plans for the former hay barn, but both represent an opportunity that wouldn't involve any foot traffic into the courtyard.'

'But planning takes forever, and I'd have to get an architect to draw up plans first. I like to think I'm sensible enough to know my limits, Riley.'

'There are a number of independent operators who tour the outlying villages in mobile vans. You can get virtually anything from fresh fish and vegetables to a mini supermarket. Even fish and chips. Work out a rota. All they need is a place to park up and willing clients. You have both. I'm not sure where the council stands on that, but it's easy enough to go along to their offices and ask the question. It's your land and I can't imagine they'd have a problem. It's just a thought.'

Now my head is buzzing with ideas. This could be the perfect solution.

'What I'd like is for the farmyard complex to feel cosy. Not necessarily a place people come from far and wide to visit, but our holidaymakers feel adds value to their stay.'

'Then go with your gut instincts. A little bakery would be perfect.'

In my head, I'm remembering various holidays in France and first thing every morning, Lola, Ben and I would take a gentle stroll to the local boulangerie. Ben would end up with a carrier bag full of croissants and pain aux raisins, and often scented apricots we'd buy from baskets at the end of tracks leading up to the most rustic of stone cottages. On the trek back, Lola and I would pinch chunks off the end of a large baguette, usually wrapped in a single sheet of greaseproof paper tucked under Ben's arm.

'I need to employ a baker,' I proclaim. Riley gives me a hesitant look.

'That wasn't quite what I meant, Jess.'

'I know, but it's a great solution. I mean, imagine waking up in a field bordering on the edge of a vast moor. Taking a deep breath in, there's that salty tang in the air and the next smell to hit the nose is that of freshly baked, artisan bread, scones and saffron buns, to name a few of the Cornish favourites.'

'It does sound enticing,' Riley admits, cagily.

'People come away for a rest, a break in their routine. What I need is to provide fresh, locally grown produce and cottage industry delights, like Erica's stews, pasties and quiches. It's cheaper than taking the family to a restaurant and who wants to cook a meal from scratch when they're on holiday? I bet the answer to that is no one.'

'Tins of beans and frozen meals are out?'

'There are supermarkets in Polreweek, but I like your idea about trying to entice some of the mobile shops here.'

Riley looks pleased with himself. 'Market days were quite a thing at the farm in the past, from what I've read. I know the intention is to have various stalls in the small barn once it's been transformed, but the large hay barn would be the perfect all-weather space to hold an old-fashioned farmers' market.'

'It's structurally sound, too, which is a huge bonus. The intention was always to use the small barn to house boutique-style booths, featuring handmade items rather than mass produced things you can buy anywhere. Maybe we could set up some bistro tables in the centre of the courtyard and the bakery could sell teas and coffees during the peak season.'

I'm thinking off the top of my head here, and getting way ahead of myself, but suddenly I'm buzzing.

'You're probably looking at four to five grand at least, to kit the bakery out with ovens, fridges, freezers and racking. And someone with enough experience to tell you exactly what you need to buy.'

'That's not a problem.' My brain is chuntering away. The Farmhouse Bakery... I like the sound of that. 'I need to make a couple of phone calls. In the meantime, perhaps this evening you and I can share a bottle of wine as we look over the plans ready to begin renovating the second cottage.'

'Back in the day it was the blacksmith's cottage, of course.'

'I didn't know that. In which case, I think it should be called Smithy's Cottage.'

'The owner was definitely a master wheelwright, as there are quite a few piled up in the rafters in the old barn.'

'Perfect. Perhaps we can get them down and find a couple to put on display.'

'You love this, don't you – finding something old and worn, and breathing new life into it.'

'That's one way of putting it, but it beats the daily commute and eight hours stuck behind a desk, breaking off to take part in an endless succession of meetings that often get you nowhere. I never thought I'd hear myself say that, as my career was important to me once. Now, I seem to experience something new every day and I realise there's so much more to life than I could have imagined.'

'It just goes to show that some meetings are productive,' he jests, winking at me playfully. 'It's good to work for someone who knows their mind. Now it's my job to turn your vision into reality.' Riley reaches out to grasp my hand briefly in his to give it a reassuring squeeze; it's an honest gesture and a touching one.

'More flagstones to lift, then,' I muse, 'and another round of concreting. This time I'll leave my keys somewhere safe. I might make mistakes, but I rarely make the same one twice.' I bat my eyelashes at him and he smirks back at me.

'I've noticed.'

'Really?'

'Yes. I notice a lot of things, including the new hairstyle. It's very you.'

I start laughing, instinctively reaching out my hand to scrunch up the curls at the nape of my neck. 'It's practical is what it is,' I reply.

'All the same,' Riley retorts, 'it looks good.'

Embarrassed, I cast around for something to say, blurting out the first thing that comes into my head.

'Oh... um... one more thing. To fill in on the days I'm going to be looking after Daisy and Lola, is there any chance you can get in an extra pair of hands?'

'Really? What's the rush?'

'I'd like to get Smithy's Cottage ready to let out late autumn and also take advantage of the Christmas/New Year period. The extra income will help.'

'That's not a problem. I'm thinking it would be two months' work for one person but double up the labour and we're talking early September. I'll have to reach out to an electrician pretty sharpish though.'

I know I'm in good hands with Riley when it comes to work, but as our eyes meet there's no point kidding myself anymore. This attraction between us is unleashing feelings I'm finding hard to contain. The problem is, will it spoil everything if this is just a passing attraction?

I'd forgotten what it's like to be flirty and light-hearted, enjoying the moment simply because I'm with a man who is fun to be around. And Riley is fun. He gives his all to everything he does and he's as enthused as I am about what's to come. His ideas flow freely and suddenly I feel excited about the future; a wave of optimism is flooding back into my life. Looking back, during the last couple of years of my marriage I think I'd lost that sense of me, of the person I was when I wasn't being a wife and a mother. At times I felt so alone and, it's true to say, miserable. Suddenly, everything has changed and one person is responsible for that.

Riley is kind and he's thoughtful. He doesn't take anything for granted and it's poignant to realise that life has taught him that in a very harsh way. I'm lucky in ways I didn't even realise before; hearing his story was a real wake-up call and made me count my blessings. I feel guilty now about feeling resentful when Ben told me that Naomi had moved in with him. She's the new love in Ben's life and, at the time, it hurt. Yes, her role in our blended family has to be managed smoothly for Lola's sake, but Lola is having a great time with her dad. The few occasions she has mentioned Naomi, it's been very casual and that has impressed me.

I reread Lola's last text sent late afternoon.

Dad and I went to see Cappy. He sends you a big hug and said he wants to come and visit us very soon. Love you, Mum. I do miss you and Misty. Dad gave me a photo of you to put under my pillow. Night, night. Don't let the bed bugs bight. xxxxx

I love the way she spelt bite, bless her!

'Is there anything I can do to get you to put down your phone?' Riley asks, extending his hand to pull me up off the sofa.

'That depends. What did you have in mind?'

'I'll think of something between here and the bedroom. It's all beginning to come back to me now.'

I burst out laughing. 'You know what they say: if you don't use it, you lose it.'

He shakes his head at me. 'Jess, I can't believe you said that!'

Neither can I.

SEPTEMBER

20

A Change of Direction

'Only me. How was Lola's first day back at school?'

'Hi, Ivy. She was anxious this morning, but she was singing like a diva in the car on the way home, which is a good sign. It's a pity they split her year group up, as Daisy isn't in the same class anymore, but Lola did mention that they played together at lunchtime.'

'I bet she wasn't the only anxious one. How did you sleep last night?'

Ivy knows me so well. 'Fitfully. I purposely avoided questioning her in case she picked up on my concern. Lola sat next to a new girl. It was her first day at the school and the teacher asked them to buddy up. Lola helped her to get her bearings. It's also the first time Lola's had a male form tutor, so she wasn't sure what to expect. It helps that Cappy is arriving tomorrow mid-morning and when Lola gets home he'll be here. He's only staying for three days, but he's going to take her to the Eden Project on Saturday.'

'That's nice. You're not going with them?'

'No. I'm way behind with the paperwork and the new bathroom suite and some of the furniture for Smithy's Cottage is being delivered. Unfortunately, it's been one problem after another and we're behind schedule anyway.'

'Ah, that's a shame. Your mum said you had a structural problem?'

'Yes. When Riley got up into the roof space, most of the joists had dry rot and had to be replaced. It wasn't an easy job.'

'And how is your *arrangement* with Riley working out?'

'Everything is just fine,' I reply, laughing. 'How's it going at your end?'

'Busy. I'm just getting some leaflets printed up showcasing a range of winter hampers, hoping to tap into the Christmas gift market. After a slow start I managed to get one of the local free newspapers to do a little feature on us. I had to take out a half-page ad, but it was worth it. We've even had a few phone orders, so it's not just passing trade looking at our window display or sit-down customers grabbing a leaflet.'

'That's brilliant, Ivy. And Adam?'

'He's still doing labouring jobs at least three days a week. It's not ideal, but he doesn't complain. He's done several quotes in the last week and a couple of them were bigger jobs. A replacement kitchen in a townhouse and installing a bathroom suite in a bungalow.'

'Things could be on the up, at last.'

'Fingers crossed. Anyway, Adam is having a drink with an old mate in the hope that it might produce a few leads and I'm about to slip into a hot bath.'

'Hang in there, Ivy. Just take it one day at a time and we must arrange to get together again very soon.'

'Cappy! It's so good to see you. You're looking well.'

'Thanks, Jess, I feel it. And you're looking extremely business-like today. I can't see a speck of paint anywhere on that rather elegant trouser suit of yours.'

I follow him around to the boot of his car as he lifts out his holdall.

'That's because I have a meeting. I was hoping you'd come with me.'

'Me?'

'Come on inside. Misty's in the window watching us and I don't want her getting into mischief because she's excited to see you.'

'Mischief?'

'Climbing the curtains.'

'It's about time you installed a cat flap, you can't keep her in forever. I told you she's a hunter by nature.'

'I do appreciate that, and it is on Riley's to-do list.'

'Where is he?'

'Taking a couple of days off. His son's school had an inset day yesterday and he drove up to spend a little time with him.'

'He did? Gracious, that's a first. His ex must want something. She'd all but cut him off from having any access at all.'

'Apparently, he wanted to do a couple of little jobs around the house, anyway.' Riley didn't make it sound like it was at Fiona's request. I presumed while he was there he just wanted to check everything was in working order.

Cappy puts down his case as Misty starts jumping around and suddenly launches herself at him. He stoops to scoop her up. 'My, you've grown, little miss. And climbing curtains? You should be climbing trees.'

Riley said more or less the same thing. 'Lola's scared that Misty will go out one night and not come back.'

'That's all a part of life, Jess. There's no getting away from it, I'm afraid. Anyway, first things first, let me put Misty down and give me a hug. Then show me what you've been up to.'

'I love the name. Smithy's Cottage, it's very fitting.'

We wander around and Cappy does an inspection; he seems pleased, I know I am despite the delays.

'Yes. It's taking a lot longer than the bakery but having to replace the joists and now a problem with what seemed like a bargain delivery of handmade Italian tiles for the bathroom and cloakroom, has totally messed up the schedule.'

'But it's all going in the right direction. I'm impressed.'

'Riley had an extra pair of hands when I wasn't able to help out and it was just as well. I wouldn't have had the muscle power to help him lift the new joists into place.'

'And is business ticking over okay?' he checks.

'Thankfully, it was a bumper June, July and August. Things are beginning to slow down on the campsite, obviously.'

'Ah, it'll be the off-season crowd next and then the hardy Christmas lot not that far behind them.' He grins at me.

'Yep. I'll be closing the second field soon and opening it up for caravan and campervan storage over winter. And there are big plans to generate some additional income from the hay barn.'

He looks at me, questioningly. 'Let me guess… you've talked Riley into building you a hotel.'

I nudge Cappy's arm, playfully.

'Are you implying that I'm demanding?'

'No. Just a woman on a mission. Are you going to show me around the farm shop? I thought you'd have had that up and running by now.'

'I've had a rethink on that. And I wonder where I get my *demanding* attitude from?' I laugh as he follows me back downstairs.

Swinging open the door to The Farmhouse Bakery, Cappy stops to stare at the handmade wooden sign. 'You changed your mind about it being a general store, then. Did Riley make this?'

'He did. Wait until you see inside. We're almost ready to open the doors and that's where I'm taking you this morning, we're having a cake and bread tasting session.'

His eyes widen. 'I thought the idea was to rent it out, not get yourself into the catering industry?' Cappy's frown is perturbing.

'I'm not. For a trial period of two months, we're linking up with a family bakery in Polreweek. They will man the bakery from nine in the morning until three in the afternoon, Monday through to Saturday. We've had a thousand flyers distributed and we'll see how it goes from there.'

'If you both make money out of it, I assume they'll take up a lease?'

'That's the general idea. On balance, I felt that having a general shop here would have been too much of a disruption. It just looks like a row of pretty stone cottages from the outside and only the sign gives it away. Anyone renting it as a convenience store would want to stay open long hours and possibly until quite late, particularly in the peak season.'

Cappy scratches his head. 'You've got a point there, but will it make enough profit to be a viable option?'

'Well, we're about to find out. It made more sense though, as even when there's less trade from the campsite, hopefully we'll still attract the locals to save them a trip in to Polreweek. Come on, let me show you the brilliant idea that Riley came up with. I'll just grab my coat, it's a bit nippy out there today.'

We walk over to the courtyard gate, and I pull it shut behind us. When we round the corner Vyvyan, an older woman and a young man are standing in the entrance to the hay barn, deep in conversation.

Cappy glances at me, his interest piqued, and I shrug my shoulders.

'Hi Vyvyan,' I call out and she turns, her face lighting up.

'Jess... and Cappy. Right on cue. Mrs Carne here was just saying that she has fond memories of her mother bringing her here every Saturday for market day when she was a child.'

The woman turns to look at Cappy and he puts out his hand. 'Prudie! It's good to see you. It's been a few years since our paths crossed, hasn't it?' He places both of his hands over hers, as if they're old friends.

'It has that. Me daughter always kept me up with the local news, even after I moved away. I was heart-broken to hear about your Maggie.'

'But you're back now?'

'I am,' Prudie replies.

'Then I'm happy for you. It's where you belong.'

I glance at Vyvyan, who clears her throat. 'And this is Mr Marshall.'

We all shake hands, and I can see Cappy is curious about what's going on.

'We were um… just talking about the stalls, Jess. As I was saying, Tuesday is the designated day to begin with. If you're interested in reserving a space let me know as the pitches are going fast. I'm happy to answer any questions you might have.'

'It's a marvellous thing you're doing bringing back market day to the farm,' Mrs Carne says, turning to face me. 'Not many new opportunities opening up these days and it's good to see something positive happening. Maggie would have been thrilled to bits.'

'Thank you, Mrs Carne, it means a lot to hear you say that. Anyway, uh… we'll let you get on, Vyvyan.' I start walking off in the direction of the campsite and Cappy turns, rather reluctantly, to follow me.

'This was Riley's idea?' he asks when he catches up with me.

'It was. If it's a success, it might become a regular thing. I'm also thinking about inviting mobile businesses to book regular slots next summer to provide our campers with everything from dairy produce to general groceries and even takeaways. It's all extra income and goodness knows there are more than enough small businesses around here desperate for somewhere to sell their goods.'

Cappy is dragging his feet though and turns to look over his shoulder.

'I don't want to cut you short my dear, but do you mind if I saunter back and have a chat with Prudie when she's done with Vyvyan?'

'No. Of course not. If you like, why don't you take Mrs Carne into The Farmhouse for a cup of tea? I want to have a word with Vyvyan afterwards, anyway.'

'Perfect. Thanks, Jess. It's a surprise I wasn't expecting; she was an old friend of your grandma's.'

And yours, too, Cappy? I wonder. He certainly seems delighted to see her.

'Cappy! How are the bees doing?' Lola throws her arms around his shoulders with such force his chair rocks a little.

'How's my sparkly girl doing? I swear you've grown another inch in what... six weeks?'

'Bees?' I query.

'When Dad and I visited Cappy he took us to see his friend who has beehives. It was amazing, Mum. You have no idea how noisy bees are! I had to put my fingers in my ears.'

'And what did I promise you?' Cappy looks at her, putting his thumb under her chin and tilting her head back to stare down into those sweet little eyes of hers.

'Honey!' Lola exclaims.

'Come on, let's go look in the boot of the car. But we have to be very careful not to drop the jars. The bees work jolly hard to turn the pollen into honey and it takes teamwork to do it.'

As Lola skips out the door, encouraging Cappy to speed up, I'm still buzzing – I guess the bees aren't the only ones who can pull that off. The fact that Vyvyan has already signed up fourteen pitches for the first market day is an amazing start. Hopefully, she'll get a few more but it's a diverse selection ranging from a mobile farm van selling meat, a greengrocery stall, a woman who makes handmade candles and small gifts, and Mrs Carne who, Cappy informed me, is an artist. And she teaches, too.

'Mum, Mum! This is a special wooden thing to scoop the honey out of the jar!'

Lola runs through the hallway holding up a wooden honey dipper. 'That's lovely. I hope you said thank you.'

'She did,' Cappy says, hot on her heels. He's carrying a pretty wicker basket with three jars of honey nestled among what looks like sachets of dried lavender.

'Is this from the lavender farm in the Cotswolds?'

'It is. The taste is subtle, but it's there. You can tell the bees are kept busy and they don't have to go far to get their fill.'

'That's a lovely gift, isn't it Lola? And you saw the bees hard at work?'

'I did, Mum. We bought a jar for Naomi.'

Cappy's head turns in my direction, and I give him a brief smile. 'I bet she loved that, Lola. Who doesn't like honey? Maybe we can drizzle some over ice cream and have that for dessert.'

'Yes, please! Cappy, can we play a board game while Mum does lunch?'

'Of course we can. Go and get it all set up and I'll join you in a few minutes.'

When she's out of earshot, he turns to me. 'You don't mind that Naomi was there that day?'

'No. I'm fine with it. I do have something to tell you, though.'

Cappy cocks an eyebrow. 'Fire away.'

'I'm not going to sell Renweneth Manor.' I hold up my hands to stop him before he can start speaking. 'I know you and Grandma had a dream, but Lola and I have one too. I'm well aware that it's not going to be easy and Mum and Dad won't be happy about it, either. Riley explained that we won't know what the problems are until we start ripping out the interior.'

'And that's not enough to put you off?' Cappy questions, as if he thinks I've taken leave of my senses.

'I know it should, but it doesn't. It's the heart of the farm, isn't it? And it would break mine to see a stranger living in it.'

He's very quiet as he processes the information. 'Jess, not all dreams are achievable, you know that. Often it's because of things that simply aren't within our control. What if all you're left with is the outer shell once it's stripped back?'

'Then it's going to be a long project. With things really coming together now and new income streams I never even considered at the very start about to become a reality, I have a real shot at this.'

'And Riley's up for it?'

'He is, although he's been very honest with me. But I know it's a project that excites him.'

'As it did your grandma and me, Jess. But I'll be honest, I had my doubts about it but seeing your grandma wandering around the manor I trusted that if it was meant to be, it would happen. I'm glad you're doing it for the right reasons and not some misplaced sense of duty. There's a lot of serious work ahead of you.'

'I know, and thanks for understanding. My head says one thing, my heart another. I just don't want to live my life wondering *what if?* Imagine how wonderful it would be to have everyone under one roof to celebrate the festive holidays and see in the new year?'

Cappy smiles at me warmly. 'Then go for it!'

'As for this year's festive season... Vyvyan talked me into letting out Penti Growan over the Christmas/New Year period and now I'm panicking about where I'm going to put everyone. Mum and Dad were supposed to be staying there.'

'You can put them up here.'

'Lola will be gutted if you're not around on Christmas morning, you know that. Do you think they'd mind if I suggest they come down in their campervan as I also invited Adam and Ivy to stay. If all goes well they'll be able to use Smithy's Cottage.' I make a face. 'I know, I got carried away with the vision of us all sitting around the scrubbed pine table in The Farmhouse and making merry!'

'They'll understand. It's not exactly roughing it, is it?'

I think longingly of Renweneth Manor standing empty and I tell myself *maybe next year*.

'No, not really. I didn't want to put Adam and Ivy off because they've had a rough time of it lately. They usually spend one day with his parents and one with hers, alternating it. Ivy confided in me that they dread it. They're using me and Lola as an excuse to break what has become a bit of a routine, in preparation for next year. They intend to spend it home alone, and why shouldn't they?'

'I see.'

'The plan is that by then they'll have a place of their own.'

'Good for them. I'm sure it will work out just fine, Jess. What's important is that we're all together. It's good when you young 'uns don't mind having the oldies around.'

'I'm nearly thirty, Cappy. That's not young.'

He does a belly laugh now, shaking his head at me. 'It is when you're seventy-two.'

'Age is just a number. You'll no doubt sit cross-legged on the floor opposite Lola in the sitting room. Even I can't do that without getting up with stiff legs.'

'That's because you don't do yoga. It keeps everything in working order, Jess, and you really should give it a try.'

My brain goes ping! Evening candlelit yoga classes in the small barn.

'Cappy, you're a genius. That's exactly what I need.'

He looks at me, rolls his eyes and shouts out to Lola, 'I'm coming, sparkly girl. Talking to your mother makes my brain ache sometimes.'

I don't mention his chat with Mrs Carne this morning. Rather than disturb them, I briefly looked in to say that I'd be back later and made myself scarce. I went off to do the tasting session alone. I did, however, walk away with a large box of assorted cakes, pastries and a rosemary and sea salt Cornish kitchen loaf. There are no preservatives, enhancers, or emulsifiers and the difference in the taste is unbelievable. I'll be trying them out on Cappy and Lola later if they have any room left after some freshly caught cod and mashed potatoes.

Maybe I can tempt Lola with a good old-fashioned gingerbread man and suggest we postpone having ice cream and honey until tomorrow, when they get back from their day out together.

21

Troubled Waters Run Deep

'Just to let you know that I'm on my way back, Jess.'

'How are you doing? Is Ollie okay?'

'Yes, he's fine. I'm just... uh... well, it was a bit stressful.'

'Look, Cappy and Lola are at the Eden Project and won't be back until late afternoon. You're very welcome to call in for a chat if you want.'

'I might take you up on that. I'm a good two hours away, but if by then I decide to just slink off home, please forgive me. There's a lot I need to process right now.'

'It's no big deal, but you know where to find me if you want to talk.' Argh... why did I say that? He doesn't have to share everything with me, that's not a part of our arrangement.

'Thanks, and it is appreciated, Jess.'

A loud rap on the front door almost makes me jump out of my skin. It's the first of three deliveries due today. After the goods are dropped off at Smithy's Cottage, I hang around doing a bit of filling and sanding. For some reason I just can't settle to any one thing and when the final consignment of the day is safely stowed away, I close the door and make my way back to The Farmhouse. It's unusual for me to walk away without clearing up after myself, but my heart just isn't in it today.

It isn't long before I'm slipping into a foaming bubble bath, the scent of wild roses and tea tree fills the air rather pleasantly.

The silence as I lie back is deafening and yet outside there's the intermittent rumble of traffic passing by and the occasional noise coming from the campsite.

Being here without Lola, there's a sense of emptiness, like a void that is almost tangible. I notice every little sound around me, even the pipes creaking beneath the floorboards as the central heating boiler fires up and it sets me on edge. No laughter. No chatter. No one. Just me.

Eventually, I reach out for the bath towel. It's soft against my skin as I wrap it around me and I make my way over to the hand basin, staring at myself in the mirror.

'What's wrong?' I ask myself, but the silence hangs heavily around me.

Walking into the bedroom, even as I dress I feel that something isn't quite right. Like a sense of impending doom.

Suddenly a little mewing sound makes me look down and Misty jumps up on to the bed. Normally she races around, but maybe she's picking up on my sombre mood and she hunkers down, her cute little face staring at me with those big, soulful eyes.

'And I thought I was alone. But I wasn't, was I Misty? Come on, let's go play. Maybe Riley will call in to see us.'

When I glance at the clock a while later, I realise that Riley isn't coming. He's obviously gone straight home and a sense of gutting disappointment washes over me.

It's Monday before we know it and Cappy is packed up and ready to go. He insists on dropping Lola off at school on his way. He headed over to see Riley for a chat about half an hour ago, but when he returned a few minutes ago he didn't mention how he was.

Lola is dragging her feet this morning, but good old Cappy knows exactly what to say to put a smile on her face and speed her up.

'I forgot! There's another little surprise for you in the back of the car.'

'What is it? What is it?' Her face brightens as she slips on her coat and picks up her backpack.

'A pencil case with bees on it.' He jumps up, pretending to be a bee and chases her out of the kitchen towards the front door.

'You two are so noisy!' I moan, throwing my hands up in the air theatrically and pretending to shoo them out. 'Drive safely Cappy and have a good day at school, Lola. Remember, kindness costs nothing.'

'Got it, Mum,' she replies as I stoop to kiss her cheek.

Moving on to Cappy he gives me a hug and as I step away he looks direct at me, loosely holding my arms and making me linger.

'You take care of you, Jess. Don't overdo it, will you?'

I let out a groan. 'I'm fine. Strong as a horse.'

'I'd rather be as strong as a lion, Mum,' Lola interrupts. 'No one messes with a lion because they have big teeth.'

'You're right. I'll bear that in mind, Lola.'

I look at Cappy quizzically and he laughs. 'Strong as a horse and with the roar of a lion. Now, let's get on the road Lola, or we'll be late. I don't want to get into trouble with your new teacher.'

'It's okay, Cappy. I'll tell him that I don't get to see you very often and he'll understand.'

Aww.

'You remind me of your mum when she was young, Lola. Full of sunshine, brimming with energy and a heart full of love. A little ball of happiness.'

I wave them off, not really wanting either of them to go. It's like the bottom has suddenly fallen out of my world and I have absolutely no idea why I'm feeling like this.

It's been five days since I last saw Riley and the moment our eyes meet he crosses the space between us in three long strides, to hold me in his arms.

'I so need this,' he mutters softly, as I sink into him. 'I heard Lola laughing and Cappy's car pull away a few minutes ago. You look upset, what's wrong?'

'I'm fine. How are you doing this morning?'

He pulls away but his gaze doesn't falter. 'I'm okay, but something's not right, I can see that in your eyes.'

'It's nothing.'

'Don't patronise me, Jess. If you don't want to talk about it I understand, but don't pretend something isn't up. I know better than that.'

I walk over to the bathroom window of Smithy's Cottage, looking down on to the courtyard.

'It's sad to wave goodbye to family and friends, not knowing exactly when I'll see them again. Cappy is getting older and… oh, I don't know. It just seemed to hit me out of nowhere, yesterday. We're so far away from everyone, Lola and me. Did I do the right thing coming here?'

'Hey,' Riley appears at my side, grabbing my hand and holding it in his. His skin is warm, his grasp firm and reassuring. 'This isn't like you.'

'There are so many thoughts going around and around inside my head, Riley, that it scares me.'

'Then you need to switch off that brain of yours. You're on overload and what you need is to take a few deep breaths. Come on, I'm going to make you a strong cup of tea.'

Riley takes the seat next to me at the kitchen table in The Farmhouse, after placing a small tray in front of us.

'I'm guessing you didn't eat breakfast, am I right?'

I nod my head.

'Then here, I found some biscuits in the cupboard. You've never offered me, or Steve come to that, a gingerbread man. You keep them for special visitors, I suppose.' It's a wise crack, an attempt to lift my mood.

I turn to look at him, making a concerted effort to raise a smile. 'They're from the bakery in Polreweek. As of Wednesday you'll be able to call into The Farmhouse Bakery and buy them over the counter yourself.'

'Well, let's see how good they are.' I watch as he takes a huge bite, then rolls his eyes. 'Even better than fairings. I'm a sucker for ginger. So come on, the sugar will give you a boost. You're letting it all get to you, Jess. It happens to everyone, even you, boss lady.'

'Don't,' I bat my eyelashes at him. 'You know I don't like you calling me that. I'm not... bossy, am I? I mean... I do listen to what people have to say.'

'No,' he replies, emphatically. 'It's a form of endearment. I'm just being friendly, playful. Life's too short to go around wearing a long face like you're doing right now.'

'Sorry. And you're right, these are good.' I nibble on the biscuit, wondering why I'm feeling so wretched this morning.

In fact, sugar does help and so does the tea, as Riley changes the subject and asks what Lola thought of the domes at the Eden Project.

'She was full of it when they arrived back. She asked whether they make small ones as, according to Lola, it would make the most adorable little summer house for the garden. To which I said I'm sure that they don't.' Riley thinks that's amusing and by the time we've finished our tea I'm feeling less anxious.

'How did your trip go?'

Riley frowns, taking a minute to gather his thoughts. 'You know how Lola asks questions all the time? Well, Ollie is about the same age and Fiona said that since the dash up to the hospital, he's been asking her questions about me.'

'Oh, I see.'

'Ollie has always been under the impression that it's my work that has kept me away. He's too young to remember the early days when I did go to visit him on a regular basis. Fiona laid down the rules; she had to be there at all times, and I understood her concerns given the circumstances of my leaving.'

'But that was a falling-out with your partner and best friend that just got out of hand,' I point out.

'That's one way of looking at it, but Fiona saw it as a red flag. She was right, I did have anger issues. I blamed Will for his obsession with success – growing the business and making it big. Nothing was ever enough for him, but the blame lay with me. I was the one who blindly went along with his plans. Fiona was easily satisfied, she didn't want a better car, a better house... she just wanted us to spend more time together as a family and I let them both down.'

'It's strange to hear you say that, as it's not how I see you at all.'

Riley sighs, raising his eyebrows. 'I thought I was building a better and more secure future for my family. Will said that in a couple of years we'd be able to expand the area we covered. The goal was to have a fleet of vehicles and enough men for us to sit back and take it a little easier.'

'And did he achieve what he set out to do?'

'Yes, by all accounts, but it cost him his marriage.'

I watch as Riley chases a few stray crumbs around the table with the tip of his finger, scooping them up and placing them on the tray.

'My monthly visits were fun at first. Ollie was four years old and we would sit at the kitchen table and play games or go out into the garden and kick a football about.' Riley smiles to himself as the memories come flooding back.

I can tell from the pained expression on his face how hard this is for him to acknowledge, and I continue to sit watching him, hoping he can sense the empathy I'm feeling.

'This visit was different. All three of us sat together and we answered his questions in as honest a way as we could. It was tough, I can tell you. What do you say when your son asks why you never turn up at his birthday parties, you only send presents?'

As a parent my heart constricts in my chest for his pain. 'It's hard to explain how difficult things become when a couple go their separate ways. How can a child possibly understand the emotional turmoil that, as parents, often clouds our judgement?'

'I told Ollie that adults don't always get it right and I was sorry for letting him down. I said that I wanted to be there for him, but only if he wanted to talk to me. I just didn't know how to make that work.'

No wonder Riley went straight home afterwards. It sounds like this is some sort of turning point for them and my heart begins to pound in my chest.

'Then Fiona asked Ollie what we could do to make things better. It's funny, but the minute she said that I wondered why I hadn't asked him that before...' Riley's words tail off, his forehead pinched.

The silence is agonising.

'Ollie said that when his friends asked him about me, he had no idea exactly where I lived, or what my job was. He vaguely remembered me talking about Cornwall, the sea and the moor. Oh, and living in a house with no heating. Fiona reached out and ruffled his hair, laughing, and said that maybe it was time for a visit.'

My throat goes dry. 'A... a visit?'

'Yes. When he's ready, Fiona said Ollie can come and spend the weekend with me at the cottage.'

'That's wonderful news, Riley!' For one moment there I thought he was going to say that Fiona was coming too. Then a cold feeling begins to settle in the pit of my stomach. Is it possible she still has feelings for Riley? I wonder. Would Riley welcome a chance to start over again if it was offered to him? If that were the case, I tell myself, he wouldn't be here.

His face brightens. 'It is, but what if I can't keep him occupied? What if he gets bored?'

No, his concern is only for his son – as a couple they've moved on. As relief floods through me, I reach out to touch Riley's hand. 'Hey, you got this. You chatter away quite happily to Lola, don't you? It's going to be a huge adventure for Ollie, and he'll have a chance to finally get a glimpse of your life. Don't overthink this visit, just let it come naturally. If you want some company, Lola and I are here so you have options.'

'You're right,' he replies, sounding positive. 'Ollie is a quiet boy but he's inquisitive. I'm just not used to answering lots of questions. I hope I can keep up with him!'

'He can't ask any more than Lola does,' I grin at him.

The look we exchange is one of empathy; I can see how nervous Riley is but he's desperate to be a part of Ollie's life going forward. And I think he's earnt that, no matter what mistakes he made in the past. All credit to Fiona that she believes it too.

What I find shocking is my reaction as panic started to set in. What if instead of Ollie coming to stay, Riley had announced that he was moving back to York? I would have been happy for him if that were the case, but for a brief moment I was thrown into a state of confusion. I didn't know quite how to react because my emotions were in freefall.

I have no idea what Riley's longer-term plans are... would it be wrong of me to ask? I ponder. But for now, having him in my life is a great comfort and it's only right that he can rely upon me for the exact same thing. Friends share good news and that's precisely what this is.

The Farmhouse Bakery Is Open for Business

'Well, are you pleased?' Riley asks, his eyes searching mine in earnest.

I glance across as the queue of people snaking its way across the cobbled courtyard and out through the gates.

'It's a better turnout than we'd expected, especially given that it's a Wednesday,' I reply, feeling a little overwhelmed by the response.

He stifles a laugh. 'What's that wonderful old saying? Be careful what you wish for,' he labours. 'Still, I'd say a bakery was definitely the right way to go.'

People are walking out of the shop smiling, and a few of the locals wave when they spot us. I know it's day one and everyone from far and wide has come to check out the new shop and the free samples, but it's still a bit of a shock to the system.

Riley and I head back to Smithy's Cottage and once we're inside I feel a lot calmer.

'I thought you'd be pleased,' he says, encouragingly. 'You really are better off attracting tenants than running everything yourself, Jess. You do know that? If only a handful of people had turned up you'd have been disappointed, admit it.'

I wave my hand in the air dismissively. 'Okay. Point taken. I know it's a bit of a novelty and things will calm down, but it feels strange.'

Riley shakes his head, as he stares back at me. 'Wait until we convert the small barn. You're creating a little community here, Jess. It's going to change the landscape, but what an achievement that is. Renweneth Farm could so easily have been snapped up by someone with deep pockets who wanted a country retreat. You're opening this up to the people who have the closest ties to the farm. Where do you think I'll be buying my bread in future?'

Riley means well and it's not that I disagree with him, but baby steps suddenly turn into massive changes and each one is a huge adjustment.

'Is there any news with regard to the delivery of the replacement tiles?' I enquire, changing the subject.

'No. Oh, they're very apologetic but I still kick myself for not opening them all up to check they were the right colour. The batch numbers were the same on the outside and I think someone simply put the wrong tiles in some of the boxes.'

'Well, next time I'll think twice before ordering handmade Italian tiles, even if they are gorgeous and competitively priced. Especially if there's a chance it will hold things up. But in hindsight, it's probably doing me a favour. With family and friends coming here for Christmas I'm going to struggle for space and as soon as the cottage is finished, Vyvyan will want to put it on the website.'

'I have two spare bedrooms at my place if you get stuck.'

'Oh, Riley, that's very kind of you to offer, but I was just thinking aloud. I'm going to suggest my parents bring their campervan and stay onsite. Do you have plans for Christmas?' It's something I've been dying to ask him but didn't quite know how to broach the subject.

He looks at me, as if it's a silly question. 'No.'

'You're in touch with your brother though, aren't you?'

'Yes. Tom would help anyone out who was in need, but we rarely get together in person these days. As for the rest of them, apparently I showed my true colours. Their version of events is that I turned my back on them.'

I'm appalled. 'Your friends came to visit you to lend a hand in the early days, but your family didn't?'

It's obvious from the expression on his face that it's still a sore subject.

'Sorry, I was just... I mean, you're very welcome to join us here. I'm going all out to make it a memorable Christmas. Lots of long walks, good food and hours spent playing silly board games. Now you can't say no to that, can you?'

He breaks out into an expansive smile as our eyes meet. 'I guess I can't. It beats sitting in front of the log fire toasting marshmallows for one.'

Riley is purposely trying to make me laugh and he succeeds. 'Well, I guess I'll be putting you in charge of organising a brazier for a couple of evening sessions on the patio. Nothing says Christmas more than a mug of hot chocolate and a singed, half-melted blob of sugar on a stick!'

'I'm a dab hand at roasting chestnuts, too,' he points out. 'And I play the guitar.'

I do a double take. 'You really are a man who is full of surprises.'

Riley comes close, catching my hand in his as we stare at each other intensely.

'Won't it be a little awkward if you include me?'

Like it or not, Riley has wormed his way into my affections and I'd be devasted if he suddenly told me that he still had feelings for Fiona. What if, in the process of protecting myself from getting hurt, I end up losing him? It's time to listen to what my heart is telling me. 'I want you here, Riley... I mean if you're comfortable with that.'

As his lips touch mine I can feel the longing between us.

'I'll be on my best behaviour,' he whispers, a little breathlessly into my ear, as he pulls away.

'Me too. It won't be easy, but it's a good start.'

I get a momentary flashback of watching Riley late one night, thinking he was asleep. I half-whispered to myself, 'What would make you truly happy?' I was taken aback when he partly opened his right eye and murmured, 'Feeling that I belong somewhere, like I do when I'm here with you, so that Ollie doesn't think of me as a drifter.'

Seconds later, he was gently snoring away and my heart leapt, because his reply had been instant. He was way too sleepy to even engage his brain. I'm sure if I mentioned it now he wouldn't even remember that moment, or might even think he dreamt it. I've come to believe that Riley does belong here, by my side, but there's so much at stake that we can only move forward one step at a time.

'Jess!' The door to The Farmhouse Bakery flies open and Alice Rowse beckons to me. Glancing at my watch, I see that it's almost three o'clock and she'll be shutting the doors shortly.

'How was day one? I was glad to see that the flyers worked.'

Instead of a huge smile, what I get is a frown. 'You'd best come inside. There's been a bit of a development.'

As if someone has flicked a switch, my light-hearted mood changes in an instant as I follow her inside.

'Come on upstairs. Would you like a coffee, Jess?'

The delicious smell of yeasty bread hits my nose first, then a waft of cinnamon, quickly followed by the bitter aroma of freshly roasted beans as Alice leads me past the coffee machine.

'No, I'm good thanks.'

'Let's head up to the office.'

I smile at her assistant who is busy wiping down the empty shelves. 'Did you sell out?'

'We ran out of bread and rolls about an hour ago,' Alice confirms, sounding pleased, as I follow her upstairs. 'There are a few cakes left and I'll box some up for you. I know that Lola loves the gingerbread men. I kept a few back for her.'

'Ah, thank you.'

'Right, take a seat.'

As she walks around the desk, I can tell this isn't going to be good news and I'm puzzled.

'Like they say, timing is everything but in this case it's... unfortunate.'

'What is?'

'Oh, Jess, there's no point beating about the bush. You know how thrilled we were when you approached us about this venture. Today has been crazy and it bodes well for the future. The thing is that yesterday afternoon our landlord broke the news that the tenants in the shop next door to us in Polreweek are moving out next month. It's a one-off chance to double our floor space in a prime location.'

I find myself biting my lip. 'I see, and that's too good an opportunity to walk away from if you can get the right deal.'

'It puts us in a quandary, that's for sure,' she admits, regretfully.

'When it comes to business, Alice, you must do what's best for you. I understand that. If it were the other way around, you'd say the same thing to me.'

I can tell how conflicted she is; Alice and her husband are well respected, and their shop is considered to be the number one bakery in the area when it comes to artisan breads and traditional Cornish confectionery.

'I know, but that doesn't make it any easier,' she concedes. 'And we've had such a good day. So many smiling faces and well-wishers. The thought of being a part of what you're doing here... well, it's hard to—'

'You can't walk away from an offer like that and I wouldn't expect you to.'

'Look, nothing has been decided yet, Jess. I just wanted to level with you.'

'And I'm glad you did. If you decide to expand the shop, would you still be able to keep this place open for the trial period?'

'Oh, there's no question about that at all.' She looks at me in earnest. 'We stand by our word, but I know we were all hopeful that Jory and I would be in a position to sign a lease. Now there's a question mark over that decision as financially it would be too much of a stretch to consider both options.'

I give her a reassuring smile. 'Well, today really created a buzz here at the farm and I'm grateful for the hard work you, Jory, and your staff have put in to make it happen.'

'The two of us are going to sit down tonight and work out on paper whether expanding the shop is a viable option. A part of us really wants to be involved here, Jess, and it's a tough decision to make. We believe, as many do, that what you're doing here will create even more opportunities for the local community as a whole. Not only are you attracting an ever-increasing number of visitors to the area, your future plans to create affordable retail space for cottage industries will be a lifeline for some who are struggling to stay afloat.'

'But it always comes down to economics, Alice. You'll get a lot more footfall in town than you will out here.'

She shrugs her shoulders. 'Why did this have to happen now?' She sighs.

'Better now than a couple of months down the line.'

'Well, if that's the way we decide to go I'll make sure you have all the facts and figures from this trial run. Tomorrow it should be business as normal and it'll be interesting to see how many customers we get. I'll keep you updated – on all fronts.' Alice pulls a face as we stand. She walks around the desk to give me a hug.

'Let's not be down about this, we should be celebrating a successful launch. It will certainly allow me to decide what to do with the bakery if it turns out that taking it on isn't the right decision for you and Jory.'

'It's not a foregone conclusion and I wouldn't want you to think that, but thanks for being so understanding. We're both reeling, Jess, truly we are and it's a headache we could cheerfully do without.'

*

Lying in bed, staring up at the ceiling, I find myself wondering why what looked like a great idea should be scuppered before it's even had time to get off the ground. Then I find myself worrying about tomorrow. What if only a handful of customers turn up at The Farmhouse Bakery? And the day after that, and the day after that.

Instead of feeling down about it, I realise there's a reason Alice and Jory opted for a trial run first. No one knows for sure what level of business will be generated. If they decide for whatever reason not to go ahead, I'll be free to rethink the strategy. If it ends up that I could earn more converting the bakery into a rental cottage, this could actually turn out to be doing me a favour. They might even consider buying the equipment from me. Cappy will probably know what hoops we'd have to jump through with planning, but I can't for one minute see why it would be a problem. It might just mean the place is empty for a while until it's sorted.

Alice and I agreed that we'd keep it just between us for now and I see that as a good thing. When their time is up if they do decide to extend the shop in Polreweek, no one will be surprised as it makes total sense. It's funny, but when something happens that threatens to throw you off track, there's often a silver lining to be found somewhere, if you look for it. My gut reaction this afternoon was that it put my head in a spin. All that money spent on the renovation and in return all I'm guaranteed is two months' rental income. Now I'm thinking that I'll end up with some valuable financial information. If the bakery can't make a reasonable profit, then what's the point of converting the small barn?

With Vyvyan throwing herself into her newly expanded role as marketing manager, if Riley's idea of holding a weekly market turns out to be a draw, it could change everything.

As my eyes grow heavy, I murmur to myself, 'An obstacle is just an opportunity for change. Flexibility is the key. You got this, Jess.'

I start chuckling as I snuggle under the covers, wantonly wishing Riley was lying next to me. He's become an integral part of my life without me really noticing it. I value his opinion and I probably share more things with him than I do with Ivy, these days. Stifling a yawn, the last thing I picture is his face when I told him I don't care if it's awkward that he joins us for Christmas. For me, and I think for Lola too, it wouldn't be quite the same without him.

23

Is It True That Trouble Often Comes in Threes?

'Morning, Dad. It's early for you to call. Is everything okay?'

'Hi, Jess. I'm just giving you a heads up. When Cappy got back on Monday he found out that his best friend, Dave, had a heart attack the previous evening. It looked like he was going to be okay, but sadly he passed away quite suddenly in the early hours of Tuesday morning.'

'Oh, Dad, I'm so sorry to hear that. How's Cappy coping with the news?'

'Not well, I'm afraid. Your mum slept over at his house last night. They spent a harrowing afternoon yesterday with Dave's wife… I mean widow. She went to pieces and all three of them were in tears.'

My heart sinks in my chest. Death is so final and just like that another person disappears out of your life. Dave was Cappy's oldest friend and I know he'll be devastated.

'Is there anything I can do?'

'Not really. I've been passing messages around as no one wants to bother the family, but Dave knew a lot of people. Mum said she'll call you later, she's just frazzled at the moment. The fact that she stayed over last night isn't a good sign, but she couldn't talk so I'm not sure exactly what's going on. She suggested I leave her to it and she's due back later this afternoon.'

'All right. I'll wait for her to ring. Oh, it's such a shock when it happens out of the blue like that. Dave was a kind man, always smiling and a good listener.'

'That was Dave to a T, Jess,' Dad reflects, soberly. 'How are things at the farm?'

'Good. Don't worry about us, just focus on Mum and Cappy.'

'I will. We'll speak soon. Love you.'

'Love you, too.'

As we disconnect, an involuntary shiver travels down my spine. No matter what goes wrong, this sort of news puts everything else firmly into perspective.

A sharp rap on the door knocker turns out to be Keith. It's only just after eight o'clock and I plaster on a smile.

'Hi Jess. I'm sorry to bother you this early, but can you spare me five minutes out in the general car park?'

Lola appears at my side, leaning around me to glance at Keith, who gives her a beaming smile.

'Of course. Give me a couple of minutes to sort Lola out and I'll join you.'

'Thanks.'

Lola doesn't need any encouragement to pull on her jacket as I walk her over to Smithy's Cottage where Riley is lying on his back, plumbing in the new bath.

'Morning, Riley. Sorry I'm late with your coffee, normal service will be resumed shortly,' I grin at him. 'Would you mind talking to Lola while I have a quick word with Keith?'

He stops what he's doing to sit up. 'Of course not. Hi Lola. You'll never guess what I found in the small barn.' Her eyes light up as I turn and begin walking away.

'A bird's nest!' he declares.

Lola squeals excitedly. I find myself thinking how wonderful it will be when Riley can chat just as easily to Ollie.

I'm still smiling to myself as I round the corner and spot

Keith, who appears to be pacing out the width of the car park. He hurries over to me.

'Were you aware there was a bit of a ruckus here yesterday?'

I look at him in surprise. 'On the campsite?'

'No. With the parking arrangements.'

I hold my hand up to my forehead. 'Oh gosh... I'm terribly sorry, Keith. Was it total bedlam?'

'Not really, but there were two incidents. Someone walked off and left their car blockin' the campsite entrance. I had to find the owner and get him to move it as we had a campervan parked up on the grass verge out on the road. At the busiest point, mid-mornin', one idiot blocked the turnin' point at the far end and people had to reverse out. I hung around for a bit to direct the traffic as it was a hazard.'

I look at him aghast. 'I'm so sorry to have left you to handle that. It was a stupid oversight on my part.'

'You were busy, and it was nothin' for me to keep a general eye on things. Besides, it was a big day with the launch and I'm sure things will calm down from here on in. But I thought I should raise the subject with you, as Vyvyan hasn't given any thought at all to market days once they start.'

Me neither. 'It's a large enough space and I am a little surprised things went awry.'

Keith frowns. 'The main problem is that people don't always park sensibly. You'll need someone on duty to direct them and that should do the trick.'

'Thank you so much for sorting out the problems yesterday, Keith, and for raising it with me. I can assure you it'll go straight to the top of my priority list.'

I'm about to turn on my heels when Keith begins speaking again. 'I think most of the campers paid a visit to the new shop, Jess. Things like that are goin' to make a real difference. It's a pity Cappy missed it by a couple of days, but he'll be chuffed to bits to see it on his next visit.'

'Thanks, Keith, that's nice to know and I'm um... hoping to get Cappy down here asap, actually.'

'Great! Perhaps this time around I can take him for that pint.'

'It would be wonderful if you could. It would mean a lot to him, Keith.'

'I'll make it happen then. You'd best be thinkin' about the school run.' He glances at his watch, and I give him a grateful smile before I dash back to the courtyard.

'Oh, Jess. What an awful couple of days.' The sound of Mum's voice sets me on edge. Mum has always been the calm one in trying times and to hear her sounding so dejected is scary.

'It was like losing your grandma all over again. It's hit Cappy hard, Jess. Very hard.'

Do I tell Mum what I'm thinking, or is this the wrong moment to bring it up? I wonder.

'He reeled off three names, including Dave's wife, and remarked that he was the oldest one left now. He said they were a group of five couples originally and now it's a waiting game.' Mum dissolves into floods of tears. It must have been harrowing for her to hear Cappy talking like that. Her own parents died within eighteen months of each other, and my dad's parents always treated her like a daughter from day one. Not least because Dad isn't good with emotional stuff, and she was often their go-between.

'It was bound to knock him, Mum. Cappy mentioned Dave at the weekend. Something did cross my mind as the two of us were talking and I was waiting for the right moment to mention it to you.'

She sniffs, takes a deep breath and I wait while she blows her nose. 'That's better. Shedding a few tears always helps, doesn't it? Right, talk to me, Jess.'

There's no easy way to say this, but I'd hate myself if I didn't bring it up.

'This is just my intuition kicking in here… it's not that Cappy has said anything specific, but I get this feeling he regrets leaving Cornwall. And the farm.'

The sound of a sharp intake of breath travels down the line. 'Someone had to say it because you're right. He hates that boxy little house he bought. There's no character to it and there's nothing of your grandma there, aside from a few ornaments. But you know what I mean. I said to your dad at the time that I thought it was a big mistake. I wanted Cappy to come and stay with us for a while until he felt ready to return to Cornwall. He dismissed it out of hand, saying he didn't want to put us out. Your dad is just the same. If there's something they don't want to deal with, they walk away. It's never that simple, is it?'

It's a relief to hear Mum mirroring my own thoughts. 'What are we going to do about it?'

She sighs. 'Cappy's a stubborn old soul with a heart of gold, Jess. He believes all that stiff upper lip nonsense, you know, soldiering on regardless, but I can see the changes in him. It's a waste when there's plenty of life left in the man, he's just lost his focus, his reason for being.' Mum begins sniffling again.

'Then I have an idea, which I'd like to run past you. You're going to need to drop a few hints, though. There's a lot going on here and in all honesty I could do with his help.'

When Erica calls to suggest she picks Lola up from school so that the girls can have tea together, she can't imagine how grateful I am. I've spent most of the day painting in Smithy's Cottage, while Riley has been up to his eyes in plumbing. I know enough by now not to disturb him unless he shouts. He's already had one leak that's been a nightmare to fix, and I can now do the sprint to the stopcock in record time.

In reality, I'm on edge as I'm expecting a call from Cappy this evening if Mum manages to impress the urgency upon him. I'm going to have to choose my words very carefully indeed and I've been rehearsing what I'm going to say in my head.

However, the thought of a few hours of downtime is appealing and at four o'clock I saunter into the shower room.

'What's up? You haven't finished, have you?' Riley questions me.

'No, I'm only halfway through painting the walls in the second bedroom but I am finishing for the day. You should, too. I thought I'd cook us something nice to eat.'

'It's a bit early, isn't it?' He checks his watch, glancing across at me and wondering what's going on.

'No. We skipped lunch. A generous slice of Hevva cake from The Farmhouse Bakery and an espresso doesn't count as a meal,' I inform him. 'Besides, Lola is having tea with Daisy, and Erica isn't dropping her back until seven this evening as they're going to watch a film.'

'Ah, right. In which case, I guess I'd better do as I'm told.'

'There are um… a couple of things I need to talk to you about.'

'I guessed there was something going on. You've been ominously quiet. Give me half an hour and I'll join you.'

'Fine. Just don't keep me waiting any longer than that,' I say, waggling my finger at him. 'I might be in the shower, so I'll leave a key under the pot by the front door.'

Riley gives me a wicked smile as I turn to go and wash out my paintbrushes.

'Half an hour,' I repeat, as I descend the stairs. 'I'll be waiting.'

Lying in bed together, it feels like forever since I had Riley's arms wrapped around me. He can tell I have a lot going on and I'm not sure where to start. When I do, eventually, talk about the bakery he's a little surprised.

'Doesn't that mess up your plans? I mean, the costs of the work you're having done are mounting up and I feel bad about the delays with Smithy's Cottage.'

Riley reaches out to sweep some stray hairs from my cheek and I love it when he does something like that. It's the small things I notice because it means he's observant. Little things matter, the big things usually take care of themselves one way or another.

'Come on, Jess. I know you well enough by now to see you're holding something back from me.'

'This is serious this time,' I reply, my smile fading, and instantly I have Riley's full attention. 'It's not about money... it's way more important than that.'

When I explain my deepest fear that Cappy feels his life is on a downhill slide and that he thinks he's the next in line to follow Dave, Riley is shocked.

'He's what... seventy something?'

'Seventy-two,' I correct him. 'But it's not about age, it's about looking around and everyone you once classed as a dear friend is now gone.'

'But Cappy is a fit and active man, Jess. And his mind is razor sharp.'

'It's about what you believe in here,' I tap the side of my head. 'He's lost his sense of purpose. He's miserable living in Gloucestershire. Everything that inspired him is here at the farm. And if I don't rescue him from himself, I can't even bring myself to think about what might happen. I owe him everything. This is where he belongs.'

'Is that truly how you feel?'

'Yes, because if Cappy dies of a broken heart, then it will take the joy out of what we're trying to accomplish here. It's not just for me and Lola, I want everyone I love to be a part of this.'

Riley looks puzzled. 'You said we're...'

This is the tough part, because I have no idea whether Riley can sense the changes in me, and what if I'm reading him all wrong?

'Who else is making this happen, if not you and me?'

He stops for a moment to consider my words. 'Yes, but I'm only—'

'There's no *only* when it comes to you, Riley. It's important to me that I set Lola a good example and that's not to give up on anything. Whether that's the risk of renovating a dilapidated old manor house, or the chance of finding love a second time around. You don't know what you can achieve until you try. In this case... *we* try, because I want us to build this dream together. I know things are difficult for both of us right now, but you care about other people even when they haven't always treated you well; that tells me exactly what sort of man you are.'

'I won't let you down, Jess – this means everything to me.'

'I know. And I owe Cappy because he saved me from myself. And from a marriage that I clung on to long after it was nothing more than a shell, by leading me here to the farm. It's time for him to come home because this is where his heart is and there's room for everyone.'

Riley pushes himself up on to his elbow, looking down at me. 'So, what's the plan?'

'Cappy needs to be needed and I have a parking issue that I'm hoping Mum will convince him I'm desperate for someone to sort out for me. With the first market day scheduled for next Tuesday, fingers crossed it will motivate him to come for the weekend.'

Riley frowns. 'I didn't know there was an issue. Is it anything I can help with?'

'Um... no. That's my point. You're my next line of attack.'

His face drops. 'Me?'

'Don't worry, with a little coaching you'll be word-perfect.'

Riley closes his eyes for a brief second, before opening them again and staring at me, hesitantly. 'Okay... are you going to enlighten me as to what my role is in this?'

'Your task is to convince Cappy that you and I are so snowed under that his presence is required onsite to tackle what is, in effect, quite a serious problem.'

Riley sinks back down on to his pillow. 'Is that all I have to do?'

'Yes. He'll only believe you if he thinks you're here to stay so you have my best interests at heart.'

Riley's expression freezes. 'Am I? Here to stay, that is?'

I look at him askance. 'I know that didn't sound like a question, but I guess it was.'

'No pressure, then. Not only am I sleeping with the boss, but I'm now a permanent part of her longer-term plan?'

'It's decision time, Riley.'

'I sort of figured that out when you invited me along at Christmas and I will hold my hands up and say I've been stressing over it. The thing is, I don't have the best track record when it comes to relationships, Jess.'

'Really? You've been my rock since the moment you turned up on that inhospitable Sunday morning, when my family and friends were flagging. Please don't let the past determine your future, Riley. Lola loves spending time with you. I've discouraged it because the last thing she needs is someone new flitting into and out of her life. But I'd be proud to tell everyone we're a couple because I think you and I have what it takes to make a life together. I just don't know how you feel about that.'

The seconds tick by and it's agonising.

'Misty needs that cat flap installed tomorrow because she's a hunter and she's desperate to rid the small barn of the mice. If we can agree on that, everything else is a resounding yes. It was obvious to me that Cappy belongs here and always will. Hopefully, I do, too.'

I elbow Riley in the ribs, and he's quick to complain. 'What? I'm just speaking the truth and I don't think my demands are excessive.'

'Fine. My one caveat is that you also sort a collar and a bell for Misty, because I'm not dealing with anything she brings back from the barn.'

Riley plants a purposeful kiss on my cheek. 'You drive a hard bargain, Jess, but you know it's the right thing to do. As for

Cappy, well, the farm isn't quite the same without him here, is it?'

My eyes start to tear up, but my smile tells him everything he needs to know. 'There's one other teeny little thing I should mention. We need to get Smithy's Cottage ready for Cappy. Oh, I know it won't be totally finished but it's a part of my master plan.'

Riley groans. 'No problem.' Under his breath he murmurs something about furniture to be assembled, the main bathroom toilet to be connected and the fact that I still haven't finished painting the second bedroom.

'Let's see who finishes their jobs first, then, shall we? And I'm thinking that if you go and pick up some tiles from the builders' merchants, between us we can get the shower tiled by the end of tomorrow. I'm assuming Cappy won't get here until lunchtime on Saturday, so it's do-able.'

'Oh... I do like a challenge. I guess that's a part of the attraction between us, Jess. Neither of us are prepared to take *no* for an answer. And you're sure your mum will be able to talk him into coming?'

'Please don't underestimate Mum when she's on a mission. He'll call me tonight and of that I have no doubt at all. Come on. We have an hour to make ourselves presentable and have dinner before Lola gets home.'

'I don't know what I've done to deserve you, Jess, but it feels right.' The sincerity in Riley's tone makes my heart skip a beat.

'Well, I was thinking the exact same thing about you. It's not that I can't do this without you, Riley, it's that I don't want to do it without you by my side.'

We roll in to face each other and he reaches out to brush his fingers down my cheek.

'I want to be there for you, and for Lola, too. When I'm here I feel as if I'm a part of something and it hasn't been that way for a long time. You made it way too easy for me to fall in love with you, Jess, and I just can't help myself.'

We kiss each other hungrily and when I reluctantly pull away I whisper, 'And I love you too, Riley.'

He breaks out into an enormous grin. 'There, you said it at last!'

'It feels good to finally say it, doesn't it? You've already made a huge impact on our lives, Riley. And by the time we reach Christmas no one will bat an eyelid at the fact that you've become a part of the...'

'Fixtures and fittings?' he offers, laughingly.

'Hmm... that's one way of putting it but I was going to say *family*. Hopefully, at some point I hope you'll feel comfortable enough to bring Ollie here for a visit. If we take things slowly, anything is possible isn't it?'

The look in his eyes as they sweep over my face is full of hope and anticipation. 'I believe you're right, Jess, and that's one of the many things I love about you – you're fearless.'

Am I? Some might call me a hopeless dreamer or even foolhardy, but when the man who has so easily succeeded in capturing my heart says something like that I'm not going to argue with him.

24

The Clock Is Ticking

'Jess, are you sure you're doing the right thing? Once you share something it's out there and it can have a domino effect. Isn't it better to hold a few things back?' Riley talks as he works, pressing the newly cut, lightly veined white marble tile firmly against the wall.

'It's all or nothing, Riley. For me, that is. What about you?'

He stands back to survey his handiwork and I sidle up alongside him.

'You've got a heck of a lot more to lose than me.'

I lean into him, throwing my arm around his waist. 'The tiles are perfect and so are you. I've never been surer of anything in my life. Whether that's admitting I love spending time with you, or in pressing ahead with the plans for this place.'

'But how will you hide it from Lola? What if she overhears a snippet of conversation?'

'It's not like you're moving in today and Lola will be overwhelmed by it all, is it? I hate waving you off at the end of our working day when the three of us could so easily be sitting around the table in The Farmhouse eating and chatting. Trust me, it's the perfect way to ease you into our family.'

'Children are one thing, adults another. Cappy knows I came here with nothing; he just doesn't know why. And what will your parents think? You employ me to do some work and suddenly you're telling them I'm a part of your life. If I were in their shoes I'd be concerned about someone who is little more than a stranger getting his feet under the table.'

My heart constricts at the sense of conflict emanating from him. 'Stop! Yesterday you said you loved me. You're not getting cold feet already, are you?'

Riley turns to face me, placing his hands gingerly upon my shoulders as his fingertips have little blobs of tile adhesive on them. 'I did, didn't I?' He gives me a hesitant smile. 'It slipped out and I didn't mean for that to happen. I wasn't expecting such a positive response from you – I'm not complaining,' he emphasises, a twinkle in his eyes. 'But I suppose I am a little anxious.'

'I'm glad we were honest with each other, because up until that point I was the one doing all the talking. You don't say much. I got it wrong once and I don't want to get it wrong again.'

'You aren't wrong. I'm happy whenever I'm around you, even when we're not talking. Just working side by side. But Cappy is arriving tomorrow so your mission will be accomplished and you don't need to muddy it with talk about... us.'

I look at him aghast. 'You think I might change my mind?'

A look of panic fills his eyes. He shakes his head emphatically, grasping me a little tighter. 'No. You've been up front with me from the very start and, to be honest, I'd have been concerned if it hadn't been that way. You're a sensitive person, Jess. A clever, hard-working woman who does everything for the right reasons. I just hate the thought of disappointing you.'

'Is this about Fiona?' I ask, warily, holding his gaze.

'Why would you even think that?'

'You drop everything for her, and I get it. There was a point not that long ago when I would have welcomed Ben back into my life. Now I see that would have been the second biggest mistake I've ever made.'

'What was the first one?'

'Holding on to a marriage that had no spark left in it. But I have Lola and I wouldn't change a thing. Going forward I want that spark, the shared passion... the sort that makes my heart race. And it does, every time you're here,' I mumble into his shoulder.

We sink into each other, and words are no longer necessary.

'Are we going to stand here chatting, or press on to make Smithy's Cottage as comfortable as possible for Cappy's visit?' Riley questions.

'It's a tall order we've set ourselves, isn't it?'

'That depends. What stage are you at?' he asks, standing back and looking at me questioningly.

'There's one windowsill waiting for a final coat and then the painting is all finished.'

'Good. If you want to tackle putting up the next row of tiles, I'll measure up and go do some cutting. If we can get these hung by the time you head out to pick up Lola, I'll tidy up and we can start unpacking the furniture. It might be a late one, though. I'll be able to do the grouting first thing tomorrow morning.'

'Well, I suggest that the three of us eat together and I'll give Hendra a call next to see if she's free to come and look after Lola and put her to bed. Give me ten minutes and I'll take over here.'

'On your way through can you crank up the heating and open a few windows?'

'Great idea. You seem to have quite a few of those,' I muse, as he leans forward to kiss me softly on the lips. When Riley reluctantly pulls away there's a twinkle in his eye and we're both thinking the same thing. One kiss is never enough. Knowing someone wants you as much as you want them is a feeling I'd long forgotten. Something Grandma said to me once immediately comes to mind. If something is right you feel it deep down inside of you and now I understand exactly what she meant, because there's no mistaking it when the seemingly impossible happens.

'Don't for one moment think I don't want this as much as you do, Jess,' Riley states adamantly, as if he can read my mind. 'Because that isn't true. I'm simply worried about what people will think, that's all.'

My concerns are a little different. The only person who could possibly come between me and Riley is Fiona, but then maybe I'm being paranoid. Perhaps Naomi feels the same way about me, although she has nothing to fear because that chapter of my life is now firmly closed. However, the difference between me and Riley is that I have custody of my daughter and I intend to do right by her. Riley's future relationship with his son is in the hands of a woman who already feels she was wronged once; will she see this development as yet another blow? That thought worries me, but I shake it off.

'They'll think what a catch, Jess has finally found her Mr Right.'

Lola hasn't moved from her window seat in the bedroom for the last hour and I've been anxiously clock-watching. When, eventually, Cappy pulls into the courtyard there's a shriek from upstairs and what sounds like a herd of elephants descending the stairs.

'He's here Mum, Cappy is here!'

I grab the key for Smithy's Cottage and hurry to follow Lola as she runs on ahead to grab the handle of the car door to swing it open.

'You're a bit late,' she points out. 'I was worried.'

Cappy bursts out laughing. 'Sorry, I was stuck behind a tractor and wasn't able to pass. Safety first, always! It's good to be back but it's much sooner than I expected.' He smiles at me over the top of Lola's head.

'I know, but it's much appreciated, it really is. We'll help carry in your things. I thought you might like to use Smithy's Cottage. It's not quite fully set up so you can give it a test run and let me know whether I've forgotten anything.'

'You've been motoring along then. I thought there was a problem with the tiles?'

'I decided to go with a slightly different one. Come on, let's get you settled in.'

As usual, Cappy comes bearing gifts. He hands three small carrier bags to Lola, and I look at him pointedly. 'Not more presents.'

'It's just a little something. Go on Lola, look inside.'

'Ooh... this is for Misty! Look Mum, a collar with a tiny little bell on it.' She holds up the packet. 'And a diary with a lock and two keys. Thank you so much, Cappy. I can write all my secrets in here.'

'The name of that boy you like in school?' he half-whispers and my eyes widen as I stare at them both, but Lola just laughs.

'This must be for you, Mum.'

I take the bag from her and put my hand inside to pull out a pretty box about the size of my outstretched hand. It's really heavy. I look at Cappy, quizzically as I open it and fold back the tissue paper.

'It's a paper weight really, but I thought you might like to fix it over one of the front doors,' he explains.

It's a silver-plated horseshoe and it's beautiful. 'Oh, that's so lovely. Thank you! But you must stop buying us presents. We just love the fact that you want to spend time here.' I lean in to kiss his cheek and he holds my gaze for a few seconds.

'You know I'm always there for you, Jess. Right, let's get this little lot put away and wander over to take a quick look at the car parking issue. There's quite a bit of coming and going at the bakery, I see.'

He sounds chirpy but I know from what Mum has been telling me, he's been in the doldrums. There's no way you can fake a smile like that, I reflect, as I watch him looking at Lola. She's grabbed his laptop carry case and walks ahead of us across the courtyard.

'You should have seen the queue on launch day,' I tell Cappy as he checks out the shop. 'It's calmed down now but there's still a constant flow of customers.' As we pass the first of the two windows, there are probably five or six people inside waiting to be served.

'It seems we've both had a bit of a week. Sorry to hear about the potential complication,' he says, his voice low. 'When will you know for sure if they're staying?'

'Alice and Jory are negotiating terms at the moment, but they're honouring their commitment to the full two months. I'll probably know one way or the other in a couple of weeks' time. It's not a foregone conclusion as everything comes down to the bottom line in the end, doesn't it?'

'Yep, every time. It's something you could have done without though.'

'But in a way, once we know for sure what level of interest it's going to attract on a daily basis it'll confirm whether I was right not turning it into a general shop. With the first market day in the old hay barn kicking off on Tuesday, if we can resolve the access issues I might consider holding them twice a week. The income from that will give me breathing space if I have to look for a new tenant.'

Cappy nods his head in agreement as we step over the threshold of Smithy's Cottage, where Lola has opened the door and has already disappeared from view.

'I think we should hang the horseshoe up here.' I point to the large wooden beam above the door, as I follow him inside.

'My word! You and Riley have been hard at it. What's it been... five and a half days and it's not far off now.'

The floorboards look amazing as we walk through; keeping them covered until the painting was completed was well worth the effort. The white walls make the space look twice as big as we head through the hallway and into the sitting room.

Two, two-seater sofas sit either side of a repurposed old chest I painstakingly restored.

'My that's a nice bit of wood.'

'You don't recognise it?' I ask and Cappy frowns back at me. 'It used to sit alongside that triple wardrobe in the second bedroom at The Farmhouse.'

'Oh. Grandma covered it with some sort of cloth because it

had paint stains on it. It's certainly come up a treat, given the state it was in.'

'And that cloth is now a table-runner in the kitchen. Come and have a look.'

He chuckles as he follows me through to the rear and I swing open the door. 'The wild strawberries, how could I forget? She loved that tablecloth.'

With pale grey shaker-style kitchen units, white walls and wall units, it's not the largest of kitchens but it accommodates a five-foot square table and four chairs with ease.

'It's a pretty little place now, Jess. You and Riley have done a great job of it.'

'Cappy, where are you? I'm upstairs,' Lola calls out. 'Come and have a look at the bathroom. It's so cool.'

His face creases up into a beaming smile. 'I'm assuming there's a working toilet now, because there wasn't one last Monday.'

'Oh, there is, and early next week Riley will finish off installing the downstairs cloakroom, then it's all done.'

'Do you want me to plug in your laptop, Cappy?' Lola's getting impatient.

'Yes please.'

As I follow him upstairs his gait is light and physically he's fine, but mentally I have no idea what's going on with him. He seems a little jaded, not quite his usual jolly self.

'Oh my! What a perfect guest bedroom-cum-study. I like this.'

'We didn't have time to assemble the second bed, but I thought the desk might come in handy. Come and have a look at the master.'

It's surprising how quickly a building can be turned from a cold shell, to a warm and inviting place. 'Is that a king-size bed?'

'It is, and what do you think of the wardrobe? I picked it up in an antique shop in Polreweek a while ago. I love the curved top and painting it that soft blue seems to make the carving stand out.'

I'm over the moon with the result. I went for a very country style pale blue and white striped duvet cover and matching throw for the bed. The soft blue on the wardrobe is also reflected in the roman blind and I stand back so Cappy can saunter over to stare out the window.

'Look at that for a view. That's a piece of history brought back to life.'

Lola has disappeared again and as I go over to stand next to Cappy, I see that Riley is back from his tip run and the two of them are standing in the courtyard talking.

'Come on, let's check out the main bathroom and then head over to The Farmhouse. The grouting was done first thing this morning but Riley says it'll be dry by this evening. Will this do?'

Cappy turns to look at me. 'I didn't think this old cottage could look as marvellous as this. It's stunning, Jess. I'm going to be very comfortable indeed.'

Sitting around the pine table in The Farmhouse kitchen on a Saturday morning with Riley joining us doesn't feel at all strange.

'I have a confession to make,' I declare.

While Lola plates up some biscuits fresh from the bakery, I carry a tray of drinks over to the table.

'I'd totally forgotten that I'd arranged to pick up Daisy at noon and take her and Lola to the cinema in Polreweek.'

'Lucky girls. That's not a problem. Maybe Riley and I can have a chat and a bit of a wander around.'

'Actually,' Riley joins in. 'Keith and I were wondering whether you were up for a pint and a pub lunch at The Trawlerman's Catch, Cappy? We thought we could kick around a few ideas when it comes to the parking nightmare.'

'Poor Keith was the one who dealt with the fallout from the launch day madness,' I explain. 'He's kept an eye ever since, so between the three of you hopefully you can come up with a quick and easy solution. We won't know for sure what will happen until market day, of course, but it's quite a worry.'

'That suits me just fine!' Cappy replies, sounding delighted. 'I haven't been to The Trawlerman's for nigh on two years now. It'll be good to see a few old faces. You girls go off and have some fun and trust us to come up with something.'

I could literally punch the air, I'm so relieved, and a quick glance in Riley's direction tells me he is, too.

Sorrow at losing an old friend isn't something that goes away just like that, but as Cappy said to me not long ago, life goes on. And here, at the farm, there will always be jobs to do; life is going to get even busier with each passing day. If I can get him to stay until after market day, I'm hoping it will gradually start to sink in that coming back here for good will be like coming home. Cappy's input is invaluable, who knows this place better than him? He needs a little time and space to realise that for himself and my job is to simply to sow the seed.

'How did it go?' Mum blurts out anxiously, as I press the phone to my ear.

'Great. No problems at all so far, but obviously tonight Cappy will no doubt have a little time to himself in Smithy's Cottage. But he's going to have a busy day and with the three of them getting their heads together, by the end of it he'll feel it's been a productive one.'

'Wonderful! What's all that noise going on in the background?'

'Lola, Daisy and I are in a café. I'm queuing for ice cream sundaes for the girls as the film doesn't start for another forty minutes. They're sitting at a table playing snap and giggling away like crazy.'

'Ah, that's lovely to hear. It cheers the heart, doesn't it? On a rather sad note, I've just heard that Dave's funeral is next Friday. I haven't told Cappy yet.'

'I'm rather hoping he won't even think about driving back until Wednesday. You know what he's like. He'll want to see for himself how their grand plan works in practice. I figure that's long enough for him to settle in and I think he'd appreciate a little time on his own.'

'I still think it's the right thing to do, not to mention any of this to your dad just yet. He'll let something slip, you know what he's like.'

'But what if Cappy does decide to return to Cornwall?'

'We'll face that if and when it happens. I hope it does because the alternative doesn't bear thinking about.' I can almost feel a shudder going through her at the thought.

'Stay positive, Mum. Like it, or not, Cappy is the only one who can make that decision. But Lola is my secret weapon, isn't she?'

Mum starts laughing. 'Oh, she certainly is and she's a blessing all right! Enjoy the film.'

'Next please. What can I get you?'

I glance at the menu on the wall. 'I think three of those strawberry sundaes with chocolate flakes would be perfect, thank you!'

This is so much better than a pint and a pie at the pub, I muse to myself. Not that I was a part of the lunchtime plan anyway, as it's more of a team building exercise. The thought of Cappy, Keith and Riley sitting together making merry, laughing and chatting, and then pooling their ideas, warms my heart. It's the first in a series of steps to hopefully steer things in the right direction, but it doesn't really have anything at all to do with parking. That's just a little bonus.

25

Knights in Shining Armour...

'Hi Jess, sorry to disturb you but I have a quick question to ask.'

'Just give me one second, Ivy.' I hold the phone away from my mouth and lean in as the driver in front of me winds down his window.

'Is it okay to park in here for the bakery?'

'Yes, just follow the car in front and my colleague will direct you into the overflow area.'

'What a bonus, we didn't know you held a market day here,' the man's wife leans across and I give her a welcoming smile. 'Is it being held every week?'

'Yes, and we're hoping to add more dates. We'll be running an ad in the local gazette, so keep an eye out for that.'

'Wonderful. Thank you so much.'

I wave out to Cappy, indicating that I'm going to take a short break, and I walk off in search of a quieter spot to talk.

'Sorry about that, Ivy. I'm all yours now.'

'Um... but first tell me what's going on? It sounds chaotic at your end.'

'To say that Renweneth Farm is buzzing is an understatement,' I groan. 'It's our first day running the Tuesday market. We've already had to create a temporary overspill area. Plus, the bakery launched last Wednesday and people are still eager to come and check it out.'

'Eek. I couldn't have phoned at a worse time. I'm so sorry. Text me later when you get a quiet moment.'

'No. I'm fine for a couple of minutes. There are enough of us here. Keith, Len, Vyvyan, Riley, Cappy and me.'

'I thought Cappy went home last week?'

'He did, but he's back again. It's a long story...'

'Okay. I'll be quick. Is renewing a lease a different process entirely? I wondered whether there are any pointers you can give me, like do I wait for the landlord to send me something to look over, or do I approach him first? And what sort of timescales am I looking at?'

'I'm afraid that's something I don't know.'

'Oh, I assumed because of the bakery...'

'We haven't tied up the paperwork yet. The terms will be dependent upon the results of the trial run, I know someone who can answer most things off the top of their head. Vyvyan has years of experience when it comes to both private and commercial lettings, and she still has a lot of contacts in the business. I'll text you her number and tell her to expect a call. She'll be only too glad to help.'

'Oh... you are a gem, Jess. I feel like I'm floundering. The landlord has done quite a bit of work on my behalf and I'm worried because I have no idea whether he'll expect a hefty rise in rent. Mind you, nothing he's done so far is something that wasn't warranted in the first place. He's simply putting right the problems, like the faulty alarm and the lack of useable sockets, but I just want to know where I stand.'

'Don't worry, Vyvyan will sort you out.'

'Thank you! Now get back to work. It sounds like your little empire is growing at quite a rate!' She sounds pleased for me.

'Oh, I'm counting my blessings. The team are really pulling together to make today a success. I'm sure lessons will be learnt, but for now my knights in shining armour are suitably equipped with fluorescent yellow hi vis vests and the visitors seem happy. The stalls look amazing, I'll send a couple of photos. Anyway,

we'll catch up really soon, I promise. Give Adam my love. Bye
for now!'

The last place I expected to find myself this evening was sitting
around a scrubbed oak table at The Trawlerman's Catch. That's
the problem with team working, you can get out-voted.

Our plates are empty and our stomachs full. Nothing beats
good old-fashioned cod and chips with mushy peas. As I look
around the table it's good to have everyone together, not least to
thank them all for what was a wonderful, but stressful day. But
instead of taking the lead this evening, I'm content to take a back
seat as Cappy raises his glass.

'Right. Well, thank you, Jess, that really hit the spot. And
can I just say that I can't believe what a turnout we had at the
farm today. Admittedly, at one point it did bring everything to
a standstill as we weren't as prepared as we might have been
to handle the volume. However, it was touching when some of
the local lads parked their cars and joined in to help get things
moving again.'

He said *we*.

'Let's raise our glasses to an amazing joint effort,' he continues,
'before we start to pick it apart and think about how we're going
to resolve some of the issues. Cheers, all!'

Everyone holds up their glass and there's a chorus of 'Hear!
Hear!' A few of them are almost empty, so I gesture to the waiter
to come and sort us out.

'What a day!' Keith declares. 'Roping off that overspill area
worked really well, Cappy.'

'I thought so too, but I think we learnt a few valuable lessons
today. Let's troubleshoot the main problems.'

'The turning circle isn't big enough,' Riley points out. 'We
either need to extend it, or – dare I suggest – move the gates to
the campsite further back.'

'Point taken, Riley, and that's a good idea. There's a lot of wasted space at the entrance to the campsite and it's doing nothing. Anything else?'

Vyvyan puts her finger up, gingerly. 'People weren't sure whether it was parking for the market only, or the bakery, too.'

'I was asked the same question,' I add.

'Okay.' Cappy jots down another note on the pad in front of him. 'We need clearer signage. Anything else?'

'Is this goin' to be a permanent thing?' Keith checks and everyone turns to look at me.

'If people want a market fifty-two weeks of the year, why not?'

'Then, in my opinion you need to build a separate toilet block nearer to the hay barn, so we don't have people wanderin' into the campsite.'

I look across at Cappy. 'Is that feasible?'

'The septic tank could cope with it, so I don't see why not,' he confirms. 'Obviously, there's a cost involved. And it would make sense to be digging the trenches and making the connections in winter when the campsite is quieter.'

'In the short term why not rent a portable toilet cabin?' Riley suggests.

'That would work,' Cappy replies, positively.

'What if we move the entrance to the campsite so that the general car park and the hay barn are a totally separate entity?' I throw out there, waiting to see what reaction it gets.

Keith is straight on it. 'From my point of view in managin' the campsite, it would be the perfect solution, Jess.'

'I agree,' Cappy immediately backs him up.

'In which case, all we need is someone to sit down and work out the best way to achieve it and how much it's going to cost to get the work done.'

'If I drop everything else, then I could take it on, Jess. However, I know you're keen to get the small barn sorted as that will bring in some much-needed extra income.' Riley says it with such conviction that even though we've rehearsed this a few times, he's managed to make it sound convincing.

I let out a soft, if rather frustrated, sigh. 'Then that's a problem for me to sort out. It's clear we need an extra pair of hands. Keith has enough on his plate, and it seems the farm is now in need of a general manager. Right, I think we're finally getting somewhere.'

As two waiters carry across another round of drinks, Cappy winks at me. Both he and I are designated drivers tonight, but at least we have clear heads. But I can tell that his brain is in overdrive. Having made it clear that I have no choice but to bring in someone new, who has no links to the farm, it won't sit well with him. I keep telling myself that this is what Grandma would want. Not the love of her life living out his remaining years somewhere he simply hasn't been able to settle. It's only because of my grandparents that Lola and I have this amazing fresh start, and I wouldn't have found Riley if I hadn't run away to Cornwall. Whatever the circumstances, it simply feels right to encourage Cappy to spend more time here in the hope that at some point he'll realise this will always be his home.

Cappy offers to drive Riley and Len home and I drop Keith and Vyvyan off, which means that I'm first to arrive back at the farm. When I hear him pull up, I hurry over to see if he would like a nightcap, but he's understandably tired. I give Cappy a hug and we part ways. I watch him trudge over to Smithy's Cottage and wait until the lights in the sitting room cast their shadows across the shiny cobbles. It looks warm and inviting; I've done everything I can to entice him here, but now it's a waiting game.

Lola is up at just after six o'clock and runs in, jumping on the bed and instantly rousing me from a deep sleep. She's eager to tell me how Hendra had Misty jumping a foot in the air last night, with a feather attached to her favourite cardboard tube.

She snuggles up next to me and I know it won't be long before my other girl appears. 'Now that Misty has a collar, thanks to Cappy,' I say, stifling a yawn, 'Riley said he'll install that cat flap today.'

'Her own little entrance, what fun! Is Cappy going to drop me off at school this morning?'

'Not today, Lola. Erica and Daisy will be picking you up.'

Her face drops. 'Aww… I hate goodbyes, Mum. And Cappy always jokes around with my friends while we're waiting in the playground. We have a laugh.'

'I know and I'm sorry, but maybe he can do that next time.'

'I wish he could stay, like forever,' Lola says quietly as if she's talking to herself. I will admit that I was thinking the exact same thing.

Riley doesn't appear until shortly before ten o'clock, but he has a couple of lengths of plastic pipe attached to the roof of the van.

'I'm not running late,' he confirms, as I sidle up to say good morning. 'I wasn't sure what time Cappy was leaving and I didn't want to be a distraction. Did he say anything?'

I watch as Riley opens the back door and begins dragging out something heavy wrapped in one of his old dust sheets.

'No. He was very quiet. I'm guessing Mum got in touch about Dave's funeral. He just said he'll email me as soon as he's looked at the options for moving the campsite entrance. It will also involve a trip to the planning offices at some point, but that was about it.'

Riley gives me a quick kiss on the cheek and I watch as he pulls out a piece of old scaffold planking. 'What have you got there?'

'Wait and see. I need the sack trucks. Don't let me stop you. As soon as I get this offloaded I'll do that cat flap next. See you in a bit.'

My arms are full of clean bedding and towels for Smithy's Cottage and I leave him to it. As I saunter past the bakery, Alice beckons me over.

'Morning, Jess. Well, market day yesterday was a crowd pleaser, wasn't it? We certainly did well from it.'

'That's good news. We're working on upgrading the parking facilities, but it might take a while to get it all sorted. How are things going back at base?'

She rolls her eyes. 'We're short-staffed and it's busy. Plus, Jory has our accountant poring over the figures and when he's up to his eyes baking, he gets tetchy if he has constant interruptions. Honestly, things go to pot if I'm not there to keep an eye. This is going to be a really tough decision to make, Jess. I will admit that this does appear to have all the makings of a nice, steady little business.' She reaches out to squeeze my arm reassuringly.

'Thanks, Alice. If there's anything you need, just shout.'

'Will do!'

It isn't until I'm about to put the key in the door that I notice the horseshoe sitting above the door of Smithy's Cottage. Cappy must have put it up before he left this morning. For some silly reason my eyes begin to fill up with tears and I hurry inside.

It's time to change the linen and give it a quick once over. For some reason it almost feels as if Cappy is still here and if I call out, his head will appear at the top of the stairs. I imagine him sitting at the desk as he fiddles with a pile of papers, in between times glancing out of the window that has far-reaching views of the moor beyond the road. In the distance, probably fifteen miles as the crow flies, sits Riley's cottage and I am curious about it.

What strikes me is that Cappy didn't question the fact that Riley was here most of the weekend, or that he was a part of the team in every way. What he did notice, and that was obvious, was the rapport between the two of us, which is getting increasingly hard to disguise.

'Jess? Are you busy or can you spare me five minutes of your time?' Riley's voice calls up the stairs.

'No, I'm just about done now.'

I carry the laundry bag downstairs and he lifts it out of my arms, placing it next to the front door. 'Before we head over to The Farmhouse, I have something else to show you first.'

'The cat flap is done, already?' I ask, as I pull on my fleece.

'It is,' he confirms.

'She won't escape, will she?'

'No. It's operated by a chip; the vet would have seen to that when Misty had her injections. Until we flick a little switch on the frame, and she goes through it for the first time, it remains locked.'

'Thank goodness for that.'

'Anyway... we were talking about fire pits.' I look at him blankly. 'You know... toasting marshmallows?'

He leads me over to the sack trucks, pulling back the blanket.

'That's awesome!'

'I thought you'd like it. It's a little project I've been working on at home. I spotted it in a friend's reclamation yard and with a bit of elbow grease as they say, it came up like new. Now, where do you want it?'

Standing on its side and tied with a rope, it reaches almost to the top of the handlebars. 'I'm not sure. It's very grand.'

'Can I make a suggestion?'

'Please do.'

'How about I use some of those surplus flagstones and make a special area in front of the manor house?'

My hands fly up to my face. 'Oh Riley, that would be amazing.'

He instinctively catches my hand to whisk me off, before we both realise there are other people about and we end up laughing, and walking side by side instead.

'Sorry,' he mutters, softly.

'It's fine. We're bound to forget ourselves occasionally.'

As we step through the archway into the grounds of Renweneth Manor I always get the same reaction. It's like entering a secret garden and my spirits begin to soar.

'Okay... wander around and imagine it's Christmas and you

have people coming round. It's time to light the fire and pull on those thick winter coats and bobble hats. It's over to you.'

I head for the orchard but the grass is so velvety it would be a shame to dig a part of it up. At the rear of the manor it's more of a market garden, or it was, but now it's just raised beds that are in need of a good weeding.

'Personally, I think you're going in the wrong direction,' Riley prompts me. I turn to follow him back through to the front garden.

There's a latticework brick wall that divides the generous parking area from the path that wends its way between the flowerbeds and lawned areas leading up to the front door.

'I think this is a nice, sheltered corner. What do you think?'

I stand with my elbow resting on my arm, as I try to imagine it.

'Wait there! I won't be a moment.'

My mind conjures up a vision of a twilit evening; some pretty metal lanterns with candles in them hang from the wall and cast a gentle light over the area as the flames dance around in the fire pit. I do a three-hundred-and-sixty-degree turn, imagining it from every conceivable angle.

When Riley reappears, gingerly manoeuvring the sack truck wheels over the bumpy flagstones and on to the swathe of chippings, I rush over to help him.

'Thanks, Jess. For a moment there I thought it was going to break free of the rope.'

'I love that it's circular, but it does look a little... basic,' I comment, not wishing to take anything away from his generous gesture.

'I know, and I'm going to use some of that pile of old stones behind the hay barn to build a wall around it. I'll raise it so that kids won't be tempted to try to sit on it. Right. Let's get this monster piece of ironwork into place.'

It takes a few minutes, but when we stand back I can't restrain my smile. 'Oh... I want to fill it with wood and light it now,' I exclaim.

After a quick glance around to make sure no one can see us, I throw my arms around Riley's neck and plant a kiss firmly on his lips. He kisses me back, lingering for a few seconds, and it feels so good.

'Thank you, Riley. It's even better than I could have imagined. And thanks, too, for everything you did while Cappy was here.'

When he finally releases me we're both a little breathless.

'I didn't really do anything other than give my honest opinion, Jess. It was nice that he listened to what I had to say; I appreciated that. Right, I'll show you how to work the cat flap next.'

As we make a concerted effort to keep our hands off each other as we walk, we're both grinning. 'Are you thinking what I'm thinking?' I ask.

'That what we need is a reason to christen the fire pit,' he states firmly, trying hard not to laugh.

'Me too! It should be something special. Bonfire night is a long time away, though,' I moan, pulling a long face. 'Although what we need once you've laid the flagstones are some gorgeous old cast iron lamps. Is that something you can sort for me?'

Riley shakes his head, then winks at me. 'I'll see what I can do.'

And I know whatever rusty treasures he manages to find will be simply perfect.

TEN DAYS LATER...

26

Renweneth Farm's End of Summer Celebration

'Look who I found wandering around and wondering where everyone was,' Cappy steps through the archway beaming from ear to ear with Ivy and Adam following a few paces behind him.

I'm busy sweeping sand into the gaps between the flagstone patio that Riley finished late yesterday. I put down the brush to rush over and welcome them, homing in for a group hug. When I step back the eye contact is all smiles, so the journey down must have gone well this time.

'It feels like an eternity since you were last here! Are you ready for a fun weekend?'

Adam raises his eyebrows. 'You have no idea how much we've been looking forward to this.'

Riley appears at the entrance to the garden of the manor house, wheeling a barrow full of logs, and calls over. 'Adam, Ivy! It's good to see you.'

We all move aside as he steers his way around the fire pit and then he walks back to shake Adam's hand and give Ivy a hug. Her eyes light up, as she smiles at me over his shoulder.

'It looks like you've been extremely busy since our last visit. Jess mentioned something about a few little jobs that needed finishing off ready for the party tonight?'

Cappy gives a little chuckle. 'That's par for the course here. Look at me – ten days ago I came to sort out a little parking issue. Now, for the next six months I'm the farm manager with a list of jobs as long as my arm.'

Riley looks directly at me as he starts speaking. 'The lists keep growing, I'm afraid, and the days just aren't long enough.'

I bite my lip to stop myself breaking out into a triumphant smile.

'I'd better make it clear it isn't all down to me,' I interject. 'We have team meetings now and everyone gets to have their say.'

'The bakery looks lovely, I can't wait to take a peek inside,' Ivy remarks. 'And Smithy's Cottage. I love the horseshoe above the door!'

'That's my temporary home,' Cappy replies, proudly. 'I'll take you over and show you around.'

'That's a great idea,' I join in. 'Afterwards, if Adam and Ivy want to get settled into the guest room in The Farmhouse, perhaps we can all meet up in the kitchen in about an hour?' I glance at Riley, and he nods his head.

'Absolutely. Don't let us stop you,' Adam replies. 'I'll change into my work gear and give you a hand afterwards, Riley. What's first on the list?'

'Have you ever built a log store?' he enquires, grinning.

'No, but how hard can it be?' The two guys exchange a mischievous glance. 'Tell me how big and I'll have a go.'

'Ah, well, I won't know that until I've finished barrowing the logs across. Judging by the look on Jess's face, I'd better leave you to it and fetch the next load.'

'Panic is beginning to set in, sorry. We've at least thirty people coming tonight, and time is running out!'

Cappy immediately takes charge, whisking Adam and Ivy off. They talk as they walk, and I overhear Cappy saying: 'It's a big one tonight. It's the start of a new tradition that Jess wants to hold every year. We'll make sure it's an evening everyone will remember for a long time to come.'

Now if that isn't blind faith, I don't know what is because

every time I stop to catch my breath, something else jumps into my head to add to the to-do list.

Riley finishes emptying the wheelbarrow and as he steers it around me he stops for a moment. When everyone is out of sight he plants a big kiss on my cheek. 'Cappy's right. Don't worry, everything is going to be just fine.'

As Ivy helps me unpack the boxes of pillar candles, I can hear the sound of Adam using the electric saw in the small barn.

'This is a brilliant idea, Jess. A party is just what everyone needs. How is Cappy doing since Dave's funeral?'

I purse my lips, thinking about the tense couple of days following it before he made the decision to join us for the next phase of work at the farm. 'Mum was right, he simply needed something to fill his time and goodness knows, we need him here.'

'We?'

'Riley is a part of the full-time team now, you know, involved in the decision-making process.'

She looks startled. 'He's sleeping here at The Farmhouse?'

I roll my eyes at her. 'No, but he regularly pops in at the weekend to join us for the odd meal, or two, and sometimes stops to watch a film. Lola often asks where he is if he's not around.' I sit back on my heels. 'So much has happened, it's hard even for me to keep up. Things here went from relatively quiet, to full-on chaos once the bakery opened and the market days started. The first two were a bit of a learning curve, but we now have a temporary solution to cope with the car parking and facilities until Cappy can apply for approval for a second entrance to ease congestion.'

'It's real then, his new job?'

'It is. In all honesty, if he'd said no I would have had to find someone to step in as no one has any spare capacity. It's like the farm suddenly has a life of its own and it's only going to get busier.' I probably sound as bewildered as I'm feeling right now.

'It's good news all round, but the pressure must be enormous. What's on the agenda?'

'Mum and Dad will be arriving this afternoon; they'll be setting up an outdoor bar. The party kicks off at seven. We've got all afternoon to get things set up here, which includes erecting a curtained gazebo that we've hired and setting up some tables for the buffet.'

'Who's doing the catering?'

'Erica, and Alice from The Farmhouse Bakery, kindly took on the challenge, so it's a joint effort.'

'Ah, that's nice. How are things going for Erica?'

'She's either rushed off her feet or twiddling her thumbs and it's driving her crazy. She has a stall at tomorrow's first Autumn Fayre in the hay barn. She'll be doing hot taster pots and handing out flyers. Alice is also going to be there giving out free samples and from what Vyvyan was saying, we have something for everyone. From a candle-making demonstration with an array of aromatherapy gifts, handmade Christmas cards, various artisan crafts including wooden toys, to a van from Treeve Perran farm selling fresh vegetables and meat. Oh, and an art display.'

'It's incredible, Jess. No wonder you're feeling overwhelmed. But you look happy, despite the pressure.'

'Hmm, I am. My first year was rather lonely in so many ways. I felt everything was down to me and I was scared, Ivy. One wrong decision could have had an impact upon everything. Now it's different.'

'And that's down to Riley.'

'Yes. We're so in tune and that felt weird at first. I wasn't used to someone thinking about things from my perspective and understanding my insecurities. But he did and he didn't ask for anything, he was just there for me, Ivy. No strings attached. No agenda of his own, other than a fair day's pay for a fair day's work. And now here we are. There's no hiding the fact that we're a couple, we just don't live together.'

Ivy pulls a face. 'That's not ideal, Jess.'

'It's okay; he still has to tread warily because of his ex. He's desperate to reconnect with Ollie and he doesn't want to upset her in any way. And when I think Lola is ready, we'll figure out the right way to tackle it.'

'Riley will continue to live in his cottage for the time being, then?'

'Yes, but he's a part of everything that happens here because to me he's family now. In the meantime, we'll grab whatever alone-time we can get, but every decision going forward is one we'll make together. We're building our future and hopefully, at some point, Ollie will be able to spend some time here at the farm. By then, maybe Lola will be ready to think of Riley as more than simply our friend and her favourite builder.'

'I'm thrilled for you, Jess. How was Lola's stay with Ben last weekend?'

'Considering it was the first visit since Ben explained to her that he and Naomi are now living together, it went without a hitch. Our joint decision to keep some things low-key and wait until we think Lola is ready to deal with yet another change was the right one. Naomi has my telephone number and I told her she can call me any time. The lesson I've learnt is that I can't control everything that happens around Lola, but I trust Ben to put her interests first when she's with him.'

Ivy glances around, her eyes settling on Renweneth Manor.

'Have you made a decision about selling this place?'

'Yes. Riley and I are going to turn it into a family home.'

Ivy gives a little squeal. 'OMG... I so knew you were going to say that! Right, let's get these gorgeous metal lanterns kitted out with candles because tonight is going to be a mega celebration.'

'I hope so! And how are things going at your end?'

'Whenever we start flagging, Adam and I think of you and what you've done here, Jess. If we keep ploughing forward eventually things will come right, even if it just means going in a slightly different direction than we first envisaged. Thanks to some sterling advice from Vyvyan, I'm in talks with my landlord, so keep your fingers crossed for me. The thing is, I know we'll get there but everything takes time. Like any work in progress, it's a case of watch this space.'

The sound of raucous laughter announces the arrival of the two men who are at the centre of our lives. They're carrying some heavy wooden posts and taunting each other as it's clear they're both struggling.

'Mind your backs, ladies. Wide load coming through. We're going to be doing some hammering, but we'll try not to get in your way,' Adam warns.

'Next time you're passing, a drill and some screws would come in handy so I can put these up.' I look across at Riley, smiling sweetly as I lean back to give them some more room.

'Yes, bos...' He stops mid-sentence and grins at me. 'I'm on it, Jess!'

Everywhere I turn there are smiling faces and the light from the candles and the fire pit reflect in people's eyes, adding that little touch of magic to the evening. In the background, Renweneth Manor looms up against the darkening sky, adding a sense of country grandeur to the occasion. I don't dwell on the decay within, the empty rooms, or the years of dust waiting to be swept away. All in good time, I tell myself.

Dad sidles up to me. 'You got to be pleased, Jess. This is quite something. I love the outdoor fairy lights Riley hung from the branches of that old apple tree. It's the little touches that have made tonight such a great success.'

I smile at Dad, and we turn to take in every little detail, even the gazebo looks picture perfect. We decorated the buffet table with freshly cut greenery from the pine and eucalyptus trees bordering the campsite. Nothing can beat the scents that nature surrounds us with and tonight I think we married rustic with a touch of elegance.

'People are waiting for you to make a speech,' Dad prompts.

I look at him, pulling a face. 'Really?'

'It's sort of expected at a bash like this.'

Lola, Daisy, and Alice and Jory's seven-year-old son Jack, run past us heading for the treehouse. Their shrieks of laughter are a joy to hear, but I'm so glad that Misty is safe inside the house with the cat flap disabled, as the noise would send her scurrying.

'Would you mind getting people's attention for me?'

Dad puts his arm around my shoulders, giving me a squeeze. 'That's my girl.'

As he moves closer to the fire pit, I trail behind him, squaring my shoulders.

'Can everyone gather around please and make sure you have a glass in your hand?'

It takes a few seconds for the buzz of chatter and laughter to quieten down, and I glance around nervously as I wait.

'Um... well... I'd like to thank everyone for coming tonight to the inaugural Renweneth Farm end of summer party. Everyone here has been instrumental in some way in getting us to this point and tonight we have so much to celebrate. I'm not one for speeches, so I feel it's fitting to hand you over to the person whose vision is being brought to life... Cappy?'

He appears next to me, leaning in to kiss my cheek, and I can see he's touched.

'Goodness me, I'm not prepared for this!' he exclaims and there's a little round of laughter.

'Go on, Cappy. You got it,' Adam calls out.

'Well, oh well,' he pauses, and I can feel the emotion in the air as everyone is thinking about my grandma. 'I knew I was leaving the place in good hands with Jess. When all is said and done we're just custodians, doing the best we can to ensure the farm remains standing for many years to come. I'm proud of the way my granddaughter has worked solidly since the day she and Lola first arrived.

'Did I think that Jess would end up roping me in? No.' There's another little ripple of laughter and sounds of encouragement. 'But I'm here and it's good to be back, because I'm more than happy to do whatever I can. Jess is right, everyone here is a part of this in some way or other. The thing is, it just goes to show that when people come together good things can happen. It feels wrong to single anyone out, as this really has been a team effort involving both friends and family, but a party isn't a party without a feast. Erica, Alice and Jory – you've done us proud.'

A little 'Ah,' filters through from behind me and there are lots of nodding heads as I glance around.

'Let's raise our glasses. Here's to more joint ventures and more celebrations to come as we make Renweneth Farm the true beating heart of our little community. Thank you all!'

I don't think I'm the only person feeling a tad emotional tonight. To see everyone gathered here tonight having fun is almost surreal and it does make me realise how far we've come. An arm slides around my waist and Riley whispers into my ear. 'You can't cry, Jess, not tonight.'

I sniff hard as he puts a little distance between us. This time next year I hope things will be very different indeed. 'I know.'

In the background the buzz is back, and the night is still young.

'Do you fancy a stroll?' he asks.

'Yes. Why not.'

'Come on, I have a little surprise waiting.'

We slope off unnoticed, to wander over to the small barn; inside it's pitch-black and I wait patiently while Riley uses the light from his phone to locate the switch for the overhead lights.

I love coming in here; yes it's a mess, with building materials everywhere and padlocked cabinets full of a growing collection of tools, but it won't be like it forever.

Riley walks over to a mound covered in an old tarpaulin.

'Are you ready?'

'Yes.'

'Right. Three, two, one…'

I stride forward and my breath catches in my throat as I gaze entranced at the two cast iron stags standing in front of me. They're about three feet high and each one stands on a solid base.

'What do you think?'

'They're adorable! Where did you find them?'

'I've got my sources. It's taken me a while as you don't often find a pair, so I put out some feelers and my contact came up trumps. I knew you'd love them.'

I throw my arms around Riley's neck. 'I do, but I love you even more!'

Never in my wildest dreams could I have envisioned us all here, in the garden of Renweneth Manor spending a candlelit evening under the stars with the people who make my life feel complete.

Suddenly, it's as if everything is finally falling into place and instead of that sense of gnawing loneliness that was eating away at me, I feel a part of something. But it's more than that, I'm grateful for the safety net that comes from knowing people are there for me, as I am for them.

I'm excited about a future with Riley at my side but, as Grandma often said, all good things come to those who wait. We have the rest of our lives to get it right, because *forever* means exactly that.

Acknowledgements

Cornwall has always been an enchanting destination for me and whenever I visit, I return home feeling renewed and uplifted. The coastline is enchanting, but the landscape too holds a powerful draw for me. And how I wish Renweneth Farm really existed, because it's a place I'd love to call home. One day, perhaps I will find my perfect Cornish retreat... in the meantime, writing a series of three books in this setting feels delightfully indulgent.

I'd like to give a virtual hug to my inspirational commissioning editor, Martina Arzu – it's a sheer delight working with you! And to everyone involved in the process: from the creation of the stunning cover to the diligent eyes of the copy and line editors who polish the manuscript so expertly, without you this story wouldn't sparkle.

Grateful thanks also go to my agent, Sara Keane, for her sterling advice, professionalism, and friendship. It means so much to me.

The wider Aria team and Head of Zeus are a truly awesome group of people, and I can't thank you enough for your amazing support and encouragement.

To my wonderful husband, Lawrence – you truly are my rock!

There are so many family members and long-term friends who understand that my passion to write is all-consuming. They forgive me for the long silences and when we next catch up, it's as if I haven't been absent at all.

Publishing a new book means that there is an even longer list of people to thank for publicising it. The amazing kindness of my lovely author friends, readers and reviewers is truly humbling. You continue to delight, amaze and astound me with your generosity and support.

Wishing everyone peace, love, and happiness.

Linn x

About the Author

LINN B. HALTON is a #1 bestselling author of contemporary romantic fiction. In 2013 she won the UK Festival of Romance: Innovation in Romantic Fiction Award.

For Linn, life is all about family, friends, and writing. She is a self-confessed hopeless romantic and an eternal optimist. When Linn is not writing, she spends time in the garden weeding or practising Tai Chi. And she is often found with a paintbrush in her hand indulging her passion for upcycling furniture.

Her novels have been translated into Italian, Czech and Croatian. She also writes as Lucy Coleman.